TIKI HORROR

Edited by

CATHERINE JORDAN

Fortress Publishing, Inc.
www.fortresspublishinginc.com

Tiki Horror

ISBN: 978-1-959797-08-1

Edited by: Catherine Jordan

This book is available for wholesale through the publisher,
Fortress Publishing, Inc.

PUBLISHED BY:
Fortress Publishing, Inc.
1200 Market Street
Unit 17 / Box 137
Lemoyne, PA 17043

WWW.FORTRESSPUBLISHINGINC.COM

CONTENTS

Foreword

Being the director of a large group of horror authors, *Moanaria's Fright Club,* I have the privilege of working with many unique talents in the field. As far as horror authors go, Catherine Jordan has repeatedly proven herself to be an exceptional addition to the group because, in spite of being a teacher herself, she can do something many authors cannot: Turn criticism into success. Sounds simple, right? It isn't. And that's why I endorse her work wholeheartedly.

For some of us, Halloween is a holiday, for some it's a product, and for others it's a way of life. Whichever side of the line you find yourself reading from, one must admit that stores do seem to be stocking their shelves with Halloween products, earlier and earlier, each year. I wouldn't go so far as to say that holiday demand is a daily universal constant, but I have observed that people sometimes don't want to wait three-hundred and sixty-four days to celebrate their favorite holiday.

I was a junior in high school when my friend Stephanie called and said, "We're having a Halloween party tonight. You in?" It was a hazy, muggy afternoon in late July, but the goths, punks, and metalheads in my circles were sick of waiting for October to arrive, and so was I! Intrigued and confused, like Fortunato to Amontillado, I hung up the phone, grabbed a costume, and hopped on the nearest bus to see if it would take me three months into the future. A few hours later, the right combination of decorations, candy, music and an empty house resulted in a very successful Halloween celebration. Some time after midnight, between a sugar-high and Ray Parker Jr. wailing that busting made him feel good, I looked out to my friends and realized it was not late July anymore. It was a warm October 31st.

From that night, at least a decade passed before I heard words like "Hulaween" or "Tiki," but in retrospect, as a former *Rue Morgue* contributor and *Pseudopod* alum, the party made a lot of sense. Today, North American horror fans persist in either rediscovering classic horror holidays like Krampus, or innovating new reasons to celebrate like Gothmas (Not to be confused with World Goth Day - May 22nd), or Creepmas. There are supernatural holidays that are celebrated in spring like Walpurgisnacht in Germany, or Asian supernatural holidays like Obon or The Hungry Ghost Month, but most spooky holidays are located in the autumn and winter sections of the global calendar. Therefore, the sub-genre's cultural roots notwithstanding, tiki horror is a special (and potentially powerful) sub-genre because it caters to Halloween and horror audiences who enjoy tropical surroundings.

In terms of literature, the tiki horror sub-genre (as well as tiki noir and vacation horror) provides lenses that have no shortage of topics to draw from for quality yarns. Their rich elements can be traced back before Suwannee Hulaweens in Florida; pine-apple jack-o'-lanterns from Australia; or tall, ceramic mugs in the tiki-style of whatever your favorite horror icon happens to be. Psychologically-speaking, I would propose that the reason why this all works is that we mentally associate ideas with media that we enjoy and identify with. For instance, one might have a Valentine's Day party (or International Single's Day party) with a viewing of *My Bloody Valentine*. At *Rue Morgue* Magazine, Friday the 13th film-viewing parties happened on Friday the 13th. So, it should come as no surprise that - especially in horror - these celebrations come in all shapes and sizes. However, in order for there to be a successful association, one must have great works to tangent to, and it is here that we come to Catherine Jordan's latest anthology, *Tiki Horror*, which I am confident will keep demand going for tiki horror fiction.

In addition to writing one of the best caveat emptor tales I've read in a while, Catherine has carefully curated an entourage of seasoned writers including Lisa Morton and Jonathan Maberry as well as *Fright Club* authors, Jacque Day, Dianna Sinovic, and Diane Sismour (i.e. members of the powerful writing group known as "The Hive"). In "Just One Bite," Dianna Sinovic particularly shines for her usage of Japanese mythology and Yokai. Carnage House co-editor, Jacque Day, does a wonderful job reminding us all about how complicated family affairs can be. And my good friend, Diane Sismour dazzles us with a reimagining of a Poe-tic classic set against a Kona backdrop. In short,

Dear Reader, you're going to have a lot of fun. But before you pour over the pages, maybe pour yourself a chilled lychee wine or mai tai to help you come back when your pulse goes up! Enjoy!

Your Beastly Brother-in-Horror,
Moaner T. Lawrence

BIO:
Moaner T. Lawrence

Born on Long Island, raised in Queens, and marooned in Germany, Moaner T. Lawrence is obsessed with everything Halloween, and made a career out of it. 2011, Moaner became the face of Germany's *Rue Morgue* Magazine for over a decade. By 2014, Moaner was also a regular contributor to Germany's largest horror magazine, *Virus*, and ascended to the title of "Assistant Editor" to *Escape Artists' Pseudopod* from 2015 to 2018. An active member of the HWA, Moaner has published several short stories throughout the years, but is best known for being the Director of *Fright Club*, an online writing workshop for horror fiction. *Fright Club* was first developed in 2004, briefly taken to Horror Writers Association for a year, and then privatized as *Moanaria's Fright Club*. Its alumni include several high-ranking members of the HWA including former officers, trustees, and even one former HWA president. It also has other authors and ranking members from other horror fiction organizations. To learn more visit: https://www.moanaria.com/.

Preface

My heart always goes aflutter when I travel. I don't relax until I get to the destination, suitcases where they're supposed to be, everyone intact. I try not to think about what could go wrong, but let's face it, we all have our worries, and sometimes a little anxiety keeps me on my toes. I've often heard horror stories, and when traveling to Hawaii toward the end of COVID, well... Suffice it to say that even with a drink in hand, I couldn't totally relax. And that got me contemplating out-of-the norm terrors, Tiki Horror, to gain perspective.

The Tiki Horror sub-genre, sometimes referred to as Tiki Noir, blends escapism with gothic horror, the paranormal, and folklore.

Consider the movie *Voodoo Island* (1957), starring Boris Karloff and an uncredited Adam West from the *Batman* television series. Filmed in Hawaii, it's about a resort site infested with voodoo horrors, zombies and carnivorous plants.

Karen Black's iconic role in the cult classic "Amelia" from the 1975 made-for-TV *Trilogy of Terror* Anthology focuses on a woman (Black) who is terrorized by a Zuni-fetish doll. She traps it in her suitcase only to have it escape and ultimately possess her.

Published in 2011 but set in 1956, Christopher Pinto's novel *Murder on Tiki Island* features a cynical New York City detective on a Tiki Island Resort in the Florida Keys whose vacation is interrupted by a murder mystery tangled up in the occult.

And what about the *King Kong* movie where a film crew travels to a tropical island for a location shoot? There are many, many more examples of Tiki Horror.

As a member of *Moanaria's Fright Club*, a writing workshop that focuses on horror, Moaner Lawrence tapped me with an idea—an anthology focused on Tiki Horror. I penned the short story "A Kiss Is Not a Kiss" for *Symphony of the Damned* Savage Realm Press, sold it, fell in love with anthology idea, and then went after a publisher.

And now I'd like to introduce you all to Tiki Horror: Tales of Trips Gone Horribly Wrong

Camping and islanding and cruising! Oh my!

Pack your bags. You're invited on a destination anthology to paradise, but beware… you might get stranded in a nightmare. Take a zipline into despair, stay in a lonely hotel where you're not quite alone, hop a flight with a fanged fiend. And watch the tiki drinkies—those bubbles aren't fermentation.

These masterful storytellers will make you think twice before booking your next escape. Go ahead and grab your one-way ticket to terror—no return guaranteed.

– Catherine Jordan

The Best Day

Jonathan Maberry

It was the best day of Hannah Smoak's life.

That's what she told her son and his wife. She said so to the salesman at the Costco where she bought her luggage set. She told that to the cashier at CVS when she went in to buy travel-size toiletries. Hannah made that claim to the Uber driver who took her to the airport, to the cabin attendant, and the middle-aged couple in the seats adjoining hers. And to the shuttle driver in Kaua'i who drove all the tourists on her flight to the hotel. She mentioned it three separate times to the pretty young woman working the registration desk at the beachside Paradise Suites.

Everyone smiled at her because she looked like the kind of person who didn't get nearly enough smiles, and most people have some to spare. Besides, how often does someone say they're having the best day of their lives and appear to really mean it?

The best day of Hannah Smoak's life.

Sadly, *best* was a low bar.

And certain milestones are surprisingly fragile.

-2-

"Isn't this lovely?" asked Hannah.

She stood in a short line at the poolside bar, and turned to speak with the couple behind her. They were about thirty years younger, Black, and looked like they, too, were having a great time. He wore bathing trunks under a Hawaiian shirt with an outrageous pattern of hula-dancing chickens. His wife was one of those slim women who could wear anything and make it look like haut couture. The batik sarong matched her bikini top and the scrunchy that gathered her beaded braids.

"Beats the heck out of Philadelphia," said the woman.

"Most things do," murmured her husband, looking past Hannah to try and give the bartender the *look*. The bartender, a mountain of a young man with a perpetual inward smile, merely dialed up the wattage of his grin and kept making drinks at his steady pace.

"I'm in from Hermantown," said Hannah. "That's in Minnesota."

"Oh?" murmured the younger woman. "That sounds nice."

"Well, not really. I mean it's a nice enough town but not much ever seems to happen there. And the winters are very long. We got over eighty inches last year, and they say this year will be snowier."

"Philly gets its fair share of snow. But nothing like that."

The line moved one person closer to the bar.

"Are you newlyweds?" Hannah asked.

The man rolled his eyes. "I wish."

His wife punched him lightly on the arm. Not too lightly, though. "You're so bad, Derek."

"Hey, I love the kids, Trish," Derek said quickly. "But it's nice just to concentrate on you for a bit."

That one was in the bull's-eye, and Hannah chuckled. Trish stood on her toes and kissed his cheek. Then she punched him again. Even less lightly this time.

"What was that for?"

"That's for Johnny and Ayleen." To Hannah, she said, "They're twins. Two years, two months."

"The terrible twos…?" suggested Hannah.

"Like times fifty," said Derek, shifting deftly out of punching range. "You'd think there were thirty of each of them."

Trish looked at him, then shrugged. "Okay. Fair."

"Well," said Hannah, "I think it's good to get away now and then. Helps a parent get their own ducks in a row. Rest and recharge."

"Rest and recharge, hell yeah," said Derek.

When it came to Hannah's turn at the bar, she bought a margarita for herself and told the bartender to give her new friends whatever they wanted. There was the usual tussle over the generosity, but Hannah won out because she was having the best day of her life.

Drinks in hand, they headed to the pool. Derek began angling over to a pair of secluded loungers near the little waterfall at the shallow end, but Trish nudged him and asked Hannah if she wanted to join them.

"Oh, I don't want to intrude."

"We're here to escape kid noise," said Trish. "Tell the truth, we could use some adult conversation."

Derek agreed with only a smidge of bad grace, but he warmed when they were seated in the shade and three-quarters of his oversized mai tai was in his belly. He put in his earbuds and dialed up a playlist of late 90s hip-hop, put on his shades, pulled down the bill of his Eagles cap, and zoned out.

Trish and Hannah found a lot to talk about. There was none of the usual tiptoeing around race issues. Not even the usual well-intentioned caution of an older white woman who knew very few people of color. That wasn't Hannah, nor was Trish like a stranger in a strange land when she asked about life in Minnesota. Instead, they talked movies, cooking, TV, and books. As it turned out they agreed that Idris Elba and Henry Cavill were both beautiful men, and if either wanted to abduct them they would be packed and ready.

They clinked over that and Trish went to fetch the next round.

The conversation drifted to kids and, with the grace of being at minimum safe distance from the twins, Trish felt empowered to bring out her phone and show pictures. Hannah, in her turn, showed pictures of her two dogs – Rosie the Rat Terrier/Cavalier King Charles mix and Daisy, the Heinz 57-variety mutt from a shelter.

It was a very good day.

For Trish it was the best day since she found out she was pregnant – best defined as relaxed, with no morning sickness, contractions, or baby vomit in her hair. And, as Hannah kept telling everyone, it was the best day of her life.

And that stayed true, because it was well after midnight and into the early hours of the *next* day when all the screaming began.

That next was no one's best day.

-3-

Hannah ate dinner with Trish and Derek, then took a glass of white zinfandel out to a patio that commanded a magnificent view of the ocean. The sun set on the far side of the hotel, but the spilled paintbox of sunset colors still splashed reds and vermilions, oranges and purples onto the gentle waves.

She nearly wept at the simple beauty of it all.

Then she went to her room, showered, dressed in blue cotton pajamas with little pink flowers on them, said her prayers, and climbed into bed. She read a book of poems by Anne Walsh, then turned over and went to sleep.

Hannah often remembered her dreams and mostly they were of the kind she called 'junk drawer' – collections of odds and ends from recent memory, collated into an improbable chronology that was often silly, baffling, and strange.

In one dream, she and Trish were eating a decorative novelty cake that was shaped like Derek. Hannah had three helpings because she loved red velvet cake and her diet was back in Minnesota.

In another dream, she was wandering down the beach in her pajamas – something she would not have done at gunpoint while awake – and all around her people were dancing. But they danced strangely… more like swaying and stumbling. "Well," she said in the dream, "I guess I wasn't the only one who had too much to drink."

She did not remember any other dreams. Sleep pulled her too deep for that and Hannah did not resist. She floated down to such a deep place that she slept through the first screams.

-4-

It was a heavy thump against the wall that woke her.

She came awake in total darkness, confused and a little scared. Sometimes it took a few moments for her to remember that she wore a blackout sleep mask. When she did and pulled it down, Hannah was startled because it was light out. A red, rosy sunrise glow behind the sheer curtains.

It made her smile.

Her first Hawaiian sunrise.

Her first sunrise over an ocean ever.

The smile turned into a small frown of confusion. So, she wondered, why did the sunrise flicker like that? For nearly twenty seconds she tried to convince herself it was the movement of the curtains.

Except her bedroom window was of the kind that could not be opened. Only the balcony had sliding French doors, and that was in the living room of her suite.

So…

There was a flash of panic as she thought she'd left something on the stove. But the suite had only a microwave and a coffeemaker. No burners, no oven.

Hannah got out of bed with the kind of caution people sometimes use when they aren't sure if they're really awake. It had a similar vibe to getting up in the middle of the night when she heard a noise downstairs and both of her dogs were in the bedroom with her. Not fear exactly, but a cautious and heightened awareness.

"Oh dear," she said softly as she toe-fished for her slippers. Found them, put them on and stood. Arthritis sent its usual morning greetings, though Hannah was beginning to doubt that this *was* morning. She turned and looked at the closed bedroom door, assuring herself that it was closed, and therefore no balcony breeze could be stirring the curtains.

Then she found her glasses in their case on the bedside, and put them on.

The frown she wore deepened. She could feel it pulling the corners of her mouth down, but she still resisted putting a label on the emotions she felt.

The sheer curtains that she had pulled closed across the window were not rippling.

It was the light from outside that seemed to move.

"Oh dear," she said again.

Sunrises did not ripple. Not even on islands like Kaua'i.

And the color out there had too little of sunrise red and too much of fireplace orange. That was something she did not like at all. Fireplace orange rippled because it was fire. So… why was the sunrise rippling?

It took more courage than Hannah thought she possessed to cross the nine steps from the side of the bed to the window. If it had been the noise of a car accident or neighbors yelling – things she was familiar with from where she lived back east – she would have already been at the window.

Now, though, she crept across the room.

Not really wanting to know what was going on. Not there in paradise.

Not after the perfect day yesterday. Her best day ever.

Yet the questions had to be answered.

She reached the window and had one hand out to grab the white plastic curtain pull. That was where she stopped and that was when she realized that today was not going to be a good day. Not at all.

-5-

Everything outside was on fire.

That was what she saw. It was how she saw it.

Everything out there burned.

She said, "Oh dear," again.

Only then did she summon the strength of will to pull the sheers open and see the full truth.

Paradise Suites was built like a big horseshoe, with the pool and a games area between the arms and a magnificent vista of the eastern Pacific. There were hundreds of boats in the water—some snugged against piers in the marinas on either side of the hotel, and twice as many more anchored out in the roads.

As Hannah stood there, she saw that there was one more vessel – an eighty-foot luxury motorsailer – lying half on its side on the beach. The masts were cracked and leaned drunkenly, and the sails were nothing but tattered rags. It looked like a derelict washed up on the hotel's beach. That alone would be cause for dismay, for excitement.

The fact that the boat was on fire seemed almost to matter less.

Because so many other things were on fire. The rows of beach umbrellas folded for the night burned like torches. Beneath them, the nylon strapping of the loungers were melted. The trash cans were ablaze, as was the poolside bar and all the decorative plants outside of the restaurant.

There were people on fire, too.

Some of them lay sprawled like baked starfish on the terrazzo. Others ran screaming as they burned. And some people were on fire but still walking. Slowly. Awkwardly, but they did not seem to be in pain.

"Oh...," she began to say, but the 'dear' never materialized.

She was too busy looking at the rest of the hotel. Across the pool area, the entire left-hand arm of Paradise Suites was fully involved. Arms of flame clawed at the night sky as if trying to catch the stars.

There was a heavy *thump* against the wall and Hannah turned sharply, suddenly remembering that a sound just like this was what woke her in the first place. She stared at the wall. The seascape painting above the bed now hung slightly askew. It had been a very hard thump.

"What...?" she asked the empty room.

There was another thump.

Louder than the first.

She hurried over to the wall and placed a palm tentatively against it, feeling for heat. For fire.

The wallpaper was cool.

There were sounds, though, and Hannah leaned close to listen, though she could barely hear anything over the hammering of her heart. She even realized on some level that she was not reacting correctly. There was a massive fire outside. People were dying. People, she was sure, were dead. The other half of the hotel was on fire.

Yet here she was listening to what the people in the next room were doing and hoping it was only two people being very naughty. As absurd as that thought was, given the disaster.

Then she heard a sound that was definitely not someone else's headboard banging the intervening wall. It was a human sound.

A scream.

Not one of passion or even of surprise. This was a scream that started deep inside someone's soul and rose, gathering momentum and volume and exploding with far too much intensity. It sounded ghastly and urgent and wet. The scream rose and rose and then…

Stopped.

So abruptly.

So wrong in so many ways.

As Hannah backed away from the wall, her hip bumped the nightstand and the jolt made the telephone give a startled half-ring. She stared at it and then snatched up the receiver. There was no dial tone, but most hotel phones didn't have one. Hannah bent close and squinted through gloom at the buttons, found the one for the front desk, and punched it.

It rang twenty times. No one answered it.

She tried housekeeping, but again, nothing. Same with concierge, valet parking, and laundry services.

No one answered.

Another sound made her turn. Loud, sharp. Familiar from watching all those TV crime dramas.

A gunshot, she was sure of it.

It was close, too.

She hurried out to the living room, pausing only for a moment to see if there was smoke coming in under the door. There wasn't. So she went to the French doors, felt *them* for heat, found none, unlocked them and pulled one open. The wind was blowing south to north, but she could smell the smoke anyway. Her room was on the thirty-first floor, but she hid behind the heavy drapes for a long time, trying to determine if it was even safe to step outside.

Another shot. Two more.

Distant, though. Somewhere down there.

She crouched as low as her knees would allow as she stepped out onto the balcony. It was five feet deep and wide enough for four chairs and a little glass-topped table. With the balcony doors open, she could hear many more things than she could from inside. All the screams. The dragon-roar of the fire. Sirens.

And gunfire.

More of it.

The quick *pop-pop-pop* of handguns. The sharper crack of a rifle. A boom of a shotgun. And here and there the *krak-a-kraka-krak* of automatic rifles. She lived in a state where hunting was popular. She knew the sound of guns.

"Have we been invaded?" she asked the noisy air.

Her eye was drawn back to the beached motorsailer. There was something about it that compelled her attention. It looked very expensive, or had been before whatever happened to it ruined the sails and the hull. It had an abandoned feel to it.

As she thought that, her mind automatically rejected that adjective. Not abandoned.

Dead.

It felt dead.

And yet, she swore she could sense some kind of vitality. Dead, but somehow not completely.

Or, dead but not *dead*. At least not dead in the right way.

There was a persistence about it. As if dead could not properly define it. Hannah knew that she was not actually personifying the boat. What she felt was about whoever came to Kaua'i *on* that boat.

That puzzled her, though. How could someone – anyone – be dead and not dead?

That made no sense.

"Hey!" called a voice and Hannah yeeped and jumped back into her room. "Hey, lady! Wait. Please."

It was a man's voice.

Hannah peeked around the window frame and saw a man standing on the balcony two down from hers. He wore boxer shorts and a teal t-shirt with ALOHA written across it in a fanciful script. His hair was sleep-tousled and his face was bright with shock. As soon as he spotted her, he waved furiously.

"Lady, do you know what's going on?"

"I… I mean… no…"

"The hotel phones are out." He showed her his cell. "I tried calling 9-1-1, but they said the lines are busy. How can cops' lines be busy? I mean… what's happening?"

He looked to be about thirty but in the moment he sounded twelve.

"I… don't know, I'm sorry." Even she thought it sounded strange to apologize, but habits die hard. "I just woke up and—"

She didn't have to explain more than that.

There was the sound of helicopter blades and they both looked up to see two news choppers and a police helo flying almost in formation. Then the police helicopter veered off and dropped low toward a group of people who seemed to be fighting. Wrestling, really, though at thirty-one stories up it was hard to tell. Some of them had arms locked around one-another, while others were rolling around on the ground.

"Hey, the cops are here," said the man. "They'll get this shit sorted out and—"

The rest of his words were smashed away by the sound of gunfire as the helicopter opened up on the struggling crowd.

-6-

"Jesus Christ!" screamed the man.

Hannah said, "Oh dear," but for her it meant the same thing.

The police chopper hovered about fifty feet above the crowd. There were two officers kneeling in the open doorway, both of them pouring automatic fire down, with no obvious attempt to pick specific targets. They emptied magazines, dropped the magazines, slapped in new ones and kept firing.

Over and over.

The news helos were on either side of it, their cameras pointed at the cops and at what the cops were doing. Hannah could not believe what she was seeing. This was not riot control, it was mass murder.

In the pool area, bodies now floated in the water, surrounded by spreading red clouds. On the deck, people lay still or crawled brokenly. Mostly they kept fighting.

"Shit, did you see that? Lady, did you see that?"

She glanced at the man and then followed his pointing finger. There were police on the ground down there now. At least a dozen of them, and they moved forward in a shooting line, using rifles, shotguns, and handguns. They, too, fired into the crowd. They, too, did not seem to aim and instead shot anyone close.

Men.

Women.

Children.

Hannah screamed when she realized they were also *shooting the children*.

"No, dear lord, no!" She turned to the man. "They're shooting everyone."

"Jesus fuck. I can't… I mean, I just can't."

They both fell silent as the choreography far below abruptly changed. As they watched, a lot of the people who had been wrestling were now moving toward the police. Slow at first, their bodies twitching and stumbling as the cops fired at them, but despite the barrage, they began to jog and then to run.

All at once everyone seemed to be running.

Masses of people, some of whom were lying motionless only moments before, were running toward the police. Running directly into the teeth of that fusillade. They should have fallen. At that range the police couldn't possibly miss. Not a chance. And yet the people – scores of them now – kept advancing.

They saw some people go down, but from that distance it was impossible to tell what stopped them while the others kept advancing. Hannah thought she saw one get shot in the head and go down, but the melee was too wild to be sure.

The police tried to hold their line, but there was no chance. Not as the attacking crowd grew larger and larger. People in party clothes and people in sleepwear; people wearing torn rags and people totally naked. Running into the gunfire, accepting it, their flesh seeming to absorb the bullets.

Then they washed up against the line of officers like a tsunami. The sheer weight of them slammed the police back, breaking their line. From then on the people broke into smaller packs to chase individual cops and tackle them, drag them down, pile atop them, and…

And…

"Oh dear," whispered Hannah.

The gunfire continued from the helicopter and from a few islands of resistance, but most of the shooting was over, the police unable to make even a token defense.

A few seconds later the police snipers in the helicopter stopped firing. Whether they were out of ammunition or out of hope was impossible to determine. The helo rose in a high, climbing turn and fled from sight, their rotors pulling smoke from the burning half of the hotel.

Hannah and the young man stared at each other.

"What's happening?" he asked again.

"I don't know," she answered.

She went inside and fetched her cell, which had been charging on the bedside table. She brought it back to the balcony and by the light of the blaze punched the buttons to load Google and search for news.

She did not have to search for local news.

There was no need for that.

Whatever was happening there in Kaua'i was happening everywhere. San Diego and Los Angeles. Seattle. Tucson. Chicago. Philadelphia and New York. Minneapolis.

Not only in the States. London, Paris, Moscow, Rome…

They were all burning.

They were all dying.

Whatever this was, it was consuming the whole world.

When she looked up, intending to tell the young man, she saw that he had copied her. He was also looking at his cell. She saw how wide his eyes were. In the fire's glow, she could see the tears on his cheeks.

She heard him say, "Mom. Dad. Carly…"

It was on that last name where his voice broke. Carly. A sister? A girlfriend? Wife?

Then he abruptly turned and looked into his room. He cut her a quick look. "Someone's at the door. Maybe they can help."

He dashed inside even as Hannah tried to tell him not to go.

-7-

Hannah waited out there, beginning to cough a little as the wind changed, bringing smoke her way. The news helicopters were gone, moved off into someone else's sky. There were almost no screams coming up from below. Not from the pool area, at least. From elsewhere, yes. From open balcony windows.

And then from the open window of the balcony two down from hers.

It was a blend of two screams, really. A man's scream. The young man, shrieking in pain and in terror. And then a duller cry. More feral, more animalistic. A sound not of fear or panic but of need. A hungry moan.

A moment later a figure stepped out on the balcony.

It wasn't the young man. It was Trish, the woman she'd met and dined with last night. Trish wore a filmy red negligée that hung heavy with red wetness. Her small breasts were visible through the sheer fabric, and the medium brown skin was streaked with crimson. The skin looked wrong. Irregular. Bruised and torn.

Bitten.

As Trish stepped out onto the balcony, she held something to her mouth that dripped fat scarlet drops. Hannah gagged.

It was a hand and part of a forearm. A jagged end of bone protruded from the ripped flesh. The hand was closed, the fingers still clutching the cell phone.

Trish tore off a piece of meat and chewed it with the slow, steady rhythm of a metronome. There was no expression at all on her face. Her eyes were vacant. The sounds she made were of chewing and moans of hunger.

Hannah screamed then.

It was the first loud sound she'd made. She was not prone to screaming under any circumstance.

This was different. She screamed very loud and she screamed very long.

Trish's head snapped up and she lost her grip on her grisly meal. The hand fell, hit the railing and bounced off, falling all the way to the ground far below. Trish's dull eyes seemed to reclaim focus as she stared at Hannah. Drawn by the noise. Drawn by other things as well.

She lunged forward, hands reaching, fingers clawing at the air between them even as her hips struck the balcony rail. It was too high for her to spill over, but she kept lunging, kept reaching, kept rebounding from the rail and repeating exactly the same actions. It was relentless.

There was a sound behind Hannah. In her room?

She turned fast, but no…the sound had not come from her suite. It was a thud as if something heavy and soft had struck her door. It came again. And again. Like a hand striking while limp. Sloppy but urgent.

Hannah looked at the door. It was a strong hotel door with the locked secured.

She looked at Trish, who was two balconies away and unable to reach her.

She looked down at the feeding frenzy around the pool.

She looked at her cell.

"Oh dear," she murmured.

Hannah could feel something inside of her change. Snap. Break.

"Oh dear."

Without knowing she was going to do it, she moved inside the room and slid the French door shut. She stood in the living room, still as a statue, while her fracturing mind tried to find a way forward. A way out.

The balcony was too high. She could not bear the thought of leaping. She didn't have the courage, even now, for that.

So she walked into her bedroom and through to her ensuite. Her makeup kit was there, and next to it a small, zippered bag with her medications. There was simvastatin and Lisinopril, Levothyroxine and Omeprazole, Hydrochlorothiazide and baby aspirin. There was almost a full bottle of eszopiclone. Sleeping pills. She also had half a bottle of Vicodin.

Hannah took all of it over to the bed and sat down with it.

The pounding continued.

The smoke outside was getting so thick now that everything beyond her sheer curtains was a uniform orange-gray. The gunfire was all but gone.

There was a full bottle of spring water – a courtesy of the hotel – on her nightstand.

"Oh dear," she said once more. Then she poured the sleeping pills and Vicodin into her palm, took a breath, held it, let it out, then popped the whole pile of them into her mouth, quickly washing it all down with water.

Through the open doorway to her living room she saw the first wisps of smoke that had to be coming in under her door. The pounding was louder. Two people now. Maybe three.

Hannah lay down on her bed and pulled the covers up to her chin.

How long will it take, she wondered.

Minutes later, as the room slowly began to lose focus, she nodded. Quicker than she thought. The pounding went on, but the door held. The smoke crawled along the ceiling now.

She thought of poor Trish. And that young man.

She thought about the previous day.

It really had been the best day of her life.

As sleep took her down, she hoped that was what she would dream about. For as long as she could dream.

There was a smile on Hannah's face as she slipped down and down and down.

STORY INSPIRATION: I travel quite a bit, usually on book-related business, but sometimes for pleasure and relaxation. We

writers never take our creative process off line. Not really. As a writer of horror, apocalyptic SF, and similar themes, I have many times wondered what would happen if a disaster or an apocalyptic event happened while we were all stuck in a hotel or resort somewhere. There are so many stories that could be told. And often – while lounging by the pool or dining in a hotel bar – I've played the "what if?" game of looking at my fellow vacationers and conjuring up details about who they are, why they're there, and what would happen if things went suddenly and completely wrong. The central character of my story, "The Best Day" (©2025 Jonathan Maberry Productions) was someone I observed while in Kaua'i as keynote for a writers conference. I overheard her tell the couple seated next to her at the bar that this was her best day ever. It was all I heard of the conversation, but it stuck with me. What if it really *was* her best day ever. What did that say about her, her life, and her future? TIKI HORROR is the perfect vehicle for telling that story.

Wish You Weren't Here

Lisa Morton

Gabe stared at the creature before him, with its spear held in one bulky fist, mouth wide and ringed with thick fangs, eyes glowering at him, and he thought, *I am so over this shit.*

He had to admit that the wood carving possessed some artistry; he could see how it might have inspired fear in an adversary. He had no idea if it was supposed to represent a particular deity, but he could imagine the general idea was, *My god is fiercer than your god.*

"Lucky, party of two."

His brother jumped in front of him, following the petite Asian waitress as she led them from the restaurant's waiting area, which was little more than a booth in front of an unmarked door with only the single tiki figure standing guard beside it, hinting at what lay beyond. They were led down a dim corridor lined with more man-sized tiki figures into a central dining room ringed with bamboo-divided booths. Life-sized papier-mâché parrots on swings and artificial leis hung overhead, with light provided by Japanese glass floats in nets illuminated from within, and the forty-gallon aquariums above every booth glowing violet under their black light hoods. The walls were covered in abalone shells and vintage travel posters, the air smelled of roasting pork and rum. Lucky was grinning from ear to ear as they sat, the stoic server placing menus before them, and then leaning in to light a candle in a faux coconut shell holder. The only other customers were two men at a booth opposite them, laughing and talking too loudly for Gabe's taste.

After the waitress stepped away, Lucky said, "Okay, I know how you feel about all this, but even you gotta admit this place fucking rocks."

Gabe nearly grimaced. So Lucky *did* know this whole trip hadn't exactly been a high adventure for his little brother. The whole tiki thing was definitely Lucky's vibe, not Gabe's. Gabe, in fact, had never confessed how he almost dreaded visits to Lucky's apartment, decked out as it was in floor to ceiling Polynesian fantasy. When Gabe had suggested this vacation together – "C'mon, it's just three days! We haven't done anything crazy together in ages and maybe you'll actually decide the whole tiki thing is pretty cool after all." – Gabe's immediate inclination had been a firm and resounding, "No."

But Paul – er, "Lucky," the name his brother had chosen for himself because he somehow thought it exotic – had been right: they *hadn't* done anything together since they'd buried Mom.

My mom, Gabe inwardly corrected, *not Paul's.*

His mom, Lidia, was their father's second wife; Lucky had been six when they'd married, Gabe had come along a year later. Because Lidia had been Filipino, Lucky loved introducing Gabe as his "Pacific Islander half-brother." Gabe knew that Lucky thought that somehow gave him whatever passed for street cred in tiki culture. He found that idea particularly repellent and hoped it wasn't true, even while his gut told him it was.

But he'd said yes when Lucky had invited him to ConTiki25, "A three-day celebration of all things TIki!" What the hell – the convention was held in San Diego, an easy two-hour drive south of their respective L.A. homes, and since Eric had left, Gabe's social calendar wasn't exactly full.

Gabe tried to focus on the menu, but the pang of losing Eric a month ago had been especially intense over the last day, as Gabe had tried to find enjoyment in the endless parade of Hawaiian shirts and exotica music that Lucky lived for. "Your mom's great but your bro," Eric used to say after get-togethers with Gabe's family, "has serious white savior issues and is a bully to boot."

Gabe had always giggled in agreement in the sanctity of their own tiki-free apartment where they'd lived and loved together, until that night that Eric had abruptly announced he'd met someone else and moved out, leaving Gabe shell-shocked, grief-stricken, trying (unsuccessfully) to drown his grief in Cosmopolitans.

"Hey," Lucky said, drawing Gabe's attention back to the present, "whattaya say we split the Scorpion for two?"

Gabe hadn't even looked at the menu yet. When he did, he saw, amidst all the graphics of palm trees and half-naked villagers, one side of the single page was drinks, the other food. The final item under the cocktails was the "Scorpion Bowl: the classic tiki drink of rum, brandy, gin, orgeat, simple syrup, and fresh lime and orange juices, served in a bowl with two straws." It was probably meant to be a couple's drink, but he shrugged, agreeing. "Sounds fun."

Flipping the menu to the other side, Lucky sniggered and said, "And we *gotta* get a puupuu platter."

"Sure." It was only a little past four in the afternoon, the drink would be strong, but Gabe figured what the fuck – he didn't have to drive, and chilling here in the dark, cool restaurant, was better than being in the throngs of tiki conventioneers outside.

The waitress reappeared, took the order, and vanished. Gabe found himself gazing at the aquariums that surrounded them: there had to be two-dozen of them, purring away with soft bubbling sounds. Something about the aquariums nagged at Gabe until he finally realized: "That's weird – there are no fish in any of the fish-tanks."

Lucky looked around. "You're right," he replied after a few seconds, "Although a better question might be: how did they get all these aquariums set up in a pop-up restaurant?"

"I'll bet," Gabe replied, "that it's not really a pop-up. We're still in the hotel, right? This is probably something they're about to roll out as a new permanent restaurant. I mean, with only one café they totally need it, right?"

Lucky shrugged. "I guess." He eyed the clutter around them appreciatively. "It's a lot of stuff for a pop-up."

They'd found out about this place only because a dealer in the vendor's room had leaned forward, handed them a flyer, and smiled knowingly. The flyer called it "Trader Don's: A Pop-Up TikiSpeakEasy"; at the bottom of the ad, a cheesy, recycled '60's-style cartoon of a girl in a grass skirt was accompanied by the slogan, "Don't you wish you were here?"

No, Gabe thought. *I wish I* wasn't *here.*

Lucky had pulled his phone out and booked them a reservation within seconds of receiving the flyer.

The waitress entered the room bearing a tray of mai tais, which she set down before the men in the other booth. As she walked away, they eyed her lasciviously. One, a burly man with a grizzled beard and overgrown brows, said, "No wonder they call it a 'pop-up'."

The other man, smaller, wearing glasses, with a narrow face, snorted.

Gabe inwardly groaned. If he'd heard that, he knew the waitress must have. But she gave no sign, remaining impassive as she exited through a swinging door that led to the kitchen.

Leaning across the table, Lucky whispered, "Those guys over there…see the one in the blue shirt?"

Glancing over, Gabe verified that the smaller, beardless and bespectacled man wore a blue Hawaiian shirt patterned with flying musical notes and records. "Yeah."

"He's known as Doctor Vinyl, supposed to have the world's biggest collection of exotica LP's."

Looking the man over, Gabe could easily imagine him in a den surrounded by cases crammed with old albums, ignoring his wife's calls to come out and help her with something as he turned up the volume on the ukulele music.

"Who's the joker with him?"

"Oh," Lucky answered, "that guy's a record dealer, Fred something. He's probably hoping to score a big sale with the Doc."

After a beat, Gabe asked, "Does it seem weird that there's only four of us here? I mean, it's a tiki pop-up bar at a tiki convention."

"Maybe we're just here early and the place will be mobbed for dinner."

"Probably," Gabe agreed. But something increasingly tugged at the back of his head, a sense of *wrongness* that went beyond the loud, ogling dick in the other booth.

Gabe turned his attention back to the aquariums, which he realized unnerved him more than the sexism on display. Why stage an elaborate set-up with dozens of *empty* tanks? Then he realized the tanks weren't strictly empty: each one had a number of odd, fleshy, tubular stalks within, like sea anemones without the flower-like tops. As he watched the one located above their booth, one of the stalks expanded, beginning at the base and moving up. The top opened and burped out a thumbnail-sized semi-translucent white sphere that floated to the surface like a weightless pearl.

"What the fuck..."

Lucky followed his gaze, saw nothing. "What?"

"Okay, so, Mr. Tiki Expert, you tell me: what the fuck are those things in the aquariums?"

Peering at the one above their booth, Lucky frowned. "I don't know." Half-rising to get closer, he leaned forward and peered in. "Are those things alive –" He broke off, surprised, as another one of the creatures produced a colorless ball. "What the fuck..." He dug inside his pocket for his phone, thumbed the camera app, started recording.

Gabe sat, trying to remain impassive, but the tanks made him uneasy in some ancient, instinctive way.

Lucky finished recording, stopped the app, and then left the booth to walk the room. He strode around the entire periphery, hunched over to look into each tank, before returning to their booth. "That," he said, sliding across the leatherette bench, "is weird as fuck. Every one of those tanks is full of those things, all burping out those little... whatever the fuck they are."

A door behind the bar opened and a man stepped out; he was built like an ox, wearing a Trader Don's tank top, with a wrestler's huge upper arms, and when he glanced at them Gabe saw that his face was heavily tattooed around the chin, as were his shoulders. The word *Maori* leapt into Gabe's head.

The Maori man carried a carved wooden bowl in one hand and a large spoon in the other, and, starting with the first aquarium, he tilted up the hood, reached in with the spoon, and lovingly scooped out all the globules floating on the surface of the water, moving with tender care. Lowering the hood, he walked on, repeating his actions at each aquarium until he'd retrieved the spheres from all of them. When he marched past Lucky and Gabe's booth, skipping their aquarium, Gabe asked, "Are you from New Zealand?"

The man answered only, "Aotearoa," before moving on. At the kitchen door, he paused and offered a scowl so fierce that for an instant Gabe feared for his safety. Then, wordlessly, he retreated, the door swinging shut behind him.

"Maybe we should go," Gabe said.

Before Lucky could answer, the waitress – who Gabe now realized also had chin tattoos and was likely Maori – deposited the Scorpion on the table between them; served in a ceramic bowl sculpted with crouching, grimacing figures, it featured a floating center garnish of mint and orchid blossom, and two long bamboo straws. "Your drink, gentlemen. I'll be back with your appetizers."

She was about to turn when Lucky said, "Oh, excuse me, miss…" He waited until she looked down at him, then he asked, "We were wondering about what's in the aquariums…"

A slight frown crossed her features. "Oh, we bring those with us from our home."

"What are the little balls they blurp out?"

She appeared to consider for a few seconds before answering, "It's hard to explain." She turned and walked out, once again watched by the grinning bearded man in the other booth.

"Let's drink," Lucky said as he grasped a straw.

Gabe took the other between his fingers, surprised at its heft – it was bamboo and wider than most drink straws. "Cheers," he said, lifting the straw.

Lucky touched his straw to Gabe's and they both maneuvered the bamboo past the floating arrangement of leaves and blossoms. Gabe took a sip but found the straw blocked by something. He pulled away, tapped it, tried again.

Blocked.

He sucked harder.

Something rushed through the straw and into his mouth.

He blinked in surprise before examining the object with his tongue. It was soft and spongy like boba, about the same size. When he bit into it, his mouth filled with an unidentifiable sweetness; not sugary but a taste like the scent of the orchid.

"Whoa," Lucky said, grimacing as he pulled back in surprise. "That's like the stuff in bubble tea at the bottom but it tastes like meat."

Gabe was about to question him when a cry sounded out from across the room. It was the bearded man – Fred something – lurching up from the table, unsteady. "Fuck," he said, his arms extending to steady himself.

The tattooed man who'd passed along the aquariums rushed into the room and was instantly at Fred's side, as if he'd been waiting for this. He wedged a shoulder under Fred, put a beefy arm around the man's waist, and steered him toward the main entrance, down the long, dim corridor lined with tiki statues.

Lucky chuckled, said, "I wonder how many of those mai tais he had."

Glancing at the man's table, where his companion now sat alone, nursing his drink, Gabe said, "There's only one glass on his side, and it's still half full."

"Maybe they've had to clear the table a few times."

"Maybe." But Gabe wasn't convinced. The guy had been loud and obnoxious when they'd entered, but he hadn't been drunk.

Lucky took another pull on his straw and frowned, chewing, speaking around the mouthful. "The drink's great, but what the fuck is *this* stuff?" He grabbed a cocktail napkin and spit out a glob of whitish material

"You said it tastes like meat?" Gabe asked.

"Yeah. Did you get one?"

Nodding, Gabe said, "I did, but...well, there must be different flavors then because mine was sweet. Not quite like boba, but not that far off."

"Damn, bro, I had two and mine both tasted like an undercooked burger."

Gabe broke off his response to watch the tattooed man (*the bouncer*, he guessed) re-enter the room…alone. He wondered where he'd taken Fred; he hadn't been gone long enough to accompany him all the way to a hotel room or a car. Surely he hadn't simply taken the man outside and left him somewhere.

The drunk's friend, who Lucky had called Doc, sat in the booth, unmoving, staring forward and down. The bouncer went to him, pulled him out of the booth, and marched him out of the room, legs moving stiffly, no response except…as they walked past Gabe on their way out, Gabe saw the collector's eyes were frozen, unblinking, wide in terror.

Then they were gone.

"Okay, bro, ya know what? I think we should…" Gabe's suggestion died as he saw Lucky quivering silently, a whole-body tremor.

"Lucky?"

His brother didn't respond but tears escaped his eyes.

Gabe stood, moved around the table and leaned over his brother, hands on his shoulders. "Hey, bro, c'mon, don't scare me like this…"

Lucky didn't answer, just quietly shook.

Gabe shouted his brother's name, tried tugging on his arm, but nothing worked. He turned, cried out, "Help! Something's wrong with my brother! HELP!"

No one came.

Intending to call 911, he pulled out his phone, but when it fell from his fingers he watched as if the world had shifted into slow motion: the phone fell, fell, taking minutes to hit the floor, miles distant, screen glowing in the gloom. He thought about retrieving it but found the prospect daunting, impossible. He spun, staggering, and came to a halt before one of the aquariums where the small stalk-like creatures continued to release white spheres (*eggs*) and he knew what had been in the bottom of the drink.

Poisoned. We've been poisoned.

He willed his feet to lead him away, any direction, and he thankfully found himself in the entry corridor, lined with wooden tiki figures, but illuminated now in vivid colors…or was it his vision that had changed? He found himself facing one that was broader than some of the others, with wide brows and a carving at the bottom of the head that looked like a long beard. Beside that figure stood a smaller one with clawed fingers clutching a round…shield?

No…it was a record. A vinyl album.

The larger of the two figures shuddered.

Gabe heard himself screaming – or uttering a choked cry – and then the bouncer was there, taking him back to his booth. He was placed there, no control of his body left. He couldn't fight or stand or even move his head. He could only see that the other side of the booth was empty now, his brother gone.

He wondered if he was dying, but he wasn't in pain. He could only wait, expecting to feel something soon, something awful, and he tried to prepare himself, but…

Instead, he felt *good*. Liberated from his body, his consciousness expanding past the bounds of flesh. His entire life replayed in his head (*Isn't this what they say happens when you die?*):

He saw himself as a child, beloved by his mother, ignored by his father, and bullied by his half-brother when he was still Paul, the only child deprived of that status by the arrival of this invader. Away from home, Paul had teased him, beat him, surrounded by cruel friends who laughed at him. Gabriel had retreated, a shy child who opened up only around his mother, relieved when adulthood had arrived and he could move out, away from his brother. College, graduation, jobs all flashed by; he saw his friends and partners, he saw Eric, whom he'd loved more fiercely than he'd thought possible. He saw Paul-now-Lucky, steamrolling through a series of meaningless jobs and short affairs before the women realized he had no interest in *them,* and Lucky had found the obsession that gave his life some meaning, the consuming passion for a fantasy culture that had never truly existed.

Except…in some way it *had,* and now Gabe was here, living *that* fantasy, where "tiki" could be a figure or the name of the First Man, another world's Adam, and that was *him.* He, half-Islander, had somehow been judged and found worthy. His brother, and all the others, would be wooden warriors, forever brooding and protective, but protective of *him,* of Gabriel/Tiki, of He who had been promised, who would take back a kingdom for his chosen people.

When he could turn his head again, he saw the waitress and bouncer kneeling before him, their heads lowered in respect. Testing his legs, he found his willpower had returned and he felt *strong,* even powerful. He blessed his people, watched as they rose and looked at him with shining eyes.

He wondered where to start, and remembered what lay just outside this room. It was time to go.

He had a lot of work in front of him, after all.

STORY INSPIRATION: My inspiration was a restaurant - now sadly long gone - here in Southern California called Bahooka. Even though it was far to the east (in Rosemead), we used to occasionally make the trip and it was always worth it. It was a tiki-themed restaurant with over 100 aquariums, and had a famous grouper

named Rufus who lived in a very large tank near the front. They kept it (of course) quite dark, so it felt like it was lit by the purplish glow from the aquariums, giving the whole place a strange feel.

A Theme Room for the Lost At Heart

Gwendolyn Kiste

It's nearly sundown, the Pacific tide lapping nervously at the beach, when I pull into the motel parking lot. There are only two other cars here and not much else, not unless you count cracks in the pavement and weeds sprouting up in every corner as signs of life.

Nearby, a banner sags from a burned-out neon marquee. *New Theme Rooms Now Open*

Theme rooms. I didn't know hotels still did that sort of thing. It seems like the kind of kitsch that went out of style along with heart-shaped bathtubs and shag carpet. A relic of last century when little roadside spots like this one had to do something to compete.

Now there's nothing left to compete for. So far, the only other business that still looks open is a bar across the street. I console myself that at least it's not a dry town.

As I climb out of the car, I gaze down Highway 101, squinting up at the next curve. It's a road that never seems to end. That's not all bad. This is my first time on this road, but I already like it on the coast at night, the way the redwoods tower overhead, guarding the gloom. Guarding you. I don't know what I need protecting from, but I'm sure those trees will do the job right.

My phone buzzes in my purse. A new text message from Carrie.

Still at work. Promise I'll be leaving soon. Don't have too much fun without me!

My chest tightens, because I already know I won't have any fun at all. Not here, not by myself. This was supposed to be a girls' trip, but that's hard to do when your traveling companion never bothers to leave work. Carrie, the most determined girl I've ever met. She's my so -called best friend, the only person who's put up with me since elementary school. Through caps and gowns and college degrees we never use. We stood by each other for afternoon strolls down the aisle as well as Monday morning trips to the courtroom when our happily ever afters didn't work out.

Carrie got there first both times, marrying her husband Del three years before I married Chad, and because she's always the trendsetter of the two of us, she got divorced three years earlier, too.

It's my turn now, my marriage officially deposited in the dumpster as of last Friday. My Prince Charming who turned out to be a false alarm.

That's why I'm here. This whole vacation was Carrie's idea, a consolation prize in the shape of a vacation.

"To get your mind off things for a while," she said, and to be fair, it's already done just that. Finding my way here took all my concentration. This town isn't on any map, at least not that I found.

"Just use the nearest zip code," Carrie told me. "It'll get you there. Or it'll get you close enough."

Close enough. That's not exactly how I want to start this vacation – with no more than a good guess. But I never argue with Carrie. There isn't much point. Once she's made up her mind, there's no going back. She decided we were relaxing in an oceanside town nobody's ever heard of, and that was that.

With my head down, I slip into the motel office. Inside, there's a woman loitering behind the registration desk. She looks about forty, about my age, her brow knit, her red hair pinned back from her face.

I hesitate in the doorway. "This is Santa Mar, right?"

The woman nods, her eyes gone gray.

I shrug. "I guess this is where we're staying."

"It sure is," she says, and gives me a toothy grin. "We're the only motel in town."

I can't help but wonder if that's a good thing or a bad thing.

I hand over my credit card for incidentals, trying not to stare at the stain on the ceiling. "I've never been to California before," I murmur.

She raises a thin eyebrow at me. "Is that so?" She asks the question almost like a challenge.

I fold and unfold my hands in front of me. "I always thought I'd visit sooner than this," I say, as if I owe her an explanation. "I just never got around to it."

"Well, you're here now. That's what counts." She passes me my room key. "My name's Angie, if you need anything."

I force a smile. "I'm Sarah."

"I know," she says, before disappearing into the back room.

Clowns. My theme room is all about clowns. Clowns on the light switch, clowns on the bedsheets, a whole family of clowns in a mural on the wall. They're smiling and they're frowning, their lips curled up or their mouths agape in silent laughter or maybe silent screams. There's red hair and green hair and even some blue hair, all of it sprouting out like clouds.

I've never liked clowns. I've never met one person who did. And I can't imagine why they gave me this room. There's got to be a better theme than a nightmare.

But it's nearly nine o'clock in the evening, and it's too late to argue. My stomach gurgling, I walk across the street to the half-derelict bar. It's got a banner of its own slung across the awning.

Now Serving Our New Menu

I wonder what was wrong with the old menu. I also wonder why everything is being renovated when it seems like this town is ready to close up permanently at any moment.

Inside, the place is even worse than I expect. Crushed peanut shells on the floor, a broken jukebox in the corner. On the far wall, there's a single circular window like the porthole of a ship. It's small and smudged, but you can still see right through it. Out into the moonlight. Out across the sand and toward the ocean.

My hands in my pockets, I order a burger at the counter. Then I slide into the booth closest to the window and tap out a message to Carrie.

any updates?

I wait ten whole minutes, staring blankly at my phone the entire time, but she never replies. My shoulders sagging, I lean back, my hand over my eyes, and regret every choice I've ever made. Especially the choices that ended up with me sitting in this gritty bar with only the lone bartender to keep me company.

As always, I've got Carrie to thank for this. She lives in California now, about an hour north of here. Her gift to herself when she got divorced.

"I need a change of scenery," she told me, and then moved all the way across the whole damn country.

"You know if you wanted a change, you could have just gone to a neighboring city," I said, but by then, it was too late. She'd lost her husband, and I'd lost my best friend.

"You should come visit," she kept telling me. That is, until my divorce was finalized, and that *should* suddenly became *need to*. So this morning, I drove up from the south, from San Francisco with an airport that's so sprawling it'll make your nose bleed. I don't travel much these days – until last night's red eye, I hadn't been on a plane since college. But Carrie's always pushed me to try new things, to try to be someone I'm not. I should tell her no, but sometimes, it's fun to pretend.

The bartender brings me my burger. It's rarer than I like, red juices pooling on the plate, but I don't bother to complain. From the looks of it, there's nowhere else to eat in this town anyway.

Meanwhile, the bartender's still lingering at my table, his eyes set on the smudged window. "Santa Mar used to be quite the town," he says. "Department stores and diners on every corner and even a year-round carnival. All kinds of magic in a place like this."

I shiver suddenly for no reason. "Where did all the magic go?"

"Maybe you can tell me," he says before wandering off.

I have no idea what he means by that, and I'm not too eager to find out. I inhale my burger, the nearly raw meat curdling in my belly, before dropping a twenty on the table and darting out the door.

On the other side of the street, Angie's hanging out near the motel office, smoking a cigarette down to the filter. I scurry across the highway, and I'm almost standing right next to her by the time I notice it. How there's one fewer car in the parking lot now.

All at once, I'm shivering again. "It's so lonely here."

Angie lets out a small laugh. "You'd know something about that, wouldn't you?"

My jaw sets. "I'm not lonely," I say. "I'm staying with someone. My best friend. She's supposed to meet me here soon."

"That's nice," Angie says and crushes out her cigarette.

Disappointment clenches inside me. I don't know what kind of reaction I expected. Was she supposed to congratulate me on having a friend? The truth is I just don't want her to look at me and see what everyone else sees. A broken heart. A lost cause.

Angie starts back toward the office door.

"You'll be here all night?" I call after her.

"I sure will be," she says, not even bothering to look back. "Don't worry about your friend. I'll give her a key just as soon as she gets here."

The clowns are different now. I'm sure of it. The moment I open the door to my room, it's like I interrupted them, like I caught them in the act, the echo of their strident giggles still reverberating through the walls.

I seize up in the middle of the room, watching them from every angle, turning slowly in circles, as though I might see them move again out of the corner of my eye. Sneaking back to their places on the light switch and the bedsheets.

But everything's gone entirely still in the room.

My skin prickles, as I crawl into bed. "It's nothing," I whisper, and close my eyes. Sometimes, the darkness is safer than turning on the light.

All night, I dream of carnivals. Popcorn butter smeared on my fingers, a mouthful of cloying cotton candy clogging up my throat.

And the clowns. They're everywhere, their laughter ringing in my ears like a curse. Their clumsy hands reaching out for me, desperate to take hold of my body. Desperate to pull me into the dark.

I open my mouth to scream, but no sound comes out.

The next morning, I wake up alone. Carrie never arrived in the night. I check my phone, and there she is, making her useless excuses.

Work got the best of me.

I'm so sorry, Sarah.

I've tried calling the motel. Nobody's answering. Don't you get service out there?

I can't help but roll my eyes. *i'm texting you now, aren't i?*

Right. Yeah. Of course.

A long moment passes, and I keep watching for the three little dots to pop up on the screen. But she doesn't type another message.

I wheeze in a heavy breath and tap out the only question that matters to me right now.

where are you?

Working again is all she says.

and when will you be done working?

Soon.

how soon?

Soon. I promise.

I can already guess what that means. Another night alone in this place.

With my hands shaking, I toss my phone on the nightstand, and for an instant, the clowns on the lampshade look like they're smiling a little bit wider. As though there's nothing funnier in the world than me and my trainwreck of a vacation.

My eyes blur with tears, and I promise myself I won't cry, I can't cry, I have no reason to cry.

I pull on yesterday's clothes and trudge down to the motel office. Angie's behind the desk again. Part of me is curious if she ever gets a single shift off.

"My best friend's been calling the motel," I say. "Why didn't you tell me?"

"Nobody's called here." She tilts her head at me. "In fact, nobody's called here all week."

"That's not what she told me."

Angie shrugs. "Maybe she's got the wrong number."

Rage rises up the back of my throat. She won't admit she's wrong, that she hasn't been bothering to answer her own phone.

I lean against the counter, my fingernails digging into the phony woodgrain. "I can't stay in my room."

Angie flips through the pages of an out-of-date magazine, the pages curled and yellowed. "What's the problem?"

"The décor," I say. "It's impossible to sleep somewhere like that."

She shakes her head. "There's only one other unit available right now."

"I'll take it."

"I'm not sure you're going to like it any better."

"I'm sure it'll be fine," I say, and as she passes me a new room key, all I can think is how this vacation can't get any worse.

Mermaids. My new room is decked out in mermaids.

This shouldn't be so bad. After all, mermaids tend to be a whole lot friendlier than clowns. Or so you'd think. But these aren't your typical Disney mermaids. Sure, a few of them are smiling, their perky visages gazing out at me from yet another mural on the wall.

A couple of the mermaids, however, aren't quite as gregarious. They're the kind of beasts from folklore. The ones with teeth and claws and a song that could lure you to your doom. There are two of them on the nightstand, small stone statues with their mouths open wide, everything about them looking ready and ravenous.

I tell myself it's nothing, just a trick of the light. But when I close my eyes, I swear I hear them calling to me.

Breakfast. I need breakfast. That's why I'm thinking these things: because I'm hungry. It's that simple.

Across the street, the bar is open early, and I order a plate of scrambled eggs before taking a seat in the same booth as last night. I'm starting to think of it as my booth. As if I've lived here for ages and have a right to claim things as my own.

The same bartender is working again today, and I wonder if nobody gets a day off in this town. He brings me a lukewarm plate of slop, but even as I pick up a smudged fork, he doesn't walk away. He's back to gazing out the window.

"You know the townsfolk chose this place because of the ocean," he says. "The views are supposedly the most beautiful along the whole coast."

I grip my fork tighter. "If that's true," I say, "then why isn't this town on the map?"

"Because it's a secret." He turns to me, a smile creeping across his face. "*Our* secret."

And with that, he shuffles across the floor and into the backroom. My eyes wide, I shovel rubbery eggs into my mouth and toss a ten on the table before bolting for the door.

I hate it here. I hate everything about this strange little town. But even as I make my way down the empty sidewalk, I keep thinking how this place wouldn't be so bad if Carrie was here. She and I could always make the best of the worst things in life. The dorm room the size of a broom closet. The cocktails that were more water than whiskey. The men that came and went from our lives like they were no more than passing fads.

"I'll figure out where we belong one day," I told her once, and she just threw her head back and laughed.

"Not if I figure it out first," she said, and then it was my turn to smile.

But now all Carrie can think about are spreadsheets and timesheets, deadlines and dead eyes from working too many hours. I'm not even sure exactly what she does. Something with accounting at an arts nonprofit.

"It's a living," she always tells me with a sigh, and I wish I knew what that was like. My last job as an adjunct laid me off three months ago, and nobody will do more than glance at my resume these days. The world's moved on. I wish someone had told me how to move on with it.

Nobody told this town to move on either. It's simply withered away in plain sight. I go walking through the remnants of downtown, peering up at the abandoned buildings, trying to guess what they once were. A courthouse, a barbershop, a proper diner. I hesitate in front of one of the store windows. If I focus long enough, I can almost see the outlines of gaunt faces staring back at me. They're not ghosts, not exactly. More like echoes. Like memories.

These are the townspeople who came before, the ones that time forgot. It's like they're waiting to wake up again, the same way those mermaids are waiting back in my room.

With a shiver, I keep moving, telling myself I hear nothing behind me. Telling myself I certainly don't hear them calling my name.

I spend the rest of the morning on the beach, my feet sinking into the sand, the ocean murmuring melodies I almost recognize. Then in the afternoon, I hike along a narrow path, up into a grove of towering redwoods, so glorious it makes your heart ache.

Safe. I'm safe here. That's what I tell myself. At least until I retreat back to my motel room. Back to the mermaids who never stop hungering.

Tonight I dream of them, those long fingers like claws, those teeth like fresh razorblades. Their tails whip out of the water like the lash of a riding crop, and they croon to me in voices sweeter than cotton candy.

I'm here, I say to them, wandering through a fog. *I'm here, and I want to stay with you.*

But all the mermaids just giggle and swim off into the darkness, never looking back.

Even the monsters don't want me now.

When I open my eyes, there's something buzzing on the nightstand.

I manage to sit up, my head heavy, my hands grasping for the phone. It's Carrie again. Of course it is. Nobody else texts me. I squint at the screen, reading and reading her message, my stomach stitched in two.

I'm so so sorry, but I don't think I'm going to make it. But try to enjoy your vacation! You deserve it, Sarah. You really do.

I sink backward onto the bed, my shoulders slumped, my body gone numb. This is the last thing I wanted. To spend four nights alone, and in the middle of nowhere. My flight doesn't leave for another two days, and I can't even drive back down to San Francisco and find another room. I used up all my savings to fly out to California. I'm broke and broken-hearted and I'm stuck here until the end of the week.

"How did you find this town at all?" I asked Carrie last Friday when I called her for directions.

"I was just driving around one day and stumbled across it," she said. "It's really special. You'll see when you get there."

Special. That's one word for it. But that doesn't mean I need to like it. And it also doesn't mean I need to spend another moment here with this silly décor. With these mermaids that laugh at me even in my dreams.

"I want another room," I say, bursting into the motel office.

It's Angie behind the desk again. Who else would it be? "I'm not sure we've got anything to your liking," she says and turns the page of that same ancient magazine.

"I want another room," I repeat.

"What if I don't have another room?" she asks.

I motion outside to the empty parking lot. "There's nobody else here, Angie. You and I both know it."

She doesn't say another word. Instead, she reaches for a key she keeps under the desk. Then she points out the window to the very last room, tucked back in the far corner of the motel.

Outside, the air is chilled as I take the long walk across the parking lot. I want to see this place. I want to see what new nightmares await me.

With my breath twisted in my chest, I put the key in the door and sneak into the room like a criminal.

Except it isn't at all what I expect. There's nothing here. No clowns on the walls or mermaids on the lampshade. Everything's white and bland as oatmeal. Like an unblemished canvas.

When I march back to the office, Angie doesn't even bother to look up. "Still not happy?"

I gaze at her, dread churning in me. "Why is the room empty?"

"You don't like clowns or mermaids, so this was the next best thing."

"That's fine," I say, fidgeting in front of her. "I just don't understand why it's empty."

"It isn't finished yet."

I blink back at her. "Why did you give me an unfinished room?"

"Because," she starts to say, but the phone on the wall rings once, and she answers it.

I seize up, waiting to see if it's Carrie, waiting to see if she's changed her mind, but I can tell by the smile on Angie's face that it's an old friend. Not my friend. Not that I really seem to have any friends now.

On my way out the door, I glance up at the ceiling. That dark stain from before is gone.

I wander across the street and out onto the beach. The weather is cooler today, and my flesh prickles against the saltwater spray.

My phone is still in my pocket. I take it out and ask Carrie one more question. The only other thing I can think of.

why did you choose this place?

I expect I won't hear from her for hours, but she answers right away.

Because I thought you'd like it there. A long moment before she adds, *Don't you like it, Sarah?*

I want to write back to her, to explain what's been happening here, but then my head whirls and I suddenly can't keep my eyes open. My phone wilting in my hand, I curl up on the sand, and the world falls away from me.

I don't dream of the empty room this time. I dream of Carrie instead. Of what it was like when we were girls, back when we had hopes and dreams and a future. Back when we would stay up late and whisper about unseen worlds where we'd go one day.

"Anything will be possible there," Carrie would whisper in the dark. "We'll find circuses open year-round and water as blue as the sky. And there will be monsters around every corner."

I'd always shudder next to her. "That sounds scary," I'd say, but she'd just wave me off.

"Don't worry." She'd give me that perfect smile of hers. "They'll be our kind of monsters."

When I awaken on the beach, it's nearly sunset. There's fog everywhere, and there's something else too, a flicker of magic in the air. The carnival still lives in the bones of this town. The people who faded into oblivion still live here, too. I can feel it, the way they were the outcasts. The way they were like me.

Across the street, all the doors of every motel room are hanging open. As I stumble past, I peek inside, a different theme coming alive inside each one. Clowns and mermaids and faeries, whispering from the walls and climbing out of the bedsheets.

But I don't stop, not even for a moment, as I head to the far corner of the motel, already knowing I won't be alone. That's because Angie is lingering in the empty room. *My* room.

"There you are," she says as I walk in, and at last, I see her for what she really is. A ferryman of sorts, a guide into the underworld.

Has this place been lost on the coast, waiting all these years? Waiting for someone like me to arrive?

"I still don't understand why the room is empty," I say.

"I told you it isn't finished yet." She takes a long, impossible step toward me. "You have to help us finish it."

I should tell her no. I should run out the door. But it's too late for that now. Besides, that's not what I want anyhow. I want to help complete this.

Breathing deep, I think how I've already seen the other rooms. I know what they look like. This theme needs to be my own.

My mind flashes back to my trip up the coast, the way the redwoods towered overhead on Highway 101, guarding the gloom. Guarding me. The forest keeps me safe, and now I'll keep the forest safe, too. All at once, I feel the rumble beneath me. It only takes a moment, before the trees are sprouting up through the floor, a new mural painting itself on the nearest wall. Me and Carrie, reclining among the redwoods, finally discovering a place where we belong.

And we're not the only ones who belong. Outside, I can sense it, the way the town is awakening. The locals are calling out my name again, louder than before. Every room in the motel is calling out to me.

But all I can do is fall back into the corner and smile, as the bark of a sequoia envelops me.

"I'll leave you to it," Angie says and vanishes out into the night, locking the door behind her.

It's long past sunrise when a car lumbers into the parking lot. I listen through the gloom, hearing that familiar click of high heels on pavement. Carrie. She decided to show up after all. I already know where she'll head first: to the registration desk where Angie will be waiting for her. Angie's always been waiting for us.

It only takes a minute before the door to my room creaks open. "Hey," Carrie calls to me, "I was able to sneak out early."

"Is that so?" I whisper from the shadows.

Carrie edges into the room, her eyes open wide. "Sarah, where are you?" she asks.

"I'm right here," I say with a giggle, because in a way, I've always been here. Or at least I've always been looking for this place. I'm no longer a broken heart or a lost cause. I'm right where I belong.

But Carrie can't see me, not yet. That's why I have to come to her. With a careful step, I emerge from the darkness, the bark and branches and the thin verdant leaves threaded through my body. I hold my breath, waiting for it. The moment my best friend screams at what I've become.

But instead, she only beams back at me. She sees me as I'm meant to be, and it doesn't scare her at all.

I inch toward her. "I told you I'd figure out where we belonged one day."

"Except I figured it out first." She reaches out and takes my hand, her skin warm against mine. "I hoped to arrive sooner, but I wanted you to get to know the place first. I wanted to make sure you liked it here."

The truth washes over me all at once. This was part of her plan from the beginning. Carrie kept her promise. She was determined to discover a place for us. She just wanted to make sure the choice was all mine.

And now that we're together, the roots in the floor are creeping closer to her, ready to draw her into a long embrace.

"Don't you like it, Sarah?" she asks.

"I do," I say, and with a grin, Carrie closes the door behind her, as the greenery devours us whole.

STORY INSPIRATION: I've always been such a huge fan of theme motels. I love discovering old pictures from the 1960s of these types of resorts, and I'm always looking for any modern-day locations. A theme motel also seems like a perfect setting for a horror story, so that's where the idea for my tale started. From there, it was so much fun meeting these characters and seeing just how terrifying a remote theme motel could be.

Blood on the Shore

Chris McAuley

They rolled into Manitou Beach with the windows cranked down, the radio turned so low it was barely there. The July air slid into the car in heavy breaths, thick with the smell of mineral water, pine resin, and something faintly metallic that caught in the back of the throat.

Ahead, the lake stretched wide and dark, a pane of poured slate. The light slid over it in dull sheets, refusing to settle.

"It's like a mirror left out in the rain," Kat said, her eyes following the small ripples that puckered its surface.

Jules didn't look at her. "It's an eye," she said softly. "A pupil, black, patient, always opening wider."

The trip was meant to be a reset button. Two nights peeled away from their lives: no emails, no office crises, no rattling arguments in their cramped apartment that had turned the place into a warehouse for unsaid things. While they packed, they'd sworn to each other no digging up old wounds, no rehearsing the same accusations. Just swimsuits, paperbacks, and the hope of finding the versions of themselves they used to love.

By dusk, they were fighting anyway.

Not with shouting but something much sharper and quieter. The kind of silence that made every word a blade you could accidentally cut yourself on. Kat stirred her drink with one finger, her eyes on the condensation trailing down the glass, fishing for a neutral topic. Even talking about the weather felt like opening a door to the wrong room.

Jules kept glancing at the lake, watching a slick of pale foam gather and drift across the surface. Her gaze tracked it like it was a message being carried somewhere.

Finally Kat said, "Let's walk the shoreline. Before it gets dark."

Jules's mouth twitched into something that wasn't quite a smile. "Sure."

The beach was a long jawbone of worn stones and driftwood ribs. Gulls drifted overhead, tracing circles that never closed. They walked side by side, steps falling into a reluctant rhythm. Kat reached for Jules's hand. Jules let her, but her palm was cold and limp, a dead weight between them.

Kat felt the absence in it. It made her wonder if they'd come here to salvage what was left or to watch it die.

The wind shifted, sliding off the lake. It was cold for July, threaded with a hiss that wasn't quite the sound of water. Rolling pebbles, water folding over itself, ordinary sounds at first, but there was a cadence, a suggestion of repetition. Almost words.

Jules closed her eyes and let it pour into her. For a moment, the sound untied something tight in her chest, easing the constant ache of their last few months' arguments about bills, the way Kat's silences could be worse than her shouting, the daily accounting of disappointments.

The wind grew stronger, and in it, she thought she heard her name. Clear. Low. Certain.

Her eyes opened, slow and dazed. "Did you hear that?"

Kat glanced at her. "What?"

"My name. Someone… calling me." Jules's tone was halfway between wonder and dread.

Kat's brow tightened. "It's only the waves. They can sound like anything if you listen too hard."

Jules didn't answer.

"Jules?"

She finally turned her head, her eyes not quite meeting Kat's. "What if it isn't just the waves?"

"It is." Kat squeezed her hand harder, a reflex, something meant to reassure. "We're tired, that's all."

Jules didn't squeeze back. Instead, she looked past Kat, back toward the lake. The foam was moving again, slowly, as if drawn toward a point on the horizon. She couldn't explain it, but she had the sudden conviction that the water had been waiting for her and that she had just been late in noticing.

The boardwalk lights blinked in and out through the mist as they crossed the road towards the pub. The sound of the lake stayed with them, even when the heavy wooden door shut behind them. Once inside, the air changed, it had become thicker now, warm with beer and fried food, the twang of an electric guitar buzzing through a corner amp.

The place smelled of damp wood and old summer nights. A pool table slouched in one corner, its felt pockmarked with cigarette burns. Locals leaned into their conversations like fellow conspirators and Kat felt herself unclench a little. The pub's noise was a buffer, something to stand between her and the cold stillness outside.

They found a booth by the window. The lake was just visible through the glass, a smear of darkness under the yellow lamplights flickering to life on the street. Jules sat facing it and tried to take in the stillness and natural beauty. After all, it was part of the reason they were here. The waitress came and went, Jules ordered a gin and tonic, Kat a cider. For a while they said nothing and the music shifted into a slow, crooning country ballad.

"I think we should move," Jules said suddenly.

Kat blinked. "Move?"

"Out of the apartment. Somewhere bigger. Somewhere with more space between us."

Kat heard the choice of words – '*between us*' – and set her glass down harder than she meant to. "You mean between the rooms."

Jules gave her a thin smile. "Sure."

They sat into silence again, this time one that seemed to have sharp edges. Kat was deciding what to say to soften the conversation between them when Jules slid out of the booth. "I'll get the next round."

Kat watched her cross the room, shoulders squared, head high in that way that could read as confidence or challenge, depending on the day. She lost sight of her in the press around the bar.

That was when the woman appeared.

One moment the seat across from her was empty; the next, it was occupied. No sound of footsteps, no creak of leather from the bench. Just there.

Her skin was pale, almost reflective in the pub's low light. Her hair hung damp, the color of wet earth. Her eyes were grey but deep, like there were miles of water behind them.

"You smell like metal," she said.

Kat froze, her hand still curled around her drink. "What?"

"Like something kept under water too long." The woman's voice was low, threaded with an accent Kat couldn't place.

"Look, this seat's..."

The woman leaned forward slightly. She didn't touch Kat, but it felt like she had, it was an invisible weight pressing in at the ribs, just enough to make breathing feel deliberate. Her gaze locked onto Kat's face with a patience that made her skin crawl.

Kat tried again, firmer. "This is taken."

The woman's mouth quirked upward, not in amusement but in recognition, like they shared a joke Kat didn't know she'd told. Then she said something under her breath, too soft to catch, and for a moment Kat smelled it: the lake. Damp stones, rust, the faint mineral sting of its air.

When she blinked, the seat was empty again.

The return of pub noise hit like surf after a long dive. The music, the laughter, the clink of glasses, it all rushed back at once.

Jules was standing there with two drinks, looking at her in a way Kat couldn't read.

"Who was that?" Jules asked.

"No one." The words came too fast, too thin.

Jules didn't smile. She set the gin down, sat slowly, and glanced at the window. Out beyond the glass, the foam was still drifting, purposeful in its slow glide toward shore.

The night air hit them harder than it should have. The pub's warmth had made their bodies forget the bite in the breeze, and now the lake's cold pressed itself against their skin like damp hands. The sound of the shoreline came back into focus, the slow hiss of pebbles rolling under water, the heavy exhale of waves folding over themselves.

They crossed the road in silence. Kat shoved her hands deep into her jacket pockets, fighting the urge to fill the quiet. Jules was moving quickly, her gaze fixed somewhere past the beach, as if following an invisible thread.

"Jules," Kat said softly, but Jules didn't stop.

The sand was darker now, nearly black under the clouded moon. Driftwood lay scattered in shapes that could have been ribs or collapsed scaffolding. The foam they'd seen earlier had spread wider, thin skeins of it catching faint light as they moved, as if marking a path.

Kat tried again. "You okay?"

Jules slowed, not turning her head. "You saw her."

The words landed like a stone dropped into water, small, but with weight enough to sink.

"What?" Kat asked, feigning ignorance.

"The woman." Jules's voice was flat, but there was an undercurrent there, something taut and vibrating. "I saw her at the booth with you."

"She just sat down. I told her to leave."

"You didn't tell me about the rest."

"There wasn't anything else."

Jules stopped. The wind moved between them. "You're lying."

Kat shook her head. "You're tired. We've been tense all day"

Jules's eyes flicked to the lake. "She touched you."

"She didn't..."

"You let her in."

The way Jules said it made Kat feel cold in places the wind couldn't reach.

"I'm not doing this right now," Kat said. She tried to step past, to steer the walk back toward the cabin, but Jules's hand closed around her wrist, firm, not painful yet, but with the suggestion that it could be.

"Do you hear it?" Jules asked, leaning slightly closer.

"Hear what?"

"The lake. Listen."

Against her will, Kat did. The hiss of the pebbles was there, the low push-pull of the water. But underneath, something faint, like a voice caught in the machinery of the waves. If there were words, they were too deep to surface.

"I don't hear anything," Kat said, but her voice lacked conviction.

Jules smiled faintly, as though she'd heard something in Kat's tone that Kat herself hadn't. She let go of her wrist, but not her gaze. "You will."

They kept walking. The foam trailed alongside them, carried by a slow current that didn't match the direction of the waves. Jules kept glancing at it, lips moving slightly, as though answering someone Kat couldn't hear.

By the time the lights of the cabin came into view, the cold had settled into Kat's bones. Not just the night's chill but something else, heavier, like the pressure of deep water.

She thought about the woman in the pub. About the moment she'd been gone, and the strange certainty that she hadn't simply left. About how Jules was still looking at the lake like it was promising her something worth taking.

The cabin smelled faintly of dust and lake air, even with the windows cracked. The low hum of the fridge was the only sound as they came in, the kind of silence that made every movement seem too loud. Kat dropped her jacket on the back of a chair and busied herself with the kettle, more for the noise than the tea.

Jules stayed near the door, still wearing her coat. Her eyes were fixed on the window, where the lake's black surface caught slivers of moonlight between clouds. Kat noticed her lips moving again – soundless, like she was mouthing something she didn't want overheard.

"You want tea?" Kat asked.

Jules didn't answer.

Kat turned. "Jules..."

"Why didn't you tell me?"

It was almost a whisper, but sharp enough to cut the air.

"Tell you what?" Kat kept her voice level.

"What she said to you. What she gave you."

"She didn't give me anything."

Jules's head tilted slightly, as if listening to something in the walls. "She gave you a piece of herself. I can smell it on you."

Kat's pulse picked up. "You're not making sense."

"I don't have to." Jules's eyes finally left the window and fixed on her. There was something brittle in them now, something that looked like it would splinter if you touched it. "The lake explained everything."

Kat tried to keep her face neutral. "The lake."

"It's been waiting for you." Jules stepped forward. "And you were ready to go to it. I saw it in the pub. You didn't push her away."

"She didn't even touch me."

"She didn't have to. You let her in."

Kat opened her mouth to argue, but the way Jules was looking at her stopped her cold. It wasn't just anger. There was awe there, almost reverence, the way someone might look at a flame they'd decided to step into.

"Jules," Kat said carefully, "you're tired. We've had too much to drink, and..."

The first blow wasn't with her hands. It was with her voice. "Don't patronize me." The sharpness in it made Kat flinch. Jules saw the reaction and stepped closer, closing the space between them until Kat could smell the cold on her breath.

Outside, the wind shifted, rattling the loose pane in the window. Kat thought she heard the same low hiss from the beach, but now it was clearer, more insistent, as if the water had moved closer.

Jules's hands were at her sides, fingers flexing and curling, as though she couldn't decide whether to reach out or strike.

"Do you hear it now?" Jules asked.

Kat shook her head, though she could feel it, like pressure behind her eardrums.

"You're lying again," Jules said softly. "You've been lying all night."

"Please," Kat said. "Just stop."

But Jules didn't.

The kettle began to whistle. Neither of them moved to take it off the heat.

Jules's eyes flicked toward the sound, then back to Kat. And then she stepped forward in one smooth motion, her hands seizing Kat's shoulders, spinning her toward the window.

"Look," Jules said, her voice low but shaking.

Through the glass, the lake gleamed in the moonlight, the foam moving in slow, deliberate arcs toward shore. Kat didn't want to see it, but she couldn't look away. For a heartbeat, she thought she saw a shape moving just beneath the surface, pale, long-limbed, turning in the dark.

"It wants you," Jules said. "But it's not going to have you whole."

And before Kat could process the words, Jules shoved her hard enough that her hip struck the edge of the table, the sharp pain stealing her breath. She stumbled, one hand catching the chair to keep from going down completely.

"Jules, what the hell..."

But Jules was already coming toward her, slow and deliberate, the way the foam had moved across the water earlier in the day.

Kat's back hit the wall before she could react. The jolt sent a framed print crashing to the floor, the glass splintering into jagged triangles at her feet.

"Jules!" she shouted, but it came out more like a gasp.

Jules's face was flushed and strange, half fury, half something Kat had never seen before, like she was watching someone else from behind her own eyes. She stepped over the glass, bare feet ignoring the shards, and drove her forearm into Kat's chest, pinning her hard against the wall.

The air left Kat's lungs in one hard rush.

"Stop..." she tried, but Jules was already moving, one hand shooting to Kat's throat, the other grabbing a fistful of her shirt and wrenching her forward.

Kat felt the first impact like an explosion inside her skull. Jules's fist slammed into her cheekbone, a wet pop of cartilage in her nose following a second later.

Jules didn't stop.

The second blow was harder, knuckles cracking against bone, the skin splitting across Kat's brow in a spray of red. Hot blood poured down her face, blinding one eye.

She slid down the wall, but Jules yanked her upright by the collar and drove her into it again, the back of her head bouncing off the plaster with a hollow thunk.

Kat's vision shimmered. Somewhere under the sound of her own pulse, the lake was louder now, its whisper swelling into a deep, eager hiss.

Jules's hand darted for the shattered picture frame on the floor. She came up with a jagged wedge of glass, its edge winking in the moonlight.

"Jules, don't..."

The first slash opened Kat's forearm to the bone. A hot sheet of pain ran up her arm, blood spilling fast and thick onto the floorboards. Jules stared at the wound for half a second, chest heaving, before she slashed again across Kat's ribs this time, cutting deep enough that the air itself seemed to burn.

The smell hit next, metallic, wet, warm. It was in Jules's nostrils, her mouth, her hair. She didn't flinch.

Kat stumbled sideways, clutching her arm, but Jules followed. She hooked her foot behind Kat's ankle and shoved, sending her sprawling across the table. Cups and plates scattered, one mug shattering on impact. Jules was on her in a heartbeat, glass still in hand, stabbing downward in brutal, erratic arcs.

The first plunged into Kat's thigh, the crunch of muscle giving way making Jules gasp, almost in surprise. The second buried itself in her side, the jagged edge tearing as it came back up.

Kat screamed, high and raw.

Jules's grip was slick now, the shard slippery with blood. She let it fall, reaching instead for the kettle still shrieking on the stove.

The water inside sloshed and steamed.

Kat tried to crawl, her palms slipping in her own blood, but Jules grabbed her by the hair and wrenched her head back. The kettle tipped.

Scalding water poured across Kat's back and neck, the skin blistering instantly. Her scream broke into a choking sob, steam rising in ghostly coils between them.

Jules let the kettle drop with a hollow clang and looked down at her work, hands shaking, breath ragged, blood spattering her face.

Outside, the foam on the lake had reached the shore, sliding over the stones like fingers curling toward the cabin.

Kat was on her side now, curled halfway under the table, one arm clamped tight over her stomach. Blood was pooling beneath her in a widening halo, soaking into the floorboards and trickling toward the door.

Jules stood over her, chest rising and falling in sharp, fast bursts. Her hands flexed and curled like she was trying to wring water from them, though it was only blood, slick, hot, and already cooling.

The lake's voice filled her head now, not whispering but speaking in a low, rolling rhythm, each word cresting like a wave. She didn't understand the language, but she didn't need to. The meaning was in her bones: Finish it. Give her back to us.

Jules stepped forward, her bare feet leaving sticky prints on the boards. Kat tried to pull herself further under the table, but Jules crouched low, her head tilting in a way that made her look more like the woman from the pub than herself.

"You hear it now, don't you?" she asked.

Kat's eyes were wide, wet, unblinking. She shook her head once, fast.

"You do," Jules said, her voice almost tender.

Her hand shot out, gripping Kat's ankle, and she dragged her into the open. Kat kicked weakly, heel thudding against the floor, but Jules hardly seemed to notice. She reached for the dropped shard of glass, the edge catching a glint of moonlight from the window, and drove it down into Kat's chest.

The sound was wet and final. Kat's body bucked, once, then sagged. Blood pumped out in slow, heavy pulses. Jules stabbed again and again, the glass sawing as it went in and out, until her hands were shaking too much to hold it.

When she finally let go, Kat's breathing was gone. Her mouth hung slightly open, a thin trickle of blood running from the corner, pooling dark against the boards.

The lake's voice went quiet.

Only the sound of the wind remained until it shifted, carrying with it the hiss of the shoreline. Jules turned her head toward the window.

The foam was moving again, not drifting now but spilling, climbing over the stones, curling across the wet sand toward the cabin. It reached the porch in thin, searching tendrils, then slipped under the door, winding across the floor until it touched the blood.

The moment it did, the foam thickened, darkened, and began to spread faster, following the trail to Kat's body.

Jules stepped back as the water came for her. It pooled beneath Kat, lifting her slightly, cradling her like something precious. The floorboards beneath them darkened as if the lake itself had seeped up from below.

And then, without a splash, without breaking shape, the water pulled her under. Not into the floor, not into the earth, just away. One heartbeat she was there; the next, she was gone.

The blood was gone, too.

The cabin was silent again, the only sign of what had happened was the wet prints leading from the door to where Jules stood.

She turned back to the window. Out on the black water, something pale moved beneath the surface, too big and too slow to be a fish. It circled once, then sank.

Jules pressed her palm flat against the glass. "I gave her to you," she whispered.

The lake did not answer.

It didn't have to.

Epilogue

By the time anyone checked the cabin, it was empty. No blood. No broken glass. No footprints but their own, fading into the wet sand outside. The air inside was still damp, carrying the faint tang of mineral water and rust.

Autumn thinned the tourists, leaving the boardwalk quiet. In late September, a new couple arrived—a man with a camera always at his chest and a woman who clung to his arm as though afraid he might drift out of her life entirely. They were seen at the pub that evening, his smile a little too fixed, her laughter just slightly delayed.

The next night, they walked the shoreline long after the others had gone in. A fisherman on the pier swore he saw the woman turn toward her husband, lips moving as though asking a question. The man nodded once, slowly, before taking her hand and leading her toward the darker stretch of beach where the water lapped higher on the stones.

Neither returned to the cabin.

In the morning, the door stood unlocked. The bed was unmade. The man's camera sat on the table, its battery dead but the last image still visible: the lake under a swollen moon, black water spreading in smooth rings as if something had just broken the surface and gone under.

Far out in the deep, a pale shape moved slowly beneath the ripples before dissolving into the dark.

STORY INSPIRATION: The idea for *Blood on the Shore* first came to me during my recent trip to Manitou Lake. I'd gone there for the same reason most people do, to enjoy the quiet water, the smell of pine, and the small-town charm of its boardwalk. But as I wandered the beach and sat in the pubs, I found myself noticing the undercurrents between people. Several couples caught my attention, their conversations clipped, their body language mismatched.

One pair would walk side by side without speaking for long stretches; another sat in silence over drinks, eyes fixed on anything but each other. These moments felt tense in a way that was hard to name, like something unsaid was just waiting for the right moment to surface.

There was something about the lake itself that seemed to amplify those tensions. Its surface looked calm from a distance, but up close it carried a restlessness, a subtle push and pull that felt alive. Watching those couples framed against that dark water, I

couldn't help imagining what might happen if the unspoken resentments between them were given a voice or worse, if the lake already had one, whispering its own suggestions.

That image of quiet disconnection, sharpened by the stillness of the place, became the seed for a story where love and violence meet under the watch of an ancient, patient presence.

Seven Chilis And A Lemon

Maria V. Snyder

It all started the day the man dropped dead in the surf. He did a face plant into four inches of seawater with a dramatic splash. Good Samaritans rushed to the rescue, carrying his limp body onto the sand, performing CPR as others yelled for a doctor, a nurse, a defibrillator. Considering we were on a small island in the middle of the South Pacific, they were out of luck.

You would think the cruise line, who had made some deal with the locals to rent out this island getaway, would have installed a first aid station or, considering the average age of the cruise passengers, a couple defibrillators.

Nope. Instead, cruise staff jumped onto a tender and raced to the Paul Gauguin to collect medical staff and supplies. The ship was anchored in deeper water a good fifteen minutes away.

The dead guy – of course he was dead, nobody is *that* grey in the South Pacific – attracted quite a crowd of gawkers. I among them. I've never seen a fresh dead body before. It was quite exciting. Chatting with my fellow cruise passengers in the bright afternoon sunshine, we talked about his chances – poor – of recovering.

"By the time they get back with a defibrillator, his heart will have been stopped for over thirty minutes," one guy wearing bright yellow swim trunks declared. His thick curly chest hair was pure white. "Isn't it like four to six minutes until brain death?"

A few others Googled and muttered in acknowledgement. No one remarked on the fact that we had cell service but no emergency service.

"Mr. Muscles has been doing CPR like a champ," another man said. "That's gotta count for somethin'."

"Yeah, a cracked sternum and a couple of broken ribs," quipped a woman.

Mr. Muscles was one of the Polynesian dancers employed by the cruise line. He wore a pair of board shorts and nothing else, revealing intricate tattoos on his back. Now don't go yelling at us for ogling him. We're old and haven't seen a body that fit in decades.

Help finally arrived and the new staff set up a barricade of sorts by holding up beach towels to block our view. Bored, most people wandered away.

My husband leaned closer to me and said, "I hope he doesn't die."

"It'll be a miracle if he survives."

"As long as he doesn't cause a delay or a change in our itinerary. I don't want to miss Bora Bora tomorrow."

Before you think he's a horrible person, the airline had misplaced his luggage and sent it on to Bora Bora for us to pick up. Losing your luggage is a terrible hassle. Misplacing it is on a different level of hassle. There's the uncertainty if it's really going to show up or not. You're in luggage limbo. And you can't enjoy your vacation until the matter is settled.

Besides, we didn't know the poor man. He wasn't a friend or relative or even an acquaintance. At our age we have so many others to grieve for, there just isn't room.

My flip-flops made a pleasing tip tap sound as I followed my husband down the corridor to our stateroom. The carpet was threadbare, and the walls were marked with black scuffs, grimy fingerprints, and unidentifiable stains. Paul Gauguin was an older ship, and she was in dire need of some reconstructive surgery. Amen sister.

At our stateroom, my husband huffed. "Can we pull that damn thing down now?"

That damn thing was seven chilies and a lemon that had been strung together and was hanging from the top of the door. It was supposed to ward off evil. Our stateroom attendant, Varun, was from India. He and his Indian colleagues had gotten spooked when our ship rescued a few fishermen yesterday.

A bunch of the fishermen's crew died when their ship sank, but I would think having survivors on board would bring us luck. Instead, Varun and his Hindu friends believed it was an ill omen. They hung them over everyone's stateroom door. Many people pulled them down right away, but I wouldn't let my husband. I liked and respected Varun, which, in my mind, included being accepting of his culture and religious beliefs.

"No. Leave it alone. Besides, it's kind of cute," I said.

"Cute? One of the chilies is already dried out."

I peered closer. Sure enough the top chili was wrinkled. "That was fast. We're in a climate-controlled environment."

Another annoyed huff. "The AC has been on the fritz since we arrived."

True. Humid air hung heavy in all the public areas of the ship. The scent of mold competed with the tang of salt. So why did the chili look so desiccated? There was plenty of moisture.

I shrugged and concentrated on getting ready for dinner. A herculean effort at my age. I considered throwing in the towel and ordering room service at least three different times. Each time I remembered that I could eat dinner in my pajamas at home. And we didn't spend all this money to hide out in our stateroom. We came to experience the Polynesian culture, the beautiful weather, and to spend our kids' inheritance (not sorry). Plus, my husband looked quite dapper in his borrowed clothes from the ship's container of discarded clothing.

Do you know people will purposely leave clothing behind so they have more room in their suitcase for souvenirs? Wasteful.

Gossip was at full steam by the time we joined our friends at dinner – we were eight couples all traveling together. The four fishermen had recovered from their ordeal and were sitting at the captain's table. I recognized their dress shirts from the discarded container. Pity that striped Van Heusen shirt was too small for my husband.

My friend Anna said, "I heard one of the rescued men is the captain of the ship that sank. Is that allowed?"

"Why wouldn't it be?" her husband, Steven, asked.

"Isn't the captain supposed to go down with his ship?"

"Not necessarily," my husband answered. "It's a maritime tradition that the last person to leave a sinking ship should be the captain. Once everyone else is safe. No need for him to die."

"But many of his crew died," I said.

"According to the bartender, the ship went down fast, trapping people below deck. Nothing he or anyone could do except save themselves."

Steven glanced at the men. "Our stateroom attendant said they were on that lifeboat for over a week. Pure luck that they ran into us. Do you know there aren't many ships that sail the South Pacific?" He waved his cell phone in the air. "There's this app…MarineTraffic…" Steven mansplained how it worked. I tuned him out.

The conversations at the other tables were far more interesting. Many people speculated about that poor man who collapsed. Amazing that they were already getting the details wrong. Whisper-down-the-lane at its finest.

Halfway through dinner, an announcement was made that we were delaying our departure.

"That means he died," my husband said. "They have to deal with the authorities before they can bring a corpse to another country." He scowled, no doubt thinking about Bora Bora. "Let's hope they're quick about it."

The loud rattling hum of the anchor being reeled in woke us around one A.M. We were underway. Unable to fall back to sleep, I lay in bed staring at the ceiling, listening to the ship. Paul Gauguin creaked and groaned and rattled just like I did after sitting too long. She might be old, but she was still mobile. I was growing fond of her.

The gentle rocking of the ship eventually lulled me back to sleep. Until I snapped awake with a jolt as the ship lurched to the port side. I grabbed the headboard to keep from tumbling out of bed.

Now, I'm a seasoned cruiser and have weathered some rough seas, but never have I experienced such extreme motion.

My husband crawled to the balcony and yanked the curtain back. He cursed.

The moonlight reflected off the snow-covered mountains that loomed outside. My sleep-fogged brain eventually translated the sight into big fucking waves.

Ice cold fear pooled in my chest as dread churned in my stomach. I joined my husband by the window, clutching his hand. We clung to each other as the ship pitched and rolled side to side. Loud bangs echoed on the hull. One particularly deafening crash pushed the ship so hard, we sprawled on the window.

We watched in horror as the inky black sea rushed up to meet us. We were going to capsize! I closed my eyes. As if pulled from a precipice, Paul Gauguin righted. My relief was short lived as once again I faced the ocean.

The speaker in our stateroom crackled to life. "This is Captain... Frank, please do not panic. The ship is strong, and our crew is capable. For your safety, please remain in your staterooms. If you need medical attention, please call guest services. Seasickness pills are available from your stateroom attendants for a small fee."

Even sick with fear, I laughed. This cruise line charged a small fee for everything. We thought we were getting a bargain when we booked the trip, then surprise.

Grey morning light revealed the full seascape. Huge gray-green waves dominated, and, as the ship climbed up the side of one, I spotted a dozen more lined up for their turn. The wind howled, pelting the window with the spray from the tops of the waves.

Throughout the day, Captain... Frank (I don't know why he always paused after saying captain. Did the poor man not know his own name?) reassured us that the ship was strong, and the crew were capable. After the fifth time, I suspected he was trying to convince himself instead of the passengers. I clutched my purse to my chest, waiting for the emergency signal – seven short blasts of the horn followed by one long one – which meant abandon ship.

Paul Gauguin eventually found calmer seas and we were allowed to leave our stateroom. I emerged in a daze, peering at the other people in the corridor as if I'd just escaped a natural disaster. We exchanged wide-eyed looks.

"Come on, I'm starved," my husband said, nudging me forward.

That was when I spotted the second and third chili on the string. Their wrinkled skin the complete opposite of healthy ones beneath it. Odd.

The dining room was a raucous combination of hysterical laughter, loud voices, and the exchanging of horror stories. Rumors were on the menu, and everyone received a large portion. The fishermen hunched over their meals, sitting close together but not saying a word.

The din died down when the captain made his noontime announcement. "This is Captain... Frank. Our ship has sustained some damage during the storm. No need to panic. We are not in any danger of sinking. However, we were struck by a rogue wave on our starboard side and seawater inundated the bridge and short circuited several instruments. A number of staterooms were also damaged. We... lost a few passengers. Once the instrument repairs are completed, we will be able to contact the authorities to help in the search for those who were swept out to sea."

Silence reigned for a full two seconds before people started demanding answers from the wait staff. Captain... Frank needed to give us more information, like when the Wi-Fi would be available.

One loud mouth – there's always one – stood on his seat and projected his voice over the buzz. "Hey! Shut up!"

And we did. Because obviously this man had to be a retired teacher.

"Look, we shouldn't wait for the Coast Guard. We all have binoculars in our staterooms. Let's use them to search the sea. Maybe we'll see them."

Instant agreement. I decided I would follow this man if the ship capsized just like in *The Poseidon Adventure*. Should I give him my cabin number just in case? I considered it as I scanned the bruised-colored sea. The choppy water made it difficult to spot anything. Twice, I thought I'd found a survivor only to be disappointed as the dot transformed into a seabird. A headache from eye strain threatened so I gave the binoculars to my husband while I took a walk.

You should know by now that I have a morbid curiosity. So, it shouldn't be a surprise that I nosed about the starboard side.

I walked through the passenger decks. The carpet squished underfoot, emanating the scent of the sea. No visible damage. The only sign of trouble were the red Xs and "do not enter" signs taped on the stateroom doors. Odd that the doors seemed random. I'd expected at least a solid row of them.

By the third deck, a niggling suspicion scratched. I retraced my route just to be sure, but it appeared the Xs were on only those doors without the seven chilies and a lemon. And yes, I checked. Despite the rogue wave, none of the talismans had fallen from the intact doors, but the top three chilies looked as wrinkled as mine. Did any of this mean anything? No clue. And I wasn't about to mention it to anyone. Would you?

Dinner that night was a subdued affair. No one had spotted any survivors. The fishermen kept darting glances at the passengers, their faces gaunt with strain. Names of the lost passengers were passed along with the butter.

"Even if Captain… Frank could signal an SOS, there's no one near us," Steven whispered to my husband. "I checked MarineTracker before we lost cell service."

"According to the hairstylist at the salon, the captain has no idea where we even are," Anna said.

I'd thought her hair looked extra nice tonight.

"So much for getting my luggage," my husband muttered.

We went to the show after dinner. The troupe of young Polynesian dancers put their hearts and souls into their graceful movements. I wished I was that connected to my heritage. Other than homemade spaghetti on Christmas, my family didn't have many traditions.

The lights went out during a spirited number. A body thudded onto the stage with a curse and the music dwindled to a stop. You'd think they'd have the score memorized by now. We all stayed in place, waiting for the lights to flicker back on. The glow of cellphones soon lit the area. We had plenty of alcohol, so it turned into an impromptu party.

Eventually the cruise director hopped on the stage. He held a flashlight. "I spoke with the captain. Seawater has corroded some wires, and it will take us a few hours to repair them. Members of the crew have flashlights and will escort you back to your staterooms."

The tropics were lovely this time of year except when you don't have AC. Halfway through the night I woke up on fire. Not literally. I suffered through menopause a decade ago, but those hot flashes just wouldn't quit.

Flinging the covers off me, I went to the sliding glass door. I reached to unlock it, then froze. A wet black blob the size of a Corgi sat on the balcony.

Seaweed? No. It appeared to be… moving. Tentacles shot out, propelling the blob toward the window. Octopus? It splayed its body on the glass, and I cried out. Even in the semi-darkness its long teeth shone sharp and bright.

"What the fuck?" my husband said behind me.

"Octopus?" I asked him hopefully.

"Not with all those teeth."

We watched in horror as it climbed the window and disappeared. I grabbed the phone. "We need to call…" No dial tone. No cell service. No electricity. Right. I set the receiver back down. I opened our door.

"Where are you going?" My husband gestured to the window. "Those things could be inside the ship."

"Exactly, I need to warn—" One more chili on our string had withered. Three chilies left. I shut the door and leaned on it. "You're going to think I'm crazy. But..."

"I already think you're crazy. You married me, didn't you."

True. I told him that I believed those chilies were protecting us from something bad.

"That's quite a theory. I think you're understandably upset by the last couple days and are giving these events more significance than they merit. Yeah, we're having a bad stretch, but no cruise goes perfectly."

"You saw that thing."

"I did. But we're not marine biologists. It could be a common sight in these waters. Something like a Pacific Sharkapus. Perhaps it was curious."

"A Sharkapus? Really?"

"No. A *Pacific* Sharkapus. Get it right. They're very sensitive creatures."

I laughed. However, my humor soured the next morning when I opened our door, and two more chilies were desiccated. Only one chili and the lemon were left.

Despite the lack of electricity, the beat went on. The plumbing still worked along with our key cards and the kitchen's massive freezers. Jim tried to explain why, droning on about circuit breakers, batteries, and wiring as if he'd been an electrical engineer instead of a mailman. As long as we didn't lose any more amenities, I didn't need to know the reason.

In the game room during American Mah Jongg, I asked my girlfriends if they'd seen anything strange last night.

"Two crack," Anna said, discarding the tile. "Seen? No. But I smelled a foul fishy odor on deck two. I almost puked."

"Nine bam," Bonnie said, tossing hers. "I saw a man waiting for the doctor. His arm was wrapped in a blood-soaked towel, and he had scratches on his face and neck."

Attacked by a Pacific Sharkapus or by an angry wife? Probably the wife.

"Joker," Pat said, setting the best tile in the entire game down, rendering it useless.

We all groaned.

"I don't need it," she said in her defense. "I did notice there were less people at breakfast this morning."

"Green dragon," I said. "That could be for any number of reasons."

"Four dot." Anna gestured to an unopened Mah Jongg set with her four dot. "The loud drunks haven't missed a chance to play all cruise."

True. But still…

Our conversation attracted the other foursome of our friends playing on the table next to us. They chimed in with their stories of strangeness. One after the other.

"I went to check on my friend, Susie," Deb said. "I haven't seen her since the storm. I knocked and knocked. Then this putrid gelatinous substance oozed out from underneath her door. I tried to track down her attendant, but no luck."

"I have a theory," I said and explained.

"Something bad? A demon?" Bonnie asked.

"An evil spirit," Pat said.

"I don't know, but I suspect it came with those fishermen. It spooked my attendant, and all the bad stuff happened after their arrival." I glanced around. Did these women think I was insane?

"Only one chili and a lemon left! What happens when they're used up?" Anna asked.

"You know what we need to do," Pat said.

"Tell our husbands?" Linda asked.

"No. Mine has a logical reason for everything," I said.

"Right," Pat said. "What we need to do is pin Varun down and find out more about this evil water demon."

They agreed. And with the speedy efficiency of retired teachers, administrators, and a project manager, an ambush was arranged.

"I'm sorry, ma'am, I can't clean your stateroom today. We're helping with very important repairs," Varun said.

He barely kept his tone civil. Wow, he must really be stressed. The people who work on cruise ships were the epitome of patience and were pleasant even when dealing with disgruntled passengers.

"Oh, it's not for that. We spotted smoke near the fridge, and it smells like something is burning."

Varun turned on his heel and headed toward our stateroom. Nothing like the threat of fire to motivate a sailor.

He took a few steps into the room and stopped short. "Ladies, you must evacuate this room immediately." He pushed his way to the fridge. "There might—"

"Not until we get some answers," I said as the women moved to block his path.

Pat pulled out the desk chair and patted the cushion. "Sit down, Mr. Varun. We need to chat."

He gazed at the eight of us in surprise. Bonnie pressed down on his shoulders, and he sank into the chair. Recovering from the shock, he glanced at the door with a calculating expression. Sure, he was a healthy young man and could muscle us all aside. That would require him to be violent and might cause injuries.

Varun wasn't raised to do harm to others. He wilted. "What do you want to know?"

"What scared you about those fishermen?" I asked.

He scowled. "They're not fishermen, they're trawlers."

"There's a difference?" Pat asked.

"Yes. Bottom trawlers destroy the ocean. They use a thick metal chain and a net to dredge the bottom, scooping everything up in its path. Most of what they catch is tossed overboard. Dead." He swept a hand out, indicating the water. "It's like destroying an entire forest to catch a couple of rabbits."

"I've watched a documentary that mentioned them," Anna said. "On the National Geographic channel with David Attenborough. I think it's called *Ocean*. They suck you into watching with videos of beautiful fish and reefs and then, bam! They show you the moonscape that's left after one of those trawlers comes through." She shuddered. "Awful."

"Regardless of the trawlers' morals, why the protective charms?" I asked Varun.

"Charms?"

"The seven chilies and the lemon."

"After we rescued those men, I received a call from my mother. She had a bad feeling. Told me to protect myself. But it's not just me. I have you. The people in my staterooms. For the two weeks you're on my ship, you're my family. Most of my crew mates thought I was silly."

Bonnie patted him on the shoulder. "Don't listen to them, you're a good son."

"Thanks. Apparently four others from India received the same phone calls from their mothers, so we strung the talismans and hung them up."

"What are they protecting us from?" I asked.

"We think those trawlers destroyed the home of an Aitu."

"Aitu?" Pat asked.

"A Polynesian spirit or ghost. They can be either benevolent or malevolent. This one seems determined to sink our ship." Varun wiped a hand over his face. "The Polynesian dancers believe it sank the trawler and is now trying to get to the survivors."

"What happens when the last chili and lemon are used up?" I asked.

"We'll sink."

"That'll certainly ruin our vacation." The rest of the ladies nodded in agreement.

"Can we just string up more of them?" Bonnie asked. "We'll call it a craft project and everyone on board will help."

Good idea. No one our age could resist a craft project.

"No. The Aitu is growing stronger. Once the lemons are destroyed, it will have full access to the Paul Gauguin."

I considered. "It is bent on revenge." I tapped a finger on my lips. "We can work with that."

"You can?" Varun didn't look convinced.

"Depends. How much time do we have?"

"We?"

Annoyed I gestured to the eight Mah Jongg playing women. "We may be old. We may be retired. But don't *ever* count us out. Our minds are still sharp. And together we have about three hundred and twenty years of work experience."

"And you have your husbands!" Varun exclaimed.

It was amazing that he wasn't cut to ribbons by the eight glares aimed at him.

"It would take us days to convince them," Anna said quietly. "We don't have days do we, Mr. Varun?"

He slumped in the chair. "No, ma'am. We have hours at most."

Once we determined the solution to our problem, Operation Sharkapus was put into action. Bonnie organized the crafters. Varun recruited essential crew mates. We rushed around, and in the process gained another ten ladies. They thought we were doing a scavenger hunt, so we gave them a list of supplies we needed.

If the situation wasn't so dire, I'd say I was actually having fun. Oh, who am I kidding. I'm sure, not you. Yes, I was having a blast.

It took about two hours to get everything in place. We decided to launch Operation Sharkapus right after the sun set. Which was like having cataracts—there was just enough light to see, but not too clearly.

I waited for the signal in the stuffy corridor. After finding the supplies, the scavenger hunt women were told we were playing a practical joke on someone, and they were all in. Really a fun group. I would have to get their contact information.

"Neon orange is really not my color," Bonnie said.

"It's no *one's* color," Pat said. "Why do these life jackets have to be so big and bulky? I feel like I'm wearing a box."

"A box that can save your life," I said. Although I agreed it was hot and uncomfortable.

Varun and his friend banged on the two cabins that the trawlers had been assigned.

"Abandon ship! All passengers must abandon ship!" they said.

Operation Sharkapus was a go!

When the men stepped out with their life jackets on, a line of panicked women, me included, rushed past them. We acted scared with cries of dismay. The four men joined the flow, and we raced down to the stairs. The scavenger hunt women poured out from the port side staterooms, giving our act a bit more realism.

Crew with life jackets and flashlights stood at the stairwell to direct the passengers. We thumped down the stairs to deck one. A lifeboat was idling at the gangway. In the gloom, it appeared to be almost full of people wearing orange lifejackets. It helped that the roof and windows of the lifeboat obscured part of the inside.

"There's only room for four more," yelled a security officer. She held one of the ropes, keeping the boat close.

As expected, the four men pushed their way to the front, knocking over a few women. I hit the wall pretty hard, but it was worth the bruise to watch as the trawlers dove into the lifeboat.

The security personnel dropped the ropes and shoved the lifeboat away. The engine was on, and the rudder had been rigged to keep it on a straight path until it ran out of gas in an hour.

We watched as the men straightened and glanced at their fellow passengers.

"I wish we had more time." Bonnie tsked. "At least to sew some eyes on our dummies."

"Who knew that discarded clothing bin would end up being so useful," I said.

"Those lifejackets really did save our lives," Pat said.

The men yelled in alarm and raced around the small vessel, trying to alter its course. They were smart enough to stay in the boat.

"Hey, how did the prank go?" a lady asked.

"Perfectly, thanks!"

They waved and climbed the stairs.

Anna gasped.

I spun around. Was the lifeboat coming back? It was shrinking as it receded into the night. "What's wrong?"

"We've only an hour until dinner."

Energized we raced back to our cabins to get ready. Right before leaving for dinner, I stepped out onto our balcony. The moon was almost full, and its silver light glinted off the ripples. Raising the binoculars, I scanned the horizon.

In the distance, the lifeboat resembled a walnut. It bobbed in the water. I waited. A long ropey creature climbed up the side.

"What are you doing out here?" my husband asked. "We're going to be late."

"Just watching a Polynesian Aitu."

"A Polynesian Aitu, eh?"

"Yes, much larger than your Pacific Sharkapus."

He laughed. "I've created a monster."

For those of you who were concerned, don't worry, my husband was happily reunited with his luggage in Bora Bora. Tears were shed.

STORY INSPIRATION: On a South Pacific cruise a couple years ago, everything went wrong, including missing luggage, dead guy, and big waves. This story is about 70% true!

The Canopy Tour

Jo Kaplan

After four days of lounging in the sun and floating in the pool with a variety of frozen cocktails, Owen suggested they do something exciting before the end of the vacation. He slapped a brochure on the table where Leah was sipping her café de olla over a paperback and said, "Let's do an excursion."

Her eyes drifted from the ATV tour to river rafting. "What happened to a week of rest and relaxation?"

Owen looked out at the pool and the swim-up bar and the beach beyond. "I just feel like I've had enough of sitting around at the resort. I'm ready for some adventure."

"When do we *ever* get to just sit around and relax?"

"And when do we ever get to fly around the canopy of a jungle?" He pointed to the zipline tour. "Come on, it'll be fun."

She slid her bookmark between the pages and picked up the brochure.

A bus took them and two other couples half an hour outside Puerto Vallarta, then another half hour bumping along unpaved forest roads before they met their tour guides: two skinny men in their late twenties who wore infectious smiles and spoke in deliberate, playful Spanglish. "We must hike to the first platform," said Marco as he waved them on. "Vamos!" His partner, Luis, took up the rear, promising not to let anyone fall behind to get eaten by jaguars. The blonde woman named Emily looked upset as she asked if there were really jaguars around here. Luis said, "Sí, and they are very hungry." Emily blanched while Marco and Luis laughed.

The humidity sat thick beneath the green canopy. Leah swatted fat, greedy mosquitoes from her legs. They hiked for another twenty minutes, pausing every so often for Luis or Marco to shush them, say, "Callarse. I hear a jaguar," then, just as tension began to ripple through the group, chuckle and add, "No, just a monkey!" And they would all look up just in time to see a spider monkey dart between the branches.

When they arrived at the first platform, they donned their gear – helmets, harnesses, gloves – and went over the protocols before climbing a ladder to the top. Leah's breath caught in her throat as she looked out over the forest from this height, seeing how the ground sloped away beneath them and feeling a twinge of anxiety. That was part of the excitement, she reminded herself. It wouldn't be fun if it wasn't also a little bit scary – but even this was mitigated by the attitudes of the guides, who seemed completely at ease in the canopy.

Marco demonstrated first, clipping himself to the zipline, then throwing himself off the platform and giving a howl as he spun backward to wave while he receded from them. That sort of wild abandon was so far beyond Leah that she wondered if she was even capable of it. This was Marco's job, she reminded herself – a far cry from her days in a windowless room, at a desk, staring at pixels. Their lives were so vastly different. To her, this was a crazy adventure she would likely never repeat. To him, it was a Tuesday.

When Marco waved from the other side of the zipline, Luis turned to the group and said, "Okay, who's first?"

Emily's partner, Eric, stepped up immediately. They watched as Luis clipped him to the line, reminded him how to brake with one gloved hand, and pushed him off. Eric's bulky frame soared away.

Witnessing the others go across only increased Leahs' anxiety, and she begged off until there was no choice, until everyone else had gone and Owen had kissed her on the cheek before flying away himself. She turned to Luis to tell him she simply didn't have the courage, thinking he would have a solution where she could return to the bus and wait for the others, but before she could speak he'd already clipped her in, saying, "Don't worry, don't worry, you're gonna be fine," and then he shoved her off the platform.

Air rushed into her face. Her legs kicked out over an expanse of nothing. Despite her speed, the world seemed calm as it drifted past. A swell of awe pushed back her lips so that by the time she made it to the other side – a little too hard, she slammed and swung back – she was grinning. Owen took her in his arms once Marco unclipped her, admonishing her about failing to brake, and said, "See?"

She did. There was magic in the canopy.

Luis came in hot on her heels, yelling at them to get out of his way as he flew onto the platform. He and Marco conferred in Spanish, speaking too fast for Leah to know what they were saying (all she caught was "Qué es eso?" and "No sé"), and then they were onto the next run. After three more runs, the fear that hit her each time she stepped off the platform was beginning to abate.

The next line was the longest at over 1,000 meters. Leah couldn't even see the next platform ensconced in trees in the distance. She listened to the shouts and cries of the others as they went out and knew the view must be magnificent. But when Luis clipped her in, he was frowning.

"What's wrong?"

"Nothing," he said, feigning brightness. "I don't think." He pulled the walkie talkie off his belt and said something into it, but there was no response. "No te preocupes. Let's just wait a moment to be sure they are all at the other side."

He glanced at his walkie talkie again as they waited, then up at the canopy, squinting through the branches as if hoping to catch sight of another monkey. "Is there something up there?" Leah asked, and he shook his head.

"Okay, time to go," he said as he sent her off.

Once again, Leah flew through the air, mesmerized by her speed and how slowly the surrounding jungle seemed to move, how long this line was, seeming to go on and on, until she felt a jerk, her legs flipping up with the force of the sudden stop, sending her swinging back and forth.

Nothing but open air below her as far as she could see. She was only halfway through the line, and completely stopped. Monkeys shrieked in the treetops, their voices shrilling around her.

She looked up. Something had prevented her from continuing: some thick, sticky, tar-like substance that coated the line from here on out. She gave a tug on the lanyards that connected her to the trolley to see if she could get it to slide forward, but the stuff on the line was like glue. There was no getting the trolly through it.

Panic crawled up her throat. Now that she wasn't moving, there was time to look down at her feet dangling over an abyss, to look ahead where she still couldn't quite make out the next platform in the distance, to look up at the thin line holding her tenuously in place. The carabiners clicked as she spun herself around, expecting at any moment for Luis to come barreling into her.

"Hello?" she shouted, listening to her voice echo. "Help! I'm stuck!"

Her breath came faster. Though she told herself not to hyperventilate, the idea of passing out up here, tethered to this line hundreds of feet in the air, only made her breathe harder.

"Owen!" she shouted, voice raw and desperate. "Help!"

All she had wanted was a relaxing vacation, to escape reality for a bit. That's what a vacation was to her – a form of escapism. Maybe that made her a superficial traveler, but so be it. She was just glad to be away from the office, away from gridlocked traffic and responsibilities, where she could pretend there was nothing more to life than sun and food and drinks.

This was where she and Owen diverged. Maybe it was why they didn't take many vacations – because what they valued in a trip simply did not align. On the rare occasions they traveled, he was adamant about studying beforehand so that he could learn the culture, the history, something that would make for a richer appreciation of where they were going and who lived there, who already inhabited this space that they would just be dipping their toes into before leaving. No place is a blank slate, he'd told her once. It's foolishness to think we can just impose ourselves on a place without understanding who already exists there.

To whit: Leah had chosen Puerto Vallarta simply because it seemed like a nice vacation spot. Owen had praised the choice, telling her about archaeological evidence of human habitation in the area as far back as 580 BC, and the Aztlán culture – Aztlán being a lost ancestral city of the Aztecs. "The archaeological record is limited," he'd said, "but who knows what secrets are hiding in the jungles of Jalisco?" It was why, she suspected, he'd wanted to go on an excursion: to get out into the jungle, to experience beyond the beach and the resort and all its phony escapism.

Tears burned Leah's eyes. She could be sitting by the pool right now with a piña colada. Instead, she was trapped on a zipline in the middle of the jungle, wondering why no one was coming to get her, wondering where Luis was, why he hadn't come down the line yet.

The monkeys' calls turned bloodcurdling, and she realized with a jolt that it wasn't actually monkeys at all – this whole time, it hadn't been monkeys screaming. The sounds were human.

Interminable minutes ticked away. Though the trolley held her firmly, Leah gripped the carabiners so hard her hands ached. She tried to keep herself oriented but kept swiveling one way and another, at the mercy of the wind and the harness. She imagined what would happen if the trolley failed, or the line snapped. A fall from this height would be instant death.

Already her glutes were starting to go numb sitting in the harness. She had to get off this line, but there didn't seem to be any way to get around the oozing substance blocking her from advancing. There was nowhere to go but backward.

Pulling on the straps, she raised herself a few inches until she could get a grip on the line itself behind the trolley. Her glove slipped and she tried again. Holding the thin wire, she pulled herself backward, sliding a few inches. The brief moments it had taken her to get to this point stretched out at dreadful length behind her, though, as she continued, hand-over-hand, with painstaking slowness. The platform seemed impossibly distant.

The screams had faded by now, leaving the jungle to its usual chirping and rustling and buzzing. She felt insects light on her bare legs and kicked but did not dare let go of the line, lest she slide right back to where she'd started. Even the few feet she'd progressed felt a near-insurmountable effort in the long journey that still lay behind her, and she told herself not to look, just to keep going. If she looked, she might just give into despair.

By the time she was halfway back to the platform, her arms were trembling and she had to pause, hanging on by one hand and then the other to give each arm a rest. She closed her eyes and thought of Owen taking her in his arms, massaging the tired muscles, kissing each of her eyelids, and she tried not to think of the screams she'd heard, or the silence that followed, which was somehow even worse. Her hand slipped off the line, and she slid forward half a foot before she grabbed it again, cursing herself.

The forest groaned as something moved in the canopy, shaking the leaves and sending birds squawking as they fled. Leah's muscles froze as she waited for whatever was up there to see her. When her arms began to tremble, she continued pulling herself along the line, slowing as it angled upward. She thought about trying to wrap her ankles around the line ahead of her and creeping like a sloth, but she couldn't quite kick high enough, and when her body swung back and forth it sent panic lurching through her gut. Her legs dangled uselessly. Sweat gathered beneath the helmet and dripped down to sting the corners of her eyes.

It seemed that hours had passed by the time she looked up and saw, with immense relief, the anchor at the end of the line. The platform was right there at her feet. She kicked herself onto it, stood on wobbling legs, and unhooked herself, then collapsed to the floor of the platform, exhaling shakily.

"Luis?" She looked around for him, but all she saw was a single glove sitting at the edge of the platform. Its fingers shifted, wiggling slightly, but it was only the movement of the wind.

The ground lay far below. Looking down gave her vertigo.

She realized she hadn't thought beyond making it to the platform. She hadn't even been sure she would be able to accomplish that. Now her mind began turning over the options that lay ahead. She could wait here until someone came to rescue her, but who could say how long that would be? Would she be waiting until nightfall? And what if no one came?

Or she could get to the ground and follow the lines to the end of the course.

She spotted a rope hanging off the side of the platform. Lowering herself over the edge was an exercise in terror; one wrong move and she would slip off and fall to her death. She grabbed the rope and anchored herself with her feet. Then she loosened her grip, let herself slide – tried to control it for a slow descent, but she went faster and faster, the ground rushing up, until she landed hard. Her palms burned, and when she pulled off the gloves she saw the skin was red and raw, but her feet were finally on solid ground. She could have knelt and kissed the dirt.

The most challenging part of following the line to the next platform was the unevenness of the terrain. As she hiked, she had to continually orient herself to be sure she was still following the line far above, as the dense foliage kept twisting her path. When she came to a creek, she tried to hop across on a series of stones but ended up stepping into the cold, rushing water instead. Her sneakers squelched and rubbed against the soaked socks when she made it to the other side.

Her pace quickened when she saw the base of the next platform just ahead. Endorphins hastened her to it. "Owen!" she shouted. "Hey!"

There was no response. She squinted up at the platform but couldn't make out anything at the top. The sun blared into her eyes through a break in the trees.

Of course they weren't here anymore. They must have continued on, thinking she was safe with Luis.

It wasn't until after her eyes adjusted following the dazzle of sunlight that she noticed the objects at the base of the platform, strewn over the ground. They didn't make sense to her. She could not bring her mind to recognize them for what they were, not at first, and when she did, heat and bile flooded through her.

A dingy white helmet with Emily's face looking out, strands of blonde hair dyed red. A few meters away, an arm strewing tendons from the ragged elbow. Nearby, a leg tangled up in the straps of a harness. And spattered around the limbs, dripping down the legs of the platform itself: that thick tarry substance she'd seen on the line.

Leah's stomach expelled its contents. When it was finished, she spat on the dirt, not allowing herself to look too closely at anything, welcoming the blur that overtook her eyes. If she looked too closely, she might recognize a piece of Owen among the body parts, a piece of him she had once touched, once kissed.

A wave of exhaustion kept her on her knees. All she wanted was to curl up here and wait for whatever it was to come back for her. She could lie here and pretend she was lying on the beach, pretend she had dreamed all of this during a leisurely nap on her nice vacation, where she had come to escape reality.

What she wouldn't give now to be safe at home, in her own boring little reality.

Forcing herself to her feet, she continued on, following the next zipline and trying to remember how many Marco had said were on the course. As she went, she wondered about the pickup spot, which she might have to find on her own. It wouldn't be right at the end of the line, she was sure; she would have to hike to it just as they'd hiked from the drop-off to the first platform. How, then, was she to know which direction to go? The forest was a mystery, dense trees looming in all directions.

Movement rustled the canopy above. She told herself it was the wind. Treetops swayed and bent. A deep, groaning sound unlike any creatures she knew echoed around her. She did not look up.

When she made it to the next platform, she realized it was the last one. Pressing her lips together, she tilted back her head. A shape, turned shadow by the light sinking behind the trees, crouched on the platform. Her heart went into her throat. It crawled over the edge and grabbed the rope hanging from the side, using it to rappel down.

Before Leah could make up her mind which way to run, the shape hit the ground and stood.

"Marco!"

The skinny man stared at her wide-eyed, face the color of oatmeal. She had never before seen such terror in someone's eyes.

"What happened?"

He shook his head, throat bobbing.

She tried again, the name curdling in her mouth. "…Owen?"

Marco shook his head again.

A weight plunged into Leah's belly, cold and heavy. It may have been shock that prevented her from crying right then. She felt oddly numb, her voice sounding far away and unusually calm in her ears. "We have to get out of here."

"This way," said Marco.

As they picked their way through the jungle, she tried to get him to tell her what had happened, but he seemed incapable of answering. "What was it?"

Finally, he said, "My abuela used to tell me stories of an age before this one. The first age, when giants roamed the earth. They were cast out by the gods. Maybe the gods set them free again because this age has not been working out so well." He sniffed and looked around to get his bearings, then turned to Leah, eyes wide. "No quiero morir," he whispered. Now that he was talking, he seemed inclined to continue, desperate for Leah to understand. He took her by the shoulders. "I did not see everything. I – I panicked and went down the next line before it was finished. Whatever it is… it is very large. Immenso." He let go of her with a jolt, as if just remembering, and asked, "Luis?"

She remembered the empty glove. Had it been empty? Had there been a hand still inside? "I don't know where he is. I think…"

Marco nodded, eyes gleaming. "Then there may be more than one."

The thought sent a chill through Leah despite the heat. Long shadows stretched from their feet as the sun westered through the trees. After a few minutes, Marco slowed and paused. "Do you hear that?"

Only silence. Leah shook her head.

"Exactly."

He was right: no insects, no monkeys, no other animals making their usual racket. The forest had gone dead.

Marco opened his mouth to say something else, but it was ripped from him. Something came down from above, circled his torso, and snatched him up into the air – or, no, not all of him. The lower half remained on still-standing legs, the place where his body ended oozing that tarry substance.

Stumbling away before whatever had grabbed him, too fast for her to see, could come for her, Leah tore through the trees, tripping on undergrowth and propelling herself forward on hands and knees until she regained her feet, smeared with soil. The straps of her harness dangled and pulled at her, so she tried to unhook herself from it as she blindly ran in what she hoped was the direction Marco had been leading her, though she couldn't be sure the jungle hadn't turned her on an increasingly errant path, deeper into it.

Behind her, above her, the thing groaned and shifted the trees around it. She zigzagged, remembering faintly, from some internet video, that this could help one escape a predator. The foliage just to her left swooshed with the movement of something swooping down, just feet from her. A hot glob of liquid with the consistency of snot landed on her shoulder, black and steaming, its stench fungal and rotten.

Up ahead, she saw a break in the trees – a dirt road – and that dingy white bus that had driven them to the drop-off point. A cry escaped her, and she waved her arms. "Help me!" The strap of her helmet dug into her chin, so she unclipped it and threw it behind her, where it clunked against the base of a tree.

The driver popped his head out the window of the bus and looked around at her, startled. He leapt out, hands in the air, asking what happened, qué pasó? Leah waved him back toward the vehicle, telling him to get in, they had to get out of there, and when he tried asking about the others she shook her head and said they were gone, muerto, and at that the driver finally jumped into action, ushered her into the bus, slammed the door, got in the driver's seat, revved the engine, and tore off down the dirt road kicking a cloud of it up behind them.

Leah held onto the seat as the bus rocked over the bumpy road, and through the brown haze of dirt out the back windshield she watched the trees recede faster and faster, hardly daring to exhale. When at last they emerged fully from the jungle, Leah felt her panic begin to ebb in a shuddering wave, but still she could not look away from the back windshield, even as she saw, rising over the canopy, the behemoth shape, the things like tentacles dripping away from it, reaching out to snatch birds as they scattered, and Leah had never felt so small, so dwarfed by her own awe at how much mystery still, somehow, remained in this world.

STORY INSPIRATION: My story was inspired by the first time I went ziplining, on a family vacation to Puerto Vallarta. It was

exhilarating and somewhat terrifying to fly through the canopy on a wire, and many of the details for the story were drawn from my memories of this experience. Well, except for the awful things that happened to the characters. Luckily, everyone on my tour made it out alive!

Lights Out

Aaron Rosenberg

I was fusing the Earth's core back together when I realized I could barely see straight.

I finished the job, of course. Couldn't let the whole thing calcify and fragment the way the Ice-Core Criminal League had planned, though it'd serve 'em right if it did. Why these guys never stop to do all the math and science required I'll never understand. I mean, sure, it would've brought about a new Ice Age – as the whole world froze over to the point where even penguins and harbor seals couldn't survive!

Anyway, I got the core nice and molten again, then surged back to the surface. SkaterPunk was waiting for me, like always, sitting Buddha-style on their Cosmic Board.

"Nice work, Irradiant," they offered as I popped up along the shore beside them. "All readings show we're geo-stable again." Then they cocked their head to look at me. "You okay? You're looking a little ragged."

I turned up the wattage a notch, hiding my features better, but I could tell from my oldest crimefighting partner's frown that I wasn't fooling them. "Yeah, fine. Just a bit beat, is all. You get the League in custody yet?"

"All good," they assured me. "Speed Geek and Knight Flight took 'em down, no problem." They snorted. "The Leaguers were so busy piling on fur coats and thermals, they couldn't even run away properly!"

"Nice." I let myself float up into the air a few feet, hovering there a second. "I'll meet you back at base, then." And I zoomed off before they could argue, much less bring their Board to bear.

The last thing I wanted right now was to face more questions from one of the few people who wouldn't let me get away with anything.

Back at base, I let the glow fade away and slumped into one of the chairs around our Action Table. When had it all gotten so exhausting? The Light Fantastic that powered me was still there, thrumming through my veins, lending me all these powers, so it wasn't that.

It was me. I was tired. No, more than tired. Beat. So much so that I barely lifted my head off my chest when SkaterPunk finally caught up, followed by Knight Flight. Speed Geek was last – even Danger Zone beat her to the table, and she'd been on monitor duty the whole time! – but our resident speedster did bring pizza and beer, so all was forgiven.

The second they were all there, though, SkaterPunk started in on me. "You look awful," they said, blunt as ever, leaning their Board against the wall and taking the seat across from me. "When was the last time you got a decent night's sleep?"

I frowned, giving that some real thought. "Uh, last Monday, maybe? No, there was that thing with the Zartuvians. Maybe the previous Thursday? No, hang on, we had that problem with the Transcon Terrorists, didn't we? Uh . . ."

"That's it," Knight Flight declared, removing his helmet to run a hand over his bare scalp and bushy beard. "Man, you've gotta take some me time."

"Can't," I replied. "Remember the last time I took a break?" That was to SkaterPunk, who frowned but had to nod. "The Seascape Disaster."

But my oldest friend wasn't backing down. "That was a long time ago," they reminded me. "And it was just you and me back then, patrolling the streets. Hell, you were still wearing a mask and everything. Now we've got the entire Hero Force, three ranks deep! We've got this covered." Without their helmet and goggles I could see the lines around their eyes, around their mouth, and the threads of silver glittering in their spiked pink hair. When had we all got so old? "Seriously, dude. You need a break before you burn out completely."

I raised an eyebrow at that, not sure it was a deliberate pun, and Danger Zone laughed. At least she got it! Still, she was nodding along with the rest. "Take a few days," she urged. "Go somewhere nobody knows you, someplace you won't hear about anything, and just chill out. It'll do you a world of good."

That did sound nice, but still I wasn't sure. "What if Archmonger returns?" I asked my teammates. "What if Dreadnaught comes back from the dead again? What if the Xenomites send another micro-invasion horde? What if—"

"Stop!" SkaterPunk shouted, hands up. Their Cosmic Board quivered where it rested, responding to their emotions like always. "Just stop," they repeated more softly. "IR, you're gonna make yourself nuts – and all of us with you. It'll be fine. We'll handle it." They gave me a wry little half-grin. "You're no good to anybody like this, anyway."

I had to laugh at that. "Okay, okay. I'll go. But if you need me . . ."

"We won't," Knight Flight promised. "What we do need is you back at full afterward, ready and raring to go. Go on." He grinned at me. "Get out of here."

Before I could second-guess – again – I nodded and stood. Letting the light seep back out of my skin and surround me in its protective aura, I floated up and then took off, out of base, across the water, back toward the rest of the world. I was still trying to process the idea that I had time to myself, time to get away, time to recuperate.

The question was, where should I go?

In the end, I opted for the Poconos. Yeah, not the most glamorous location, but when you've dived through a birthing star and swam across a diamidine asteroid belt under a triple sun, no Earthly view can compete. Besides, I didn't need scenery, I needed solitude, or at least distance from any major cities or sites. Those were the places that criminals, villains, aliens, and other troublemakers tended to target.

I also figured I should stay away from the oceans. It'd be too easy for me to fly across them if I did hear of any trouble. So, mountains it was. I did want to be around people, though. Isolation's never been my thing. Not too crowded but not empty, decent accommodations but nothing fancy, with lots of fresh air.

"Hi, and welcome to the Palace of the Poconos!" The woman at the desk – her nametag read "Nancy" – had probably passed "young and perky" a decade ago but I appreciated the effort nonetheless. "Room for one?"

"That's right," I answered. "Uh, three nights." A long weekend should make the others happy and give me some time to rest – but not too much time.

"Sure thing." Nancy typed and studied her screen. "Looks like we have a room available." Somehow, considering there were only a handful of people milling about in the lobby, I wasn't all that surprised. "Name?"

I almost laughed. When was the last time anybody had asked me that? It actually took me a second to even remember it, I was so used to just being Irradiant twenty-four-seven. "Uh, Bob. Bob Gaynor. Bobby."

That got a quick side glance from her and I could practically read the thoughts flashing through her head: *Oh no, is he flirting with me? Please don't let him be flirting with me!* But after a second, when I didn't say anything more, she let it slide. "Got it. I just need to see some ID, and of course a credit card."

"Right. Of course." Crap. I hoped my card was still active as I handed it over. I hadn't used the darn thing in years, not since Danger Zone and SkaterPunk had come up with the bright idea of charging countries for the right to request our help. Nothing crazy, of course. Just enough to keep the base running and make sure we had the fridge stocked, cover any replacement gear, stuff like that. Some of the others like Knight Flight had families and jobs out in the real world, but me, I was Irradiant all the time. Until now. I'd been lucky I still had some old clothes in my closet, and a battered old gym bag to stuff them in.

The card must've gone through because Nancy smiled as she handed it back, along with my ID. "Okay, you're all set. You're in three-fourteen, which is right along this hall and then up two flights. Here's your key and the Wi-Fi password. Breakfast is included and starts right over there every morning at six. If you need anything else, just call down. Enjoy your stay!" She was still bright and professional but also just as clearly done with me, so I accepted the key card, said thank you, and walked away in the direction she'd indicated.

My room proved to be perfectly decent, good-sized with its own balcony and plenty of light. There was a desk and chair, a small fridge and a tiny microwave, a decent bed, a reasonable bathroom, and a comfy couch across from the TV. I sat on the couch, leaned back, and looked around.

What did I do now?

I wasn't going to turn the TV on, I told myself. That way lay madness. Instead I headed back downstairs, wandered outside, and figured I'd go for a walk. Just me and nature. What could go wrong?

Barely out the front door, I nearly bumped into a couple. They were too busy paying attention to their phone to notice me. "Man!" the first guy was saying. "That's crazy, can you believe it? It's like somebody crossed a shark with a gladiator!"

Oh, no! That had to be Orcus Rex and his army of Fin Fighters! I could feel my body tensing automatically, the Light Fantastic already responding to my need, and forced myself to take a deep breath. I'd promised I wouldn't power up while I was gone.

"Damn, it's the Hero Force!" the second guy said, tapping the screen. "Look, that's Danger Zone! And there's Knight Flight! And that blur, that's gotta be Speed Geek! But where's Irradiant and SkaterPunk?"

"Must be doing a two-pronged attack or something," his buddy replied. "Come on, I wanna see this on a bigger screen!" They hurried off, not even noticing me or the fact that I was still trying to tamp down a residual glow.

That had been close. But Knight Flight and the others had been right. They had things handled. I could just relax and enjoy my vacation.

It took more willpower to walk away from the hotel with all its screens and Internet connections and up-to-date reports on the battle than it had for me to fend off an entire fleet of sentient torpedoes.

But I made it into the woods behind the hotel and only glanced back twice.

It was nice, just walking among the trees, nobody else around, no sounds except the wind and the leaves and the birds – and me. I was pretty sure I could actually feel myself relaxing more with each step and each breath, just unwinding. Letting Irradiant slip toward the back and good old Bobby Gaynor come to the fore.

Bobby Gaynor. Man, I hadn't thought about him in years! After the whole Lake Ponchatrain Incident, when the Light Fantastic had chosen me as its new vessel and I'd first become Irradiant, I'd rarely taken the time to power down and just be Bobby again. That had become even more true after the Galagar Exhibition, when I'd finally tapped into the Light fully. I'd barely recognized my face in the mirror when I'd let the Light dim, back at base. Who was this guy with the flyaway hair and the weak chin and the watery blue eyes? I was in crazy good shape, of course – the Light kept me that way – but I guess it hadn't done anything for my bone structure. No real point when all anyone ever saw of my face was vague features inside a cool white glow, with twin blue lights for eyes. It felt weird now, glancing down at my hands and seeing regular flesh, catching a glimpse of myself reflected and seeing a normal person.

Eventually I got tired of walking around and wound my way back toward the hotel. It was getting on toward sunset and my stomach was starting to rumble – evidently when I dimmed the Light it stopped powering me as fully, so I needed regular food again – and I turned some thought toward what I'd do about dinner. I'd seen a few places not that far away, local joints from the look of them. The problem, of course, was that I hadn't driven here. I didn't even own a car, not anymore. I'd flown in, rendering myself invisible for a change, and had landed around a corner of the parking lot. Which meant either doing the same thing now – or walking.

I opted for the latter, and half an hour later I stepped into Mel's Roadside Cafe. It was quaint, with rough-hewn timbers for the walls and sawdust on the floor, and there was some sort of country music playing but not too loud to override conversations.

Or the TVs mounted in the corners and also over the bar at the room's center.

"Bar or booth?" the server asked me. I opted for a booth, feeling a little bad about taking up a whole table for just me, but I didn't want to be right under a screen. Turned out that couldn't be helped, as I could see no less than three from my seat. Fortunately, they were each tuned to a different sporting event.

Unfortunately, those kept being interrupted by special news bulletins.

"Breaking!" a newscaster announced while I was eating my Caeser salad. "Polar Princess has just been spotted approaching Anchorage, with her squad of trained polar bears and orcas. The Hero Force has scrambled a team to respond!"

"This just in!" I heard as I was trying to enjoy my potato-leek soup. "Parts of the Autobahn have collapsed after an unexplained tremor! Local heroes are aiding authorities with evacuation, rescue, and repair."

"We've just learned," a reporter declared while I was cutting into my chicken parm, "that Main.eAK has taken the First National Trust and everyone in it hostage. The AI cyborg terrorist is threatening to vaporize the entire building unless it's given access codes to the World Bank immediately."

"A new species of killer bee has emerged from the wheatfields of Russia," the nearest TV announced while I was eating my slice of apple pie. "Given their size and apparent intelligence, authorities are wondering if the swarm is the latest eco-attack by Holly Honey and the Hive Mind."

I paid and left soon after that, barely having tasted the first real food I'd had in I don't even know how long. I didn't hear anything on my walk back to the hotel, but I couldn't get all those reports out of my head. Had the team been able to handle them all? Should I check in? Did they need me? I reached for my communicator three times, but each time I stopped myself. SkaterPunk had my number, they all did. They'd call if they needed me. And they'd specifically told me when I'd left, "Turn the darn thing off while you're gone." Which I hadn't, but at least I'd muted it.

Back at the hotel, there were more people around than before, most of them chatting in the lobby. I heard several talking about those same events but I tried not to listen or to linger, heading up to my room as quick as I could.

Once in my room, I turned on the TV and set it to the first movie I found, some recent rom-com about a mismatched pair thrown together in the middle of a botched hijacking. I tried to focus on that and a similar movie after it about a couple who learned each was a child star and never told the other about their past.

When I finally climbed into bed I was so tired my eyes could barely focus. But my dreams were filled with nightmare scenarios of my teammates tackling all those threats – and failing repeatedly because I wasn't there to help. I startled awake each and every time.

The next morning I felt worse than I had the day before, exhausted and emotionally bruised. I went downstairs for breakfast but they had the morning news on so I gathered up coffee, cereal, and some fresh fruit and fled outdoors to eat among the trees. At least there I couldn't hear about all the problems I should've been fixing.

When I ducked back inside to get my coat – I'd forgot what it was like to feel the weather – I caught sight of the morning paper. "Where Has Irradiant Gone?" it declared in big, bold letters across the top. I couldn't help snagging a copy and taking it up to my room to read.

The reporter noted that I hadn't been seen at all yesterday, despite the rest of the team working overtime. They'd even called in backup members like Gemstone Julie and Stretch Cassidy and Wildlife. Hell, Mystic Max and the Wordslinger had been sighted with the others, and nobody could stand either of them!

So naturally the reporter wondered whether there'd been some sort of falling out, whether I was on the outs with the Hero Force, or whether something had happened to me.

"No," I muttered, sitting there in my cheap hotel room looking out at the mountains. "I just needed a break."

Surely I deserved that much? It was only for a few days, then I'd be right back at it. Was that too much to ask?

When I went back downstairs, though, the TV was showing protests around the world. And the thing people were protesting now?

Me.

"Where are you, Irradiant?" I saw one sign ask. "Why did you abandon us?" another accused. "Come back, Irradiant – we need you!" a third insisted.

I all but sprinted outside after that, but not before I caught the headline above those videos:

"Irradiant Goes AWOL!"

Walking through the forest, I kept replaying those scenes in my head. And the more I did, the angrier I got.

AWOL? Really? I'd been working nonstop for the past how many years, barely sleeping, never stopping, flying all over the world to stop everything from aliens to epidemics to bombings to fairies. And now, the one time I took a break – because I'd been practically ordered to by my teammates – I was being accused of dereliction? How dare they!

I could feel the Light coiling within and knew without looking that my fists were starting to glow. The energy responded to my need, my thought, and my emotional state, which was one reason I always tried to stay calm. The last time I'd lost my temper, after Mystic Max had made some incredibly crude comments about Gemstone Julie and her wife and had then insulted the rest of us when we didn't laugh at what he claimed had been "just a little joke, jeez!", I'd had to fly out into space and pulverize a stray asteroid before I exploded and took out a city or worse. Now I forced myself to close my eyes, take deep breaths, and count to ten, quelling that energy before it could erupt.

Beneath the enforced control, however, I was seething. I'd been away one day and they'd gone from practically worshipping me to accusing and badmouthing me!

Well, if that was how they wanted to play it, fine. I'd take the rest of my planned vacation, and gladly.

Let's see how the world fared without Irradiant for an entire weekend!

The answer, as it turned out, was "not well."

Hero Force managed to stop Polar Princess and her Arctic Army, but not before they trashed half of Anchorage and snarled up shipping lanes for miles. Most of the Autobahn had to be shut down until Germany could manage emergency repairs. Kid Commando led his Combat Teens against Main.eAK – and half of them wound up in the hospital, along with about a third of the hostages. And Holly Honey and her Hive Mind started menacing ports all throughout Russia and Eastern Europe.

Naturally, the worse things got, the more people started blaming me for not being there. Everywhere I went, I heard it. People in the hotel lobby, people in the local restaurants, people on TV. Even the maids were gossiping about it as they cleaned the rooms, talking about, "Who does he think he is, letting the world down like that?"

I slept worse the second night and was bleary and stumbling all the next day. I kept being tempted to turn up the Light, to let it restore me, but resisted. I was trying to do this without resorting to my powers. Hell, at this point I was basically daring myself to survive the weekend as a normal dude. It was a point of pride now. And I was already halfway there. I could do this.

Then I walked straight into a hold-up.

I'd decided to check out the local casino. Why not, after all? Besides, I figured it was the one place that probably wouldn't have the news going, not the way casinos liked to make you forget about the outside world.

I'd been to Vegas, of course, and Monaco, and Atlantic City, and others. But always as Irradiant. Always on the job. This was the first time I'd gone to one as a regular guy. I had to blink a few times when I stepped inside, letting my eyes adjust to all the flashing lights and bright colors and moving images. It was like all of Times Square shoved into one big opera-house sized room. And the sounds! Clangs and dings and whirls and whistles and snatches of music, all mixed with people talking and laughing and shouting. I could smell cigarette smoke despite the whole place being no-smoking, and beer and booze and sweat and perfume and room deodorizer desperately trying to overpower the rest and failing miserably.

I was still standing there in the lobby just to one side of the door, trying to get my bearings, when I heard, "Get outta the way! Move or get shot!" The three men heading my way wore ski masks and black hoodies – it was like a trio of shadows spearing out from all that light. They were all armed, all clutching bags of what I guessed was money from the cashiers, and all heading my way at a dead run.

I didn't even stop to think. As they approached I let the Light Fantastic take back over, the sounds and sights and smells muted by my own rising glow, gravity and hunger and fatigue falling away as I rose into the air, hovering there in front of the three men.

Two of them just gaped at me. The third raised his gun and fired.

The bullets melted before they hit me, of course. I'd long since learned that my glow was good for a lot more than just being tough and strong. I reached out with it, sending shards of light lancing down, to vaporize their guns. Then I just tapped each of them on the forehead, knocking them out and letting them fall to the floor.

I heard gasps behind me, and a smattering of applause. Then a woman's voice cut through the rest:

"Where the hell've you been?"

I glanced around. She was maybe fifty, Hispanic, slim, well-dressed but not flashy. And her face, lean and lively, was contorted in rage.

"I said, where the hell've you been, Irradiant?" she demanded again, glaring up at me. "What, you been on a bender, big hero? Hiding out here getting drunk and hitting on waitresses while the world goes to shit?"

I started to reply, not really sure what to say, but she cut me off with a wave of her hand.

"My nephew was at First National," she informed me, her tone sharp enough to slice through steel. "He's in a medically induced coma now. Even if he wakes up, they're not sure he'll ever walk again. And why, so you could have yourself another mai tai and play another round of Blackjack? You disgust me!"

"Excuse me?" My anger was rising, and my luminescence with it. "Do you have any idea how hard I work for you people? Even I can't be everywhere at once!"

"So why're you here, then?" somebody else asked. "Why not where they need you?"

Others started shouting agreement, yelling at me to get back to work, to stop lazing about, to stop being so selfish. I could barely see them, the room had got so bright, and I flew out before I accidentally immolated them all.

But I could still hear their accusations, no matter how high I rose. I could still see that woman's anger, her hatred.

After all I'd done for the world, apparently all it took was one time not answering their call to turn me into the bad guy. A part of me wanted to shout, "Okay, fine, I'll be the bad guy!" But the rest of me was practically in tears. How could they turn on me like that? And, another part of me wailed, how could I ever make it up to them?

I didn't go back to the hotel. I didn't dare. What if somebody at the casino had seen me light up? What if they'd caught it on their security cameras? For all I knew, Bobby Gaynor's face was now all over the news, with captions like "Irradiant Hides Behind Boring Face" and "Not Much of a Hero After All." Instead I just flew as high and as far as I could and still stay within the atmosphere. Up among the clouds, nothing but a few distant planes in sight, I could at least be alone with my thoughts.

Not that they were particularly comforting.

Part of me hated those people for turning on me. But another part hated me for letting them down. None of me hated SkaterPunk and the others for making me go, at least, but I did hate myself for listening to them. Though they'd been right, too. I'd been burning out. Wearing myself down trying to do everything for everyone, trying to stop every threat, counter every disaster, save every person.

I couldn't do it. No one could. It was too much for anyone, even the Light Fantastic's champion.

Except – was it?

Because it occurred to me, slowly like the dawn breaking over the clouds, that maybe there was a way.

Maybe I'd had the answer all along.

When I'd first been granted the Light Fantastic, first let it inside me, I'd thought it was just this cool glow that protected me and let me fly and made me super strong. I'd worn a costume, all blue and white and silver, with a mask and a cape. But slowly I'd realized that the Light hadn't just surrounded me, it'd infused me. It was in every fiber of my being. And I started to learn that I could do a lot more with it. So much more.

That had culminated in the Galaxar Exhibition, when I'd been whisked away by the Promoter and made to compete against other galactic-level powers. When, to save myself, I'd been forced to let the Light Fantastic take control. It had suffused me, raising my powers to truly cosmic levels, but I'd become more energy than man, pretty much just the Light given human form.

I'd only barely been able to wrest back control after it had defeated all the other entrants and the Promoter herself. It had been a near thing, forcing the Light back down enough for my personality to take hold once more.

Now, I let myself float high up in the sky, right where the atmosphere gave way to space. Closing my eyes, I reached inside me, to that warm glow that was always there, pulsing like an enormous, brilliant heart. It welcomed my thoughts, my mind, into its embrace, wrapping around me in a soothing grip like a soft blanket.

And I let myself sink deep into its folds. I was safe and warm and cozy and didn't have to worry about anything ever again.

The Light would take care of everything.

Katie Peng – also known as the superhero SkaterPunk – started when a familiar glowing figure suddenly touched down on the base's wide back terrace. "IR, what're you doing here?" they demanded, rushing toward him. "You're not supposed to be back for another day at least!"

He glanced down at them, his eyes those eerie blue sparkles like a pair of sapphires amid a snowbank. "I am needed here," he answered, and Katie frowned. There was something off about his voice. It was flatter than usual. And colder.

"Did you get enough rest?" they asked, following him as he headed inside toward the monitor room. Danger Zone and Wordslinger had been arguing over a game of ping-pong in the rec room and hurried over upon seeing them.

"I am rested, thank you," Irradiant replied, nodding to the others as he passed them. "Now I must return to work."

"What, you figure we couldn't handle things without you?" Wordslinger drawled, hands resting over his doubled gunbelt, the twinned Literary Pistols hanging at his sides. "Shoot, pardner, we was doing just fine."

Irradiant glanced his way. "No, you were not. But I am here now. I will handle it."

Danger Zone shot a look at Katie. "You sure you're okay, Irradiant?" the big warrior woman asked. "We're happy to have you back, of course, but if you still need some time to get your mojo back to full, we understand."

Katie could just make out the hint of a frown through his glow. "I do not need more time. I am fine. I need to be busy. There are people who need my help." He'd reached the monitor wall and was studying the screens there, those vivid blue eyes scanning each image in turn. Then, with a single nod, he turned away – and blurred into motion, flying across the base and back out into the open air, disappearing in the blink of an eye.

"Whoa," Wordslinger muttered in the quiet that thudded down behind Irradiant's abrupt departure. "Guy's never been warm and fuzzy but that was next-level. Y'all replace him with a robot and not tell anybody?"

Danger Zone cuffed him upside the head, but Katie stared in the direction their friend had gone. Something was definitely wrong. They only hoped he would confide in them when he was ready.

Already miles away, Irradiant was focused entirely upon the list of upcoming tasks. Polar Princess was still at large. So were both Main.eAK and Holly Honey. Along with many others.

But no matter. He would handle them all. He no longer needed sleep, or sustenance of any kind. He could take care of every problem. Now that he was fully committed to the Light Fantastic, he never needed to stop or slow down or worry ever again.

Somewhere deep inside, the tiniest part that was still Bobby Gaynor was screaming, crying, begging. But Irradiant ignored him.

He had a job to do. Forever.

STORY INSPIRATION: I wanted to do a quieter, more internal horror, psychological rather than physical. And I thought it would be interesting to deal with someone who was outwardly so strong but inwardly so vulnerable. I always love writing superheroes, and the whole notion of a superhero trying to shut down long enough to relax and take a vacation brought it all together.

A Pirate's Life, for Me

Hildy Silverman

I can't believe how much I paid for this cruise. It better be worth it.

At least we're finally underway after the safety briefing and hundred-dollar-a-glass toast on deck. The *Barbary Coast* has around three hundred souls onboard, who each paid an exorbitant amount for the privilege. For the vast majority, it's a pittance that was paid out of a limitless Cayman Island account or will be made up by a single week's stock dividends.

I am *not* a member of that majority. I scraped together the cost of my cabin from my divorce hush money and the windfall sale of our primary home. I readily acknowledge this cruise is a foolish, wasteful, self-indulgent expense, but given the hell I've survived? Trust me, I am *owed*.

Strolling the upper deck, I size up other passengers as I pass by, offering each a brief smile or polite nod. Some return the empty gestures – the old money who still have a sense of noblesse oblige. Others look through me like I'm a ghost. Doesn't bother me much. I'm used to not being seen.

Back when I'd more regularly shared rarified air with these people – the rich, the famous, the spoiled – Nick had been with me, and all anyone ever saw was him. Fame had radiated off my then-husband, blinding everyone to all but the man at its center. At most, I was only acknowledged as an acolyte to be envied for my proximity to their idol.

No one knows the price I paid for that privilege. And now, thanks to the ironclad NDA our attorneys hammered out, no one ever would.

But hey, at least now when I jolt awake at night, my throat raw from screaming in my dream-memories, I have a fat bank account to comfort me. Enough to cover the years of therapy and medications I should have been on even before my marriage.

I'll look into those after vacation. For real this time. I *swear*.

I shake my head hard enough for my long, blonde ponytail to slap my cheeks. Go away, intrusive thoughts!

I adjust the chin strap on my straw, floppy brimmed hat ensuring it doesn't blow away in the light, steady breeze. I don't want to think about my disaster of a marriage or my upbringing or any aspect of those dead lives. I paid a fortune for this high-end cruise and I'm *damned* well going to enjoy it.

Bright sunlight glints off white-capped waves. The deck rises and falls languorously as the swells are gentled by the ship's stabilizers. Beautiful. Soothing. Lush shoreline recedes as we chug toward deeper waters. Peeking over the mahogany railing reveals dolphins or porpoises (I never remember which is which) frolicking in our wake. I draw a deep breath for what feels like the first time and relish the tickle of warm, salty moisture in my nasal passages.

The ship is magnificent. Far smaller than one of those cruise ships out of Bayonne my family vacationed on when I was a child, it is what the upper classes refer to as *well-appointed*. The wood used for the railings, decks, and decorative trim is rich, dark brownish-red. The planks below my feet have been polished to a sheen that reflects the sun blazing in the cloudless blue sky.

Arriving at the pool and jacuzzi area aft (front is *fore*, back is *aft* – Sandi and I learned that during a guided tour on the *Song of the Seas*), I appreciate the attempt, through use of lush, potted palms and tiki bars, to make the surroundings look like a beach. Yacht rock plays just loud enough to be heard but not so much to be intrusive. The pool water is a shade of turquoise that begs me to plunge in. The shallow end has a row of white padded lounge chairs arrayed within. Flat-bellied women in tiny bikinis and round-gutted men in Speedos have already taken up residence on them. Each hold umbrella-and-fruit topped drinks that gleam with pink, green, orange, and blue liqueurs. An alcoholic rainbow of indulgences.

No kids. This is a playground for adults, which is one of the things that convinced me to spend what I had for my solo berth. It's not like I hate children, it's just that seeing them reminds me of too many sad things. Infuriating things. Lost things I couldn't do anything about yet shrieked and gnawed and clawed within me, constantly demanding a retribution never taken.

As if on cue, my memory conjures up my sweet little sister, Sandi, with her golden curls that tightened into Shirley Temple-like ringlets in the humidity. She still has rosy cheeks, still visibly pulses with joy, with life. Is that what attracted him – the creeper, the monster who'd stolen her from the beach while she was out of our sight for a few minutes? He'd been fast, that son of a bitch. That… *pirate*.

Of course it was our fault, my parents' and mine, or so the authorities clearly implied. We'd gotten off our ship in a country where girls of all ages disappeared, and likely more often than was reported. Why weren't we more vigilant? He'd probably stalked us from the moment we left the ship. Two active little girls itching to run free after three days at sea, parents far too relaxed to police them like they'd been warned to during the port pre-arrival briefing. Easy prey.

Why didn't he take me? Maybe because I'd stayed in my parents' line of sight while balancing on the edge where the white sand of the local hidden beach met azure water, unsure whether to venture into the shallows where jellyfish might lurk. My folks had followed a tip from another passenger on where to go to *avoid the crowds*. I still wonder if he was a real passenger or a scout planted on board to misdirect gullible families?

My little sister had scurried off toward the jungle that surrounded and concealed the beach, fearless as ever, in search of the source of a loud bird's repeated cry. Maybe the pirate used it to lure her. Or perhaps she just got lost and trusted the first grownup to offer a hand and a promise to lead her back to mommy and daddy.

All speculation. We never found out – not who, not why, not where she wound up. Not even whether she was alive. Sometimes, I pray that she is and I'll run into her again in whatever remote part of the world she was spirited to. Other times, I pray that they killed her quickly instead of making her suffer for the past...

Huh. It's the twenty-fifth anniversary. Exactly today.

Fucking pirate. Yes, that's what I call him, whoever he was. And yes, I'm sure he was a *he*. Isn't it always? A pirate stole my sister, robbed my parents of their lightheartedness and our family of joy. We never went on another cruise, or any vacation, after that. The pirate stole my parents' souls and left behind bitter, angry husks who in turn robbed me of my freedom, all in service to *never going through that again.*

Whether Sandi's dead or not, I sure hope *he* is. Living that sort of life, someone must have gutted him by now. I hope they took their time.

I hated the pirate for making me imagine what he and his buddies did, for getting away with it. I used to imagine everything I'd do to him if I ever found him, things I learned from every book, TV show, and movie with themes of revenge I could consume. When I reached my teens, I figured out how to release some of the tension, rubbing myself while imagining the terror on his face, the light fading from his eyes, as I slowly, precisely carved…

When did I reach the bow?

It's not too crowded up here. This is nice. I can almost pretend the whole ship belongs to me. Resting my forearms against the railing, I close my eyes and let the wind, stronger and more defiant as the ship chugs into it, blow my hat back and rake salt-crusted fingers through my hair. Only the strap securing it around my neck keeps it from being lost forever.

I've lived a life of loving confinement. Sure, I would have enjoyed sleepovers with my friends, taking class trips in high school, living in a college dorm instead of my ever-shrinking (or so it seemed to me) bedroom at home. It was a miracle my parents let me go to college at all. Then again, if they hadn't, I wouldn't have met Nick back when he was just a fellow student who sang in a campus band. Back before he became NICK, writ large, name chanted by throngs of fans who soak their panties as soon as he opens his mouth or flirts from the stage with his trademark wink-and-nod.

At least being with Nick freed me from my parents' cage. He'd been a different kind of pirate – certainly styled himself like one with long black hair cascading from beneath a wide tie-dyed headband, long velvet coat with brass buttons worn open over his bare chest, and leather trousers tucked into Doc Martens. His skin was always bronze (more from tanning beds than the sun) and his features were, as the entertainment rags described them, *ruggedly handsome*. A self-styled pirate, to be sure, but he still earned the designation. He'd certainly stolen me away from my parents and career plans with promises of high-seas freedom, fortune, and unbridled passion.

He broke all those promises, of course. Tried to break me too. Came pretty damn close; maybe even succeeded. Depends on who you ask.

Nick ran our marriage like a tight ship, confining me to my post as worshipful first mate to his captain. Even after his glamor faded and my eyes finally beheld the narcissistic, insecure man-boy beneath his carefully constructed persona, he'd bound me with threats and taunts.

Sometimes his fists, especially after I caught him in our bed with yet another underage groupie.

Yeah, yeah. I shouldn't have gone after him with the butcher knife that last time. It worked out though, because he cared more about being outed and cancelled than punishing me for my insubordination. I might not have succeeded in castrating the bastard but at least I convinced him to finally let me go.

Damn it, I'm doing it again! Letting my mind suck me down into the quicksand of the past.

Time to find my cabin.

I follow a mahogany-railed marble staircase down to Deck Three where my single suite awaits. Opening the door with the keycard, I behold a compact, yet again *well-appointed* space. It might not be as luxurious as the ones on the higher decks, but there's really no bum space on this vessel. Closing the door behind me, I take a few moments to revel in the fact that it's all mine.

I toss my straw hat onto the bed, which consists of two singles bound together by tight sheets and a mattress topper to form a full. A towel fashioned into an elephant shape sits atop the pillow, cradling a card of tips for making *lifelong happy memories* on my cruise.

I peek into every drawer, cabinet, and nook. Clever construction, allowing passengers to store so much in such a confined space. My suitcase awaits on a luggage rack courtesy of my room steward. Time to unpack. This is a ten-day voyage, and I don't plan to live out of a suitcase.

Once it's empty, I tuck it into a discreet corner. And just like that, it ceases to exist. For now, this is *home*.

Contentment warms my insides like a mug of hot buttered rum. Sliding open the glass door that leads to my small private balcony, I step over the raised sill and take a seat on a white-padded lounge chair. Closing my eyes, I listen to the *shush-shush-shush* of waves as they lap against the hull. Other than that, and an occasional seagull's cry, there is silence.

Peace, elusive and unfamiliar, settles over me the way it used to when I was a kid, before the pirates invaded my life and instilled me with a rage that no amount of primal screaming or breaking things or screwing around could relieve. Well-meaning friends and doctors have looked at me with pity-filled, fearful expressions for so, so long, encouraging me to *get help, talk to someone, work through it*. At least they used to, before I learned to just avoid seeing friends and doctors.

But I heard them. When I get back, it'll be different. I just need some time to rest, to figure out what I really need. Then I'll take their advice. I'll *try*.

A mere few words from the captain of the *Barbary Coast* during our initial safety briefing float back into my consciousness. About the *highly unlikely* possibility of pirate activity in the region, accompanied by confident reassurances that the crew was *more than prepared* should the *unlikely* occur.

I sit up straight on my lounger. *Real* pirates. Not the fanciful ones from books and films and romanticized history. The kind who sought out ships full of fattened fortunates and their expensive things and cash for buying more things in exotic ports of calls. Filled with targets for ransom, rape, and slaughter.

Actual pirates don't ravish. They don't duel. There's nothing romantic, no noble codes of conduct. No, they are hungry, desperate, angry, and *real*. If they make it aboard this ship, this gleaming beacon of every single thing they'd been denied in life, not a one of us will survive. I'm as certain of this as I am that the captain wouldn't include mention of them in his safety briefing if pirate attacks weren't genuinely possible. Hell, I *watched* that Tom Hanks movie!

I can't seem to catch my breath. Of all the private cruises available, why did I choose one where fucking *pirates* could actually happen! How did I not even consider it while planning? I chose this itinerary as an indulgence I could (barely) afford due to the time of year and location. My travel agent assured me the passage was a beautiful one, with lovely ports of call and lush, gorgeous scenery few ever got to see. You would think though, given my history, I'd have at least asked, "Hm, that all sounds great, but what about the area's murderous pirates?"

I clench my fists, force myself to suck in one slower, deeper breath. Then another. I'm being ridiculous. This ship is moving constantly (unless it's in port), and it's pretty damn fast. How would pirates even get aboard from their small, rickety motorboats? I'm just paranoid. Imagining shit again. This ship is perfectly safe and secure (until it's in port).

Another thought, from the deepest, darkest part of me, extends a tentacle: *Maybe you didn't ask about the threat of pirates because that was part of the appeal.*

Enough!

Battening down the proverbial hatch on my chattering thoughts, I check the time on my diamond and gold watch. It was a gift from Nick on the occasion of our fifth anniversary, so that I wouldn't have *any more excuses for coming home so goddamn late* back when I still used to hang out with friends. Nick only cared about what I did and where I was when he was home between gigs. He needed me with him every minute around the clock so I could cater to his whims the way his roadies and groupies did during tours.

Wow, it's nearly time for dinner. I'm not sure how. When I went out on the balcony, it was around noon. It doesn't feel like much time passed, but it's been almost five hours. Admittedly, I *do* zone out sometimes – it's one of the things I mentioned to my general practitioner back when I still saw her.

It *is* annoying that I'm still losing time like this. Another thing to deal with after I return.

I take a quick shower in the cylindrical glass stall provided, using the sea salt and coconut-scented body and hair wash provided. We're all going to smell exactly the same on this trip and it amuses me for some reason – thinking about everyone smelling like we are members of an extended family that, for some reason, has to share a single soap.

Stepping out, I nearly stub my toe on the drain in the middle of the small bathroom. I guess the stewards use that to quickly drain and dry the bathroom after cleaning. Maybe to clear up any accidental floods. Clever.

I run leave-in conditioner through my hair and decide to let it air dry. It falls to just past my shoulders. In the humid, salted air, my hair will kink into long, beachy waves. I like the way they look on me. Reminds me of being a kid and letting my hair fly freely in the summer breeze, without worrying about one of my ex's fans or a paparazzo snapping and posting an unflattering photo that might embarrass him.

Fuck it. I'm not even going to wear makeup tonight!

I pull on a spaghetti-strap white maxi dress decorated with embossed green-and-gold palm fronds and a pair of low-slung strappy sandals. High heels aren't a wise choice for a cruise with the decks rolling and lurching beneath. Plus, if there's an emergency, you can't run away.

A final check in the full-length mirror hung over the closet door. My reflection scowls back at me until I relent and add a little black mascara, rosy blush, and lip gloss.

Now I'm ready.

The cavernous main dining room is ornately decorated with enormous gold and crystal chandeliers above. Below are royal-blue velvet cushioned chairs set around spotless, white cloth-covered tables with centerpieces of exotic flowers and candles in hurricane glass holders. A wide, winding mahogany staircase divides the dining room in half. A host seats me at a table with other single passengers and couples – other *low-levels* only on board because, like me, they'd gotten a deal of some sort. We make the usual small talk:

"What's your name?"

"Where are you from?"

"Is this your first cruise? Isn't it just beautiful?"

The trick when being forced to interact with strangers is to keep smiling. Now, lots of people know how to hide the fact that they don't give a shit behind a smile. But here's a tip – you have to put more than your mouth into it. *Anyone* can make their lips turn up at the corners, even show some teeth. But they forget about their eyes.

Most people look others in the eye, to size them up and decide whether they are present, genuine, invested. Safe. So, when your smile is just something you put on when circumstances call for it – like makeup – you have to make sure it reaches your eyes. Otherwise, the contrast between your empty, disconnected, uncaring gaze and your broad, toothy smile comes across as uncanny. Disturbing, even.

I make sure my eyes smile. It's simple enough to tighten the muscles across my cheeks until the corners of my eyes crinkle appropriately. I don't even need a mirror to confirm I'm doing it right anymore; God knows I've had a *lot* of practice. Simply by gauging the reactions of the other passengers, I can tell that I'm projecting my desired image: *I am engaged. What you say matters. I care.*

The food is excellent, as you would expect (if not demand) from a high-end cruise. The meal begins with an amuse-bouche of an oyster topped with horseradish foam. A petite Caesar salad follows. Next is a chilled bouillabaisse velouté, creamy and savory. Then the main course of prime rib, accompanied by cheesy scalloped potatoes and herb-seasoned broccoli steamed to a bright emerald green. Delicious, flawlessly prepared, each course is accompanied by an expertly selected wine served by a white-gloved waiter with a napkin draped over his forearm to cradle the neck of each bottle. Pours range from a crisp, dry white to a red with sharp, spicy tannins.

My tablemates and I pass a basket of pumpkin seed-studded rolls and flavorful garlic butter around the table throughout the meal, talking about ourselves in ways that reveal only the best of who we are. We make quips and laugh like we are actually friends.

One particular man, another single traveler, sits across from me. He is tall and what I would describe as ruggedly handsome. His hair, still more pepper than salt, is longer than current fashion, but perfectly coiffed. His gray eyes are alert, intelligent, and meet my gaze throughout the meal with increasing frequency. Whenever he smiles, the skin around those eyes crinkles in unison.

He has clearly practiced.

He says his name is Sam and that he is the CFO of a tech startup that's really taken off. He is a widower, his beloved wife having sadly passed away after a battle with cancer last year.

When he thinks no one is paying attention, his gaze roams around the table. It pauses on a heavyset woman wearing a glittering pendant that may or may not be a real diamond. Then on another woman wearing a white gold bracelet studded with a rainbow of sapphires, a man sporting a ruby tie clip, and an elderly woman with loops of pearls around her neck.

I notice because I am *always* paying attention. Everyone else probably thinks he's just being attentive, engaging. He keeps the conversation going whenever it ebbs, telling us how this is his first trip without his late, lamented Joan, that he is finally ready to move on with his life. He looks right at me when he says it.

For just a moment, that friendly smile plastered across his face shifts into something… predatory. Is it my watch he wants or something else?

Dessert is served. Baked Alaska, fashioned into the shape of our ship, flambéed tableside before being sliced and served with an Ethiopian coffee that is rich and darkly roasted. Together they create a delicious contrast of sweet and bitterness. Unfortunately, the course's charms are lost on me; the bite I take of sponge cake, ice cream, and merengue merely freezes my mouth and tastes like ashes.

Because I know. *This* is how they board ships despite prepared crews and high-end surveillance equipment and being in constant motion (unless we're in port). I know who Sam really is… *what* he is. Beneath the veneer of a tech bro's linen shirt and khakis, and under that expertly styled hair, he wears a single gold earring and frock coat with brass buttons.

Imitate. Insinuate. Infiltrate. That's what pirates do.

I look at my jabbering table companions, then surreptitiously around the dining room. Passengers guzzle drinks, dribble decadent rum sauce from the corners of their mouths before hastily dabbing with their white napkins staining them red. How many among the botoxed and lifted and painted faces surrounding me, representing nearly every color in humanity's palette (not all pirates are one color; I'm no racist) are hiding in plain sight?

The middle-aged woman with duck lips and perpetually wide eyes to my right gently touches my hand and asks if I'm okay. Realizing I'm hyperventilating, I direct my most friendly and confident face to her and admit I might have drunk a bit more than I'm used to. She nods understandingly and stops feigning interest. Good.

Calm down! Sam could be alone, on reconnaissance, assessing security and gauging opportunities before reporting back to his fellows on when to mount their full assault. Our first port of call isn't for two more days. It makes sense to wait until we're in port to sneak the rest on board, rather than try to surround a moving ship and take us at sea.

Yes. That's logical. My throbbing heartbeat starts to slow. It might not be too late!

From across the table, Sam is staring at me openly. When he sees my gaze shift to him, one side of his mouth crooks upward. He must have overheard what I said to Duck Lips about having drunk too much.

I can work with that.

A part of me laments, *why me*? Cold, hard experience has taught me that no one else will step up, do what has to be done. If I go to a crewmember, demand to see the captain on a matter of urgency, they'll brush me off until I tell them why. And if I do, they'll lock me in sick bay because I'm drunk or hysterical or both…which *might* be true, but also, pirates might be coming for all of us and I know what they will do, what they're capable of doing.

No one, not my parents, not my friends, not the doctors ever believed me whenever I confided in them about the pirates. Warned how dangerous they are, how they're every-*fucking*-where. So why would these strangers believe me now?

The rest of me? Might be just a *wee* bit excited by the opportunity Sam presents.

I smile at Sam, a different smile than the *polite interest* version I've been utilizing all night. I'm better at it than him, my mask more practiced and convincing. His delighted expression confirms this.

I yawn and announce to everyone that I should probably head back to my stateroom. My imitation of Nick's trademark wink-and-nod is only for Sam though. His grin widens.

I cross my utensils on my plate, heavy serrated steel steak knife over fork, and spread my napkin over. I open my beaded evening bag just below the edge of the table and fumble for a few moments as if searching for my keycard.

Sam offers to escort me back to my cabin. Doesn't want me to lose my balance on the swaying ship and twist an ankle or otherwise come to harm. A proper gentleman.

A cunning pirate.

We stroll outside, enjoying the cool ocean breeze. Sam tells me more about his persona – his loneliness over the past year, the Porche Panamera he has his eye on, the exciting future of the software startup he cofounded with Chad, his best friend since their frat days at Cornell.

I smile, nod, and talk enough to keep his interest and convince him of mine. The gentle breeze blows his scent toward me. It's different than mine, than that of the passengers who, like me, showered before dinner. True, he could have just skipped that, but more likely he smells like musk and rum because he doesn't have a cabin but rather has been hiding below decks since sneaking aboard at our port of embarkation.

It confirms my suspicions. He doesn't smell like sea salt and coconut because he isn't a passenger. He's an invader.

When we reach my cabin, Sam stares into my eyes. I recognize his hunger and take full advantage. "Would you like to come inside and tuck me in?" I purr.

"Yes. Yes I would," he replies in a voice husky with alcohol and desire.

I swipe my keycard, pretend to miss the pad once or twice, and giggle. I am sober – well, sober enough – thanks to fresh air and pumping adrenaline. I've developed a pretty high tolerance for alcohol and other substances after a decade of marriage to a rock star. Of course, Sam doesn't know that. All the better to make him believe he's controlling this situation.

As soon as the door closes, he pounces, mouth hot and moist as it engulfs mine. I taste steak and rum sauce and stale marijuana as he thrusts his tongue halfway down my throat. I try not to gag.

Why do men think jamming their slimy, thick tongues down a woman's throat is a sexy first move? Almost every guy I've ever had has made this their opener. Makes my stomach lurch every goddamn time. The fact that Sam pulls the same maneuver makes what I'm going to do even easier, emotionally and practically.

He is so distracted by my sucking and moaning and grinding against him in seeming delight that he doesn't notice what I'm doing with my hands and my evening bag behind his back.

I manage to detach my mouth from his. "Let's take this into the shower." I grab him with my free hand, giggle, and start pulling him toward the bathroom.

He hesitates. "What? Why? The stall's too tight for two."

"Tight is good." I close the gap between us, mash my breasts against his chest, and blink at him like a wide-eyed ingenue in a rom-com. "Don't you want to get *really* close to me?"

He utters a sound halfway between a growl and a moan. Drags me by the wrist into the bathroom. I keep my other hand positioned out of his eyeline. Not that he's paying attention to anything but the raging hard-on tenting his trousers anyway.

In the bathroom, his mouth once again absorbs mine. I tangle my fingers in his hair with one hand and tug. It's now or never.

He probably thinks I'm caressing his throat. Then his gray eyes fly from lusty half-mast to wide open. His face contorts with confusion and pain. He gropes at the gaping hole just below his Adam's Apple, pulls his hands away slowly, watches his blood flow through quivering fingers. He gasps like a fish for water after being yanked by a hook into a dinghy.

I could have slit his carotid, his jugular, but that would make blood jet all over the bathroom and arterial spray is a *bitch* to clean up. Amazing how many practical things you learn from years of reading and watching horror and true crime... not to mention life experiences.

That includes not stopping until you're certain.

I plunge the steak knife into his midsection. Stomach, solar plexus. Soft parts, easier to puncture fast and repeatedly than, say, the chest. And just as effective.

Sam sinks to his knees, falls forward onto the floor. His eyes are empty, ruggedly handsome features slack. Masks don't stay on after death. His blood swirls toward the drain in the center of the bathroom's tiled floor.

I walk out to the balcony and fill my lungs with crisp, clean salt air. It's cleansing; sweeps away the taste of Sam-the-Pirate. I strip off my now bloodied dress (a shame; it was a favorite), ball it up, and lob it into the sea.

Back inside, I turn on the shower, making sure to keep the glass door open, and point the nozzle at the body. Blood dilutes and disappears down the drain. Perfect. This won't be too hard to clean up at all.

Getting rid of the body is a chore, but nothing I can't handle. I do a lot of Tae Bo to keep in shape. A little dragging, a little tugging, and over the balcony rail he flops. Any splash is wholly muffled by the ship's engines and throbbing techno music blaring from the nightclub located just above my deck.

That's going to be annoying at night. I hope I remembered earplugs.

At least there's one less pirate in the world. I close my eyes and sink into my lounge chair. The release and relief surging through me is better than any orgasm.

Is that a small boat keeping pace with our ship?

I'm up and leaning far over the balcony, but it's hard to see as clouds pass across the moon. Wait… yes, there it is! Ramshackle and low-lit, like it doesn't want to be seen. I have to squint to make it out as it disappears and reappears. They must be waiting for a signal from Sam or one of the others. Will they attack us tonight, while we're isolated out at sea? Or follow until we reach port?

The steak knife rests on the glass-top table. I pick it up. Between streaks of blood and viscera, slivers of steel gleam in the fluctuating moonlight.

The thing is, pirates aren't lone creatures. Sam was just one of many. I have to find the others on my ship and deal with them before it's too late. Otherwise, they'll destroy everything and everyone. Like they always do.

STORY INSPIRATION: With regards to the story setting, I was inspired by my love of cruising and fascination with super high-end cruises (I've never taken one... yet!).

As for my character and the plot, I enjoy stories with unreliable narrators, especially those who are so lost in derangement and delusion that they genuinely don't perceive how sick they are. I tried to capture that mindset in my protagonist – that innate confidence that she is the heroine regardless of her bizarre beliefs and heinous actions.

Lookout

Mia Dalia

When Jeff says he likes all things Hawaiian, he means that one time he drunkenly stumbled into a Tiki Con at the hotel where his family reunion was being held. And The Rock. Definitely The Rock.

Still, his enthusiasm is palpable – he gets worked up easily and stays that way. That "pump it" energy does wonders for his career as a fitness trainer. Besides, we need an extra person. Craig has dropped out, and this trip is a package deal. Unless we have enough people, everyone's share goes up.

Every group of friends has a Jeff – too loud, too awkward, too much – someone kept around mostly out of nostalgia and inertia. If you think your group doesn't have one, then you're the Jeff. The glue of adult friendships is ineffable. As a kid, it's as simple as geographic proximity or a cartoon you both love. Over time, things get complicated.

Most of us have been friends since college. We've matured at different rates and moved around for various reasons, yet managed to stick together. A loosely grouped formation at best, but still.

I never thought I'd be the last to get married. Even Jeff has a failed year-long matrimonial stint marring his late twenties. I like to say I've been busy, but really, I've just been picky. My freedom has stretched on far too long, and now that I've finally found someone, my friends and I have come to the tropical paradise of O'ahu to celebrate the end of it.

A strange ritual, when you think about it, but it's what we've always done, and approaching middle age, the last thing any of us wants is change. If nothing else, it's a nice vacation, a break from the world and its looming responsibilities.

Everyone else is free to bring their significant others, while I'm to come alone. Symbolism aside, it's a crappy arrangement, but there you have it.

My bride-to-be is left behind to sort out cakes and dresses while I'm here, in the blinding sunshine, staring at the impossibly blue water, and contemplating how *White Lotus*-y my friends are. Not me, I'm technically the poorest of the bunch, but the rest have done pretty well for themselves.

Ollie is a graphic designer. Milo's old man finally retired a while back, handing over the reins of the family construction business to his son. Tom's a lawyer; personal injury, but he fronts like it's high-end litigation.

Me, I've tried many things with limited success. The realtor thing is still recent enough to have that new car smell. My future wife's family owns the company I work for. Our romance has been all too easy breezy – and just a bit sleazy, albeit in a way that guarantees my job security.

I'm not complaining, mind you. Jen's great. From what I know of love, she may well be the one. But right now, she's about five thousand miles away, and the grimy city I've left behind feels like another world.

There are barely any direct flights from Philly to O'ahu. With a layover in LA, my total travel time to get here was close to sixteen hours.

Jet lag has always hit me like a ton of bricks. This has been the worst one yet. Something about losing hours in the air while chasing the sun across the sky has left my brain feeling like an overripe banana. Time moves sluggishly through me… or perhaps I move sluggishly through time. Sometimes when I blink, I forget where I am – like a momentary signal cutout. Then I look around and remember.

Everyone else seems to have shaken off their jet lag easily enough. Although to be fair, most of them had shorter trips. Jeff, who's been in Los Angeles for the last few years, helping beautiful people get more beautiful, is positively bouncing with energy.

In the morning, while I struggle to push through the mental fog, drowning my inner cobwebs with strong black coffee, he's chugging a smoothie while flipping through a book. Without my reading glasses, I squint to make out the title – something about local lore.

Has LA made a reader out of Jeff? Not likely. He's turning the pages like he's looking for pictures.

"This place is unreal," he says, licking the smoothie mustache off his top lip. "They've got ghosts and things."

"Everywhere's got ghosts, if you believe in that sort of thing," I tell him.

"For real?"

"Sure," Milo says, entering the kitchen of our rental house. "Yo." He nudges me. "Tell him about that house in Atlantic City."

Milo's wife, Gina, plops down on the dining booth bench next to me, ready to listen, while Milo starts sorting out their breakfast.

I rub my forehead and proceed to regale them with the story of the infamous abandoned property in AC. It used to belong to some old -timey magician and is, apparently, haunted as hell. People are rumored to have disappeared there. These days, no one goes near it except for curiosity seekers and daredevil looky-loos.

Ollie and Gordy walk in, hand-in-hand, looking ridiculously loved up and well put together, like a couple from a reality TV show. They have the same build and could probably swap clothes if they wanted to, if not for their distinct styles: Ollie favors a skinny, tailored fit while Gordy prefers long, flowing pieces, what he calls "kimono chic." They've been together the longest out of any of us and have always had the audacity to look the youngest.

"Clean living," they swear. We suspect otherwise but don't argue.

The kitchen is getting full, so breakfast spills out into the dining room. There is no real separation between the two.

The rental house is nice, plain but comfortable with enough bedrooms for everyone. Colorful shrubs bloom outside. It's close to the beach. What more can you ask for?

Tom's the last one to get up, accompanied by Alisa, his latest and least likable squeeze to date.

She grabs a yogurt and glowers at me. I get the impression she doesn't like anyone here, and least of all me. Alisa has a heavy brow, thin mouth, and dark, deep-set eyes that speak of an Eastern European ancestry. Well, that and her dour outlook.

"She's a writer," Tom says. "And an editor."

It's as if he's trying to score some gravitas by proxy.

I've looked her up. Her claim to fame is a single novel that didn't set anyone's world on fire and a bunch of short stories, all on small presses. She also has a small press of her own – another nobody writer who gets off passing judgment on the talents of others.

I know her kind. I gave writing a shot once, a while back, before realizing I didn't have the stamina for the vagaries of the publishing business and the sort of people it attracts.

Alisa has an affected way of talking. Through a mouthful of Greek yogurt, she encourages me to tell more stories, probably fishing for new material.

I oblige and launch into another ghostly real estate story, this one featuring a ramshackle property in the Strawberry Mansion area of Philadelphia. A grand old house has been converted into three condos, one per floor, with an unusually high turnaround of owners. It is said to be haunted by the family who originally owned the place and was brutally murdered in their sleep by former employees.

Ghosts are all we talk about the entire breakfast, until Jeff declares it to be "beach time."

O'ahu is beautiful enough to pass for otherworldly if you get far enough from the hustle and bustle. The third-largest and most populous island of Hawaii features everything from busy urban centers to serene natural wonders. They call it "The Gathering Place" for a reason.

Being from Philly, my go-to beaches are all in Jersey. This is nothing like Jersey. The beaches in O'ahu are pristine. Breathtaking.

Jeff has rented a surfboard. The only other single person on this trip – "by choice" he beams proudly – he is treating himself to some waves. Not to be outdone, Tom has rented one, too. The rest of us are taking bets as to who will fall on their faces first.

Smothered in sunscreen and a complicated dark fabric wrap, Alisa has immersed herself in some luridly covered novel. The rest break out cards, snacks, and other beach staples.

There are mountains on O'ahu – volcanic, no less. Lush valleys to explore. And, of course, Honolulu, with all its attractions. But for this vacation, we've decided to stay put and bake ourselves in the abundant sunshine, like lizards.

We were lucky to score a place in Lanikai. Originally, we were shooting for Kailua, the more laid-back surfer town, but the house in Lanikai opened up last minute and offered an irresistibly deep discount.

Now we're here, in the lap of luxury, which mostly seems to mean fewer people. Which, in turn, translates to more isolation. The latter, amplified by the Ko'olau Mountains dramatically rising in the backdrop, has been playing havoc with my jet-lag-addled sense of reality.

Jeff wipes out first. Of course he does. Guess he hasn't picked up much surfing in LA. Tom is obnoxious with his success, but then he buys everyone a round, and, suddenly, we don't care.

At some point, I think I doze off. I dream of ghosts and wake up with a sunburn. Looking at the ocean soothes my eyes, but my skin is on fire.

In the evening, Ollie and Gordy grill fish in our backyard. I look at the night sky and think about what it must be like to live here, in this isolated place, on this isolated island, surrounded by water as far as the eye can see, the nearest land thousands of miles away. O'ahu is wide open but feels strangely claustrophobic. I wonder if that's what marriage is going to feel like.

It isn't something you can ask others, because every answer will be different. My parents persevered in semi-hostile silences for decades. My sister has been divorced twice. Milo and Gina appear to be slowly morphing into each other. Ollie and Gordy always seem deliriously – rather unbelievably – happy. But you can never tell unless you're in other people's shoes, their heads, their skin.

We barely have a week on O'ahu, but time feels muddled. My days are full of sunshine and merriment, but my nights are troubled and restless. When I can't sleep, I sit outside in the backyard and look at the stars. Back home, you're lucky to see a few. Here it looks like someone has sprinkled gold dust across a sheet of dark velvet.

Jeff joins me one night.

"Can't sleep?" I ask him.

"Just a bit jittery," he mumbles.

I have a sinking suspicion that Jeff's superhero-muscular build isn't one hundred percent organic. He used to be pudgy in school. Now, he occasionally exhibits the kind of side effects one may associate with steroid use, but no one ever says anything, because Jeff is living his best life.

He's wearing boxer shorts and flip-flops. The moonlight glistens across his ripped abdomen.

"Nightmarchers," he says, never one to enjoy silence for long.

"Night what?"

"Nightmarchers, that's the ghosts that live here," Jeff clarifies. "It's in that tourist book. They are like the spirits of fallen warriors that walk around at night and kill anyone who gets in their way."

"Anyone?"

"Yeah. I mean, I think so. I didn't read the fine print or anything, but I think unless you show them respect or something." He laughs. "Like mafia dudes."

I nod. There's a pounding in my head that is aggravated with every movement. I really should have insisted on a closer destination. I may be getting too old for long flights, and at the end of the day, one beach is – nearly – as good as another.

"I'm gonna try to find them," Jeff says.

My brain, thick and molten like the innards of a lava lamp, struggles to pick up the thread of the conversation. "Who?"

"Nightmarchers, dude. There are these places they supposedly haunt. And we're not far from one of them. You just take the Pali Highway." In the dark, he gestures to where it cuts through the mountains like a jagged scar. "About a twenty-minute drive gets you to the... Something Lookout. And there they are."

"At the Lookout?"

"Yep. At night." Jeff rolls on the balls of his feet, vibrating with kinetic energy.

"Well, good luck with that," I tell him.

He doesn't convince me to join him until the end of our short vacation, on an uncharacteristically gray day that I spend inside reading a local history book borrowed from the small living room library.

Intermittent rain pelts the sun-faded window shutters and the reddish shrubbery as I learn about O'ahu, page by page.

I find out that its ti shrubs – like the ones outside our rental with long, colorful leaves, shaped like the tips of spears and ranging from green to near blood-red – are planted around houses for luck and protection. On a day like today, the idea feels strangely ominous.

A lot of the book is dedicated to Nightmarchers; O'ahu is a place proud of its ghosts.

Not only are the ti shrubs meant to ward them off, but the houses here – including, I realize, the one we're in – are built with the front and back doors aligned in a straight line so the spirits can pass through without causing harm. The thought makes me shudder, despite the ambient warmth.

"So, you're gonna go check some ghosts out with me?" Jeff asks, his enthusiasm kid-like in its purity. Just another silly Jeff adventure to laugh about later. Who knows how many more of those I'll have after getting married? "Alisa is coming, too."

"She is?" I say, surprised. But then, perhaps I'm not. She looks like the type to go ghost-hunting, a charmless Lydia Deetz.

"Yeah, it'll be fun." Jeff rips into a power bar whose bright cover promises a protein boost. "It'll be loads of fun."

My arm doesn't take much to be twisted. We go that evening. The rain slows down to an intermittent drizzle before dying out. Others opt for a cookout, so the three of us set out on our adventure.

Nu'uanu Pali is the official name of the lookout. We get there just as the day is about to slip into night, and the scenery makes it easy to understand its popularity. Situated on a 1,186-foot mountain pass and surrounded by 3,000-foot peaks, it offers a spectacular bird's eye view of Kaneohe and its bay, Kailua, Mokoli'i Island, the magnificent Ko'olau Mountain Range, and the vast expanse of the Pacific Ocean that surrounds it all.

The wind here is strong enough to send you flying. It blows clean through us, snapping our clothes like sails.

The Lookout is officially open until six, but it's not a fortress. There's no fencing or patrolling, and gaining access is easy enough. The idea seems to be for nature to take guard duty overnight. With low visibility and precipitously steep drop-offs and wind gusts that threaten to send you careening down into the glittering darkness below, this isn't a place for the faint of heart.

"Wow," I say, staring at the panoramic splendor.

"Wow," Alisa echoes, managing to make the simple comment sound sarcastic.

Jeff starts snapping selfies.

From my book, I also know it was here that King Kamehameha I fought his last battle in the war to unite all the Hawaiian Islands. He commanded an impressive army of ten thousand soldiers. Those who dared stand in their way paid a high cost.

In 1795, several hundred warriors were forced over the edge and sent plummeting a thousand feet to their deaths by Kamehameha's men. According to the local legend, the cries of the dead warriors still pierce the air on certain nights.

I listen but all I hear are the howls of the wind. We wait for the night to fall, passing time with small talk. I remind myself that Tom's post-divorce relationships seldom last, and Alisa will be gone from our lives soon enough. With luck, I may never have to endure her grating pretension again.

I'm almost curious to read her novel and see what she's like on the page, but I can't imagine she'll be any different than in person. She already talks like she thinks she's a character in a book.

The sun sets, taking the views along with it. In the dark, the place is no longer spectacular. Mostly just uncomfortable.

There are no ghosts here, I tell myself looking around. No one but three very different people who frankly have no business hanging out together. Is there anything more tedious than bored tourists looking for some local flavor? A story to tell back home over Friday night drinks. Proof that they, too, have led a life less ordinary.

I'm about to suggest calling it a night when I hear something. It sounds like an audio distortion, like a broken radio trying to get a message across. But subtle. So very subtle. A dragging across the rocky earth, a hum that vibrates the air around us.

The smell comes next, foul and musky, like spoiled fruit and wet soil. There's a smothering heaviness to it as it clamps around your mouth and nose like a giant meaty hand.

"Look," says Jeff. His voice sounds like it's coming from over the ridge, even though he's standing right next to me.

My eyes follow his extended hand toward the distant flickers. I thought they were the lights from one of the towns below. Now I see that they are not that distant – and moving closer still with every moment.

The beat of war drums is easier to pick out through the wind now – a slow ceremonial rhythm, underscored by the mournful blows of conch shells.

"They're coming," Jeff whispers, looking like he's just hit a jackpot. "The Nightmarchers."

"Huaka'i pō," I recall their proper name from the book.

I don't feel excitement at all, only a peculiar numbness shot through with trepidation. My mind, which still hasn't fully recovered from jet lag, categorizes this as a dream. And yet I am awake.

As they come closer, I can see them. Their feet don't touch the ground as they move, floating just above. More corporeal than ghosts, the Nightmarchers are human-sized and dressed for battle, carrying spears and clubs. Some drum. Others blow into large pale shells that gleam in the moonlight. The low sound they make resonates bone-deep within me. There's an ancient menace to it, waves of sound permeating the air like heat rising off pavement.

It's meant as a warning to stay away, but I find I cannot move. My traitorous feet have anchored me in the warriors' path. There's only one thing the book says to do when this happens.

"Get down," I urge Alisa and Jeff in a panicked whisper. "Get down to the ground."

"Like hell," Alisa counters in full volume as she trains her phone on the approaching procession. "This is amazing. An authentic supernatural experience."

Jeff, at least, obeys. He follows me down, and we prostrate ourselves before the warriors, pressing our faces into the dust.

The screaming startles us. I never suspected Alisa's voice could hit such high notes; her usual register is somewhere in the sardonic, droll range.

I keep my head down, but Jeff looks up. Then back down, his face as pale as the sheets our rental house came with.

"Dude," he chokes out. "They, like, shredded her."

I don't want to know. It's bad enough I'll likely imagine it for the rest of my life, however long that may be, but I don't want to know.

Time may have stopped around us or sped up. There is no way to tell.

My mind drifts because the brain can only take so much adrenaline at once. When I snap back, I see Jeff getting up.

"Stop," I hiss at him, trying to grab his hand and pull him back down.

"It's okay now," he says, stupidly brave. "Look."

I risk a glance and see a young woman hula dancing. It makes no sense, but she's too mesmerizing to look away. She moves as gracefully as the ocean waves, lehua blossoms in her hair, maile wrapped at her waist. Long dark hair cascades down her back.

Never in my life have I seen or imagined anyone more beautiful. I could watch her forever. I start getting to my feet too, but then I see those torches again, flaring brighter. A survival instinct as old as time takes over and drops me back down to the ground.

Not Jeff, though. He stays, staring. A fool and a brash one at that, he smiles at her. That's the last thing I see.

After that, I shut my eyes tight, and there are only sounds.

A conch shell's bellow. The drumbeat speeds up. A chanting, low and primal, gathering in volume. Jeff pleading, fear warping his voice into something barely human. Then nothing but the wet ripping of flesh parted from bone and the dry snapping of bones apart. It seems to go on forever.

When it stops, there's a sudden silence as if all the sound in the world has died. The silence isn't empty – there is a certain tacit satisfaction in it. The warriors depart quietly, dragging the remnants of the bodies away. The dead take care of the dead.

Do I black out? It's difficult to say. All I know is that when I come to, I am alone, and dawn is breaking. It looks as if someone has split open the ocean's edge, leaking golden streaks into the slate stillness above. The remnants of fog still curl around the trees, like night's tentacles, reluctant to let go.

I sit up, my body stiff from hard ground and fear, and watch the sun slowly come up, setting the sky on fire.

The night retreats slowly, hiding in the tree trunks, under the rocks, and somewhere deep within me.

I sit and watch the world, awed and heartbroken by its beauty and its darkness and all the mysteries that I fear we will never truly know. Eventually, while the day burns brightly all around me, I begin finding my way back.

STORY INSPIRATION: I've never been to Hawaii. But when I was invited by our esteemed editor to contribute to a tiki horror collection, I said "Yes" immediately. Then, like a seasoned armchair traveler with access to YouTube, I promptly immersed myself for a day in all things Hawaii. What struck me the most was the legend of the Nightmarchers, so that's what I went with for my story. My wife, who had been to Hawaii, read it and said I got the setting right. But the ghosts... that's all me and my morbid imagination! And they are everywhere. Look out!

Biting God's Tongue

Viktor Bloodstone

She'd seen plenty of eviscerated bodies before, but she had never woken up next to one.

Blood pulled Calista Linquist from her sleep – the taste coated her mouth, the coppery smell filled her nose, the tackiness pulled along her right arm and leg. Eyes snapping open, she leapt from the bed, shivering in the cool air. The second her bare feet hit the hardwood floor, she immediately realized that this wasn't her room.

Her stomach rolled. All four limbs of the man in the bed were shredded to the bone, most of the muscle and skin gone. Some of his organs were gone, his torso an open pit; Cali was in no mood to ascertain how many organs were missing. But she fought enough of her hangover haze to study the part of his face *not* torn away, the dead -eye gaze more impactful than the empty socket. Sure enough, it was the guy she'd met at the mixer last night. Seeing the mangled body of someone she'd hooked up with was not a unique experience for Cali.

Naked, she wiped the blood from her arm and leg using the corner of the bed sheet, but something rattled against her chest. "What the hell?"

A necklace.

Of human teeth.

Not daring to touch the necklace, Cali grabbed her clothes and nearly popped a blood vessel trying to fight the blackness of her memory for clues as to how she went from flirting with a cute guy to waking up next to his corpse. And what about the freaky jewelry? *Nah,* her brain said, *I got nothing.*

Stretch pants and T-shirt on, everything else stuffed into her boots, she cracked the door open. Third floor, number 307 posted in black on his door. Her room, 305, was two doors away. From the resort's open circular design, she was able to see all eleven of the other rooms. Doors closed, curtains drawn together. Perfect.

Beginning in high school, she'd taken the walk-of-shame plenty of times. Now, not quite thirty yet, this was the first time she had her date's blood smeared on her. No fear of security cameras – privacy being a high priority selling-point of Apex Peak Ski Experience – Cali padded along the walkway in bare feet, making it to her room in mere seconds.

Door locked, clothes off, necklace flung aside… Something about the last tooth on the filled strand prickled her senses. Other than the reddish discoloration of the roots, the tooth was pristinely white. As white as her teeth. Cali now understood the copper taste as her tongue probed the back of her mouth and found an empty socket. As if her tongue could be lying to her, she hurried to the bathroom mirror and pulled the corner of her mouth back with her pinkie. Sure enough, there was a hole where her first molar should be.

She stepped back to examine her face, looking for swelling or bruises. Long blonde hair a mess from sleep, blue eyes rimmed with bloodshot, skin on the paler side from a hangover making every experience in the past few minutes worse, but zero injuries.

In her line of work, she'd been punched, kicked, elbowed, and kneed in the face. Always bruised and swollen afterwards, yet miraculously had never lost any teeth. Now, after waking up with a thin leather cord of teeth around her neck, and realizing one of those teeth was hers… "What the hell is going on?"

She was in no state to answer that question, or any questions, until she cleaned herself up and fought back the hangover punching her brain. Mouthwash to kill the god-awful taste of blood mixing with stale booze as well as the germs that might be congregating in her tender socket, then a handful of whatever pain meds were in the resort's medicine cabinet. A quick shower turned into a long shower, the water soothing her skin even though questions kept forming in her mind. The shower washed away the adrenaline shakes and some of her headache.

A half hour between jolting awake and now, yet no closer to remembering what happened after her third, no, fifth martini... It took way more than that to black her out. Roofie? Possible, but as always, she had watched her drinks being made.

It'd be 7:00 in the morning soon enough, so she wanted to make sure no one—

A woman's scream shredded the quiet.

Too late, body discovered.

Cali scrambled, yanking a pair of jeans and a Motorhead T-shirt from her suitcase, and hurried out the door just in time for the housekeeper in the hallway to look at her and scream again. The middle-aged, Ojibwe woman's black eyes were piercing, and Cali felt every bit of terror the housekeeper experienced. Of all people to discover the body, Cali's heart broke that it happened to be Bhumi.

Doors flung open as sleep-interrupted frowns poked into the hallway, none of them with a proper angle to see what caused the ruckus, just the hysterical housekeeper.

Clarkson – who Cali tried to hit on last night but quickly gave up after he showed no interest – bounded up the stairs and rushed down the hallway with his gun drawn. Cali thought the private security guard's weapon was overkill. Sure, she had snuck her own Glock inside her luggage, but she didn't pull it every time someone screamed. Judging by the way he was waving it around and how green his face was after he jumped out of room 307, Cali knew it was going to be a long, frustrating day.

The main room of the ski resort buzzed with the electricity of furtive conversations among the thirty people present. *No, down to twenty-nine people now.*

The massive, ever-burning fireplace cast rutilant light in the middle of the communal room for social gatherings – including last night's mixer. The light filled most of the circular room that served as bar, seating area, and dining room. The remainder of the floor consisted of the lobby, front desk, concierge, and a staging area for skis and snowboarding, though Cali couldn't see them from her seat on a thick built-in sofa by the bay windows. Those bay windows, which ran the length of the first floor, normally captured a majestic view of the mountains and scenic landscape of the Canadian side of the Great Lakes, but with the blurry squall of a blizzard looking like angry ghosts trying to get inside, visibility had been reduced to less than a foot. She stayed aloof, content to drink her Chimay blue label ale and observe.

"Beer at eight in the morning. Classy," Lincoln Masterfield said as he sat on the sofa next to Cali's outstretched feet. A slouch with his elbows propped on the back of the sofa showed how unaffected his entitlement had made him, which came with his insane good looks and billion-dollar family name.

"It's a Belgium, so it's all but a mimosa. And you're just pissed that you don't know where to look for them."

A chuckle, as deep and full as his pockets. "True. Do you know why Oswald dragged everyone out of bed? For some of us, last night ended only five hours ago."

Oswald Harwell, the owner of Apex Peak Ski Experience, a resort that catered to those with more money than brains. This place wasn't Cali's usual cup of tea, but it'd been years since she'd hit slopes of any kind, and the fact that there were only twenty-two – *no, twenty-one* – total guests for the week was appealing.

Cali took a slow pull of her bottle to rub it in, that she had what Lincoln wanted. She then pointed to the spiral staircase as Oswald ushered Sabrina and Courtney Masterfield – Lincoln's younger sisters looking every bit as hungover as most of the guests – downstairs. They'd been the last ones to arrive. "Looks like we're about to find out."

Clarkson collected the sisters and guided them to another couch beside Lincoln. The youngest brother, Everest, was nodding off in an oversized armchair nearby. Peter Rubins, a cousin of the Masterfields, also sat close by. Despite the impending awkwardness from the soon to be announced news, Cali appreciated that she had a literal front row seat to see how the siblings were going to react.

"What's going on, Clarky?" Sabrina asked, then moaned, rubbing her eyes with the heel of her hand, her fingers curled around her cellphone.

Clarckson, the mound of Army trained muscle known as the Masterfield Family Bodyguard, was surprisingly tender as he forced the sisters to sit. As he walked away to join Oswald in the center of the room, he tapped Everest's knee to jolt the young man awake.

"We have some unfortunate and quite distressing news," Oswald announced. The other guests quieted and shifted postures to become more attentive. They were mostly couples, but a few individuals like Cali looking to get away. But unlike Cali, every other guest once had their faces on magazine covers. Actors. Moguls. Power players. "There appears to have been a murder last night. At 7:00 A.M., Bhumi from housekeeping discovered the body."

Gasps. Shock. Hands covering mouths. If Cali hadn't woken up with the victim, she might have laughed – the Masterfield siblings had yet to notice one of their own was missing.

Before anyone could ask who, Clarkson cleared his throat and said, "It was Webber."

This got reactions.

Tears from Courtney and Sabrina, the latter shrieking, "What? What did you say? Webber? Did you fucking say Webber is dead?"

Everest's perpetually douchebag face twisted into frustration. Lincoln massaged his jaw, a faraway gaze befalling his face. After a minute of Sabrina's ignored hysterics, Lincoln sniffled and knuckled away burgeoning tears. He addressed Clarkson, asking, "What happened? How do you know he was murdered?"

"By the state of his body."

"And how was that?" Cali asked. Clarkson glared at her, but that only encouraged her to needle harder. "I saw you go into his room. You came out looking like you had a not-so-fresh feeling."

Everything about him looked angry, even the veins webbing his muscles, and Cali was satisfied. Through clenched teeth, he kept his voice even, obviously for the sake of the Masterfields. "His body was… mutilated."

"Mutilated?" Sabrina cried. "How?"

Clarkson rolled his neck. "His arms and legs were shredded."

More gasping.

"Has *he* checked Webster's body yet?" Cali asked, this time pointing to Dr. Vincent Perricone, the resort's medical professional.

Mid-fifties with the slenderness of a vampire, his perfectly coiffed beard tapered to a point that didn't move when he spoke. "We thought it best to gather everyone here first."

"He's right," Oswald said. "There's no point in repeating information or having it twisted by scuttlebutt and supposition."

"Have the authorities been contacted yet?" a voice asked from the pool of other guests.

"We, unfortunately, are unable to do so."

"Sure we can!" Sabrina yelled. She held up her phone, then squinted at it. She stood and raised it over her head, an offering to the gods of cell service. "No bars?"

The rustle of guests reaching into their pockets to retrieve their phones filled the circular room, followed by grumbles of "no signal." The hangovers must be bad if none of them had tried their phones until now.

"Why is there no Wi-Fi?" Lincoln asked.

"The blizzard has negatively impacted our service provider," Oswald said. He was a fidgety man in his late thirties. Too short to have been athletic in school and too dull to sparkle academically, Cali could tell that he was one of those guys who desperately wanted to hang out with the cool kids. This resort was a thinly veiled way to rub elbows with the rich and famous.

"What about a radio?" Lincoln asked. "Surely, blizzards and snowstorms can't be uncommon here, so you have to have some contingency right?"

"The radio is out."

Worry-filled murmurs raced about the room. Clarkson frowned, clearly angry with that answer. As much as Cali hated to admit it, she'd need to work with him to suss out what was happening. He was a connection between management and a portion of the guests, and he'd undoubtedly be investigating, whether anyone wanted him to or not. *Might as well be on his good side. Now, how to get him to trust me?*

"Wait," Everest said, jolting straight as if zapped by lightning. Scanning everyone who wasn't a family member, he blurted, "That means one of you killed my brother."

Everest was in his mid-twenties, though he didn't look like he'd grown out of his awkward adolescence thanks to his hooked nose and big ears. The unkempt mop of curls was permanent, not bedhead. He lived a showy life as a playboy because his money told him that he could.

The volume of voices bubbled up, becoming dangerously close to an eruption. It shouldn't have surprised Cali that the one to explode first was the one she'd been hearing the most – Sabrina.

"Her! It was the housekeeper! She killed my brother."

The resort staff had been huddled close together at dining room tables, quietly keeping to themselves. Bhumi's eyes widened. Anjali, the cook and fellow Ojibwe woman, wrapped her arm around Bhumi's shoulders and pulled her close. Annabelle Levlee, the day manager, and Tucker "Truck" Kilgore, the night manager, each slid their chairs to flank the Ojibwe women. Even the ski/pro instructor, Slick Andrews, stood from his chair and crossed his arms.

"What motivation would she possibly have?" Anjali said, shooting her words like bullets.

"Jealousy! We're rich and she's tired of cleaning up after us!"

Cali slid from her perch and strode to Sabrina. "Look, I know you're angry and hurt and you're lashing out. We've all been there, and your emotions are valid. But how about you turn to your family now. At the very least, be careful of what you say next."

From the corner of her eye, she caught Clarkson's body language and how he stared at her. He appreciated what Cali did, a move that meant he would trust working with her.

Sabrina, a young blonde woman with the baby doll features that social media found addictive, twisted her face in ways that made her look like a caricature of a toddler throwing a tantrum. Still sneering at Bhumi, she said, "The person who found the body is usually the one who did it."

"Yeah? Got any stats to back that up?"

A deeper frown. "It's common knowledge. And if it wasn't her, why was she at his room at 7:00 A.M.? I've never heard of housekeeping showing up that early. You?"

Cali had no answer, so she turned to Oswald. A headshake. "We never send housekeeping to anyone's room before 10:00."

Cali looked at Bhumi. Instead of an explanation, the housekeeper's eyes widened further and she sunk deeper into Anjali's embrace.

"That's suspicious," Sabrina said.

Cali rolled her eyes. "You're suspicious."

"Doubtful. But… Wait, I remember you flirting with Webber last night. That makes *you* suspicious."

More mumbles and murmurs, soft affirmations among the other guests, confirming with each other that they all saw Cali flirting with Webber. She took a swig of beer, all the time she needed to think of a way out of this. A good lie contains partial truths. "Look, Sabrina, I did hook up with your brother. But, please don't make me say mean things about him that I'm sure you and your siblings would rather not hear." Cali wiggled her pinkie, her non-verbal statement about his size going far beyond implication. "We went back to my room and half an hour later, he left. I then locked my door and passed out. Please don't push me to be less polite than that."

In her mind, Cali was accepting the Oscar for best actress while waiting for anyone to rebuke her story. No one proclaimed seeing the two of them go to his room, no accusations of her sneaking out of it this morning. Bonus – Sabrina backed down, flopping back onto the couch, falling into Courtney's awaiting arms.

"What are we going to do about the housekeeper?" Lincoln asked.

"We have a couple unoccupied rooms," Oswald said. "We can sequester her to one of them for the time being."

"Bhumi? Why?" Cali asked.

"She's currently our only suspect."

"She's no more of a suspect than her!" Anjali snapped, slinging her words at Cali.

Cali brought the beer bottle to her lips, needing to buy a couple seconds to formulate a response. But she didn't have to.

Bhumi whispered into Anjali's ear and then stood. Addressing everyone, she said, "I accept these terms. I believe room 207 is empty." Pure grace, she turned to Dr. Perricone and said, "Please look over Mr. Masterfield and do what you can to ease his family's pain." She turned to Cali, her dark eyes boring into her soul, but said nothing. Finally, she made her way to the stairs and started up to the second floor.

Clarkson followed Bhumi while Annabelle, Truck, and Slick followed him. Dr. Perricone took the elevator. Cousin Peter joined the Masterfield siblings, sobs emanating from the circle of grief. Some guests broke away in smaller groups – safety in numbers – while others accosted Oswald, demanding answers he didn't have.

Cali drained the bottle, weighing her options. Her stomach growled, so first…

I need another beer.

Leaning against the wall, arms crossed with a newly opened Chimay in hand, Cali waited for Clarkson to finish up in room 207. Twelve rooms on this floor as well, and she quietly watched. Not much to see, though. The power couple in 201 came up shortly after this morning's meeting as did the celebrity chef in 204. No fanfare, just closed doors and pulled curtains. Voices didn't carry in this place, even though thick wooden railing, decorated with fancy carvings, was the only thing separating the second floor from the first. A dozen guests had to have cornered Oswald, and she didn't hear a peep. Nor did she hear anything from the grieving Masterfields, still in the lounge.

Room 207's door opened and she nonchalantly peeked inside to check Bhumi's wellbeing. Hugging herself, the housekeeper was sitting on the couch, gazing out the window to the whiteout. Clarkson frowned at Cali when he exited. "Any reason why you're here?"

Cali ignored him and caught Anjali as she exited behind the security guard, shutting the door behind her. "How is she? Did this guy rough her up at all?"

Clarkson's back went rigid at the last question, but Anjali answered, "She is comfortable. I will bring her breakfast after I make it for everyone else. Eggs and fresh rabbit sausage hash in two hours."

As Anjali walked away, Cali took a swig and then asked Clarkson, "Fresh rabbit?"

"A decent sized coup with rabbits, chickens, quail, and pheasant behind the building, attached to the kitchen by a covered walkway."

"Fuckin' rich people, right?"

Clarkson folded his arms over his muscular chest and stepped closer. "What are you doing here?"

With another pull from her beer, Cali said, "How cute! You're trying to be intimidating."

"I'm curious about the same thing," Lincoln said as he strode along the curve of the walkway. "I come to check on my bodyguard and find you lurking outside the room of my brother's murder suspect."

"Shouldn't you be comforting your family?" Cali asked.

"Not as head of the family. It would be more helpful if I returned with the housekeeper's answers to Clarkson's questions."

"I think you mean you're first in line to be head of the family," Cali said. "*After* your dad passes away, that is."

Clarkson's chest flexed and Lincoln bristled. The oldest Masterfield sibling snapped, "How do you know that?"

"Because I can read. Your in-depth interview regarding the ins and outs of your family's business in *Time* magazine was just last month, dumbass."

Clarkson relaxed and the corner of his mouth twitched; Cali assumed he was trying to stifle a smile. Lincoln deflated, but quickly regained his composure and puffed up again. "That doesn't explain why you're trying to involve yourself."

"That's because Webber and I got married last night. He was second in line, right? After you? Now that I'm your sister-in-law, I have a personal stake in your company."

This time Clarkson adjusted his stance to make covering his mouth with his hand look as natural as possible. Lincoln was less than amenable to her charm. "This might be some kind of joke to you – and if it is, then shame on you – but I lost *my brother*. And suddenly there is a stranger butting into my family's personal matters."

Another swig and she swiped her thumb-knuckle across her bottom lip. "Sorry. A little hungover, a little hungry, and a little freaked out. A guy who I hooked up with last night was found dead this morning. I just want to stay in the loop before I end up locked in a room like Bhumi. That's why I was talking to Clarkson about taking a look at the radio."

"You were?"

"Yeah." Cali winked at Clarkson. "We were just saying how we both found it suspicious when Oswald said it wasn't working, and we wanted to check it out."

Lincoln's scowl asked his security guard to confirm her statement. Clarkson shrugged, then gestured to the stairs and said, "Care to join us?"

With a huff, Lincoln led the way.

A tangle of wires nested under the desk that held the radio transponder. Even to the untrained eye it was obvious that someone had grabbed and yanked everything they could get their hands on. Cali finished her beer, tossed the bottle in the office's recycle bin, and said, "You certainly undersold the direness of the situation, Oswald."

"I'm inclined to agree with her," Lincoln said, rubbing his temples while looking around the small office. A nice, cherry wood desk shared by three people, as well as two metal file cabinets. A smaller, simple desk in the corner of the room held the radio and modem. No security monitors meant that Oswald was at least telling the truth about Apex Peak Ski Experience offering pure privacy by eschewing surveillance.

"I didn't want to add any more alarm to an already alarming situation," Oswald said.

"How many people have access to this office?" Clarkson asked.

"Myself, Annabelle Levlee, and Truck Kilgore. And the housekeeper, of course."

Cali wanted to call bullshit on his list. She doubted that Oswald would trust Bhumi with a key to management's office, especially since it was obvious he didn't even know her name. Neither Annabelle nor Truck disagreed with him, both content to hover around outside the office with their arms crossed and lips sealed. Cali couldn't get a beat on what their frowns meant. Upset that their workspace had been violated? Angry that they had to remain quiet for their boss's benefit? Disturbed that there was a murderer among them? If it was the latter, then they were about to become more disturbed – Dr. Perricone arrived with the rueful look of needing to share upsetting news.

At first, he tried to be discreet with a whispered, "A moment, please," to Oswald.

"Is this about my brother?" Lincoln asked. "If it is, then Clarkson and I have every right to be present for whatever news you have to share."

A nod from Oswald.

"Very well," Perricone said. "Anyone else?"

All eyes went to Cali. She winked at Lincoln and tapped her left-hand ring finger. An eyeroll, but he acquiesced. "Yes. She's fine."

Making a quick trip to the lounge, everyone got as comfortable as possible, though Clarkson and Lincoln flanked Cali. Their scowls softened to mere frowns, so maybe she was a source of comfort? Trust? Annabelle and Truck sat at a table built for four; she absently dug at her cuticles while Truck leered at Cali. Annabelle's long sleeves hid prison tats – Cali had seen them the night before as Annabelle relaxed during the mixer. She had the nervous energy of someone worried about going back. If this place had security cameras, then no doubt that Truck would be jerking off while watching the monitors. That was the main reason Cali kept an eye on him keeping an eye on her. The doctor had a little more color to his complexion than this morning, though starting the day looking at a gutted dead guy had a way of sapping skin tone. Cali knew better than anyone. Oswald stared at the doctor the way a stage director stared at their least talented actor, hoping they didn't flub their lines.

"I need to preface this with a disclaimer that I'm ill-equipped to render a definitive opinion on the matter," Dr. Perricone started. "But after examining Mr. Masterfield, he was definitely torn apart."

Cali knew the extent of the wounds, but since Clarkson had only allowed Oswald and the doctor into Webber's room, she needed to ask her questions cautiously to avoid exposing herself. "Torn apart in what way? Like limb from limb?"

"No. But there were deep gouges in his skin. Also... he was gutted."

Disturbed grumbles were passed around and everyone looked appropriately upset. Cali wracked her brain trying to think of a way to ask if all the organs were accounted for, but the doctor continued. "And there were bitemarks."

"Bitemarks? You're saying an animal did this?" Clarkson asked.

"No. Human."

Clarkson shook his head. "There's no way a human could have done that."

"Like I said earlier, I don't have the proper training nor the proper equipment for this sort of examination, but I can assure you, humans are capable of a great many horrific things if properly motivated."

"Like shredding a man with their bare hands?"

The doctor gave a little shrug, implying he'd witnessed worse.

"Did...? Did you say that Webber was...? Ripped apart?" This questioning came from the edge of the lounge. Sabrina. Both of her quaking hands worked her cheeks, chin, and mouth, readying for another round of convulsive sobbing.

Lincoln hurried to his sister and put an arm around her, leading her closer to the group. "Sabrina, the doctor meant—"

She struggled to push away, but her brother's grip was tight. "I know what he meant, Lincoln! I heard him!"

The course changed as he now escorted her to the doctor. "Sabrina, we need to—"

Sabrina no longer fought against Lincoln, her hands now flapping like panicked bird wings. "We need to figure out who's doing this! We need to figure out *what* is doing this! Like a vampire! Or a werewolf!"

A simple glance from Lincoln was all Dr. Perricone needed to reach for his little black bag. A syringe. A vial. Sabrina offered zero resistance to her medicinally induced nap.

Cali wanted to smack Lincoln in the face. Even though Sabrina was annoying, she didn't like seeing a drugged woman go limp in a man's arms, family member or not. She asked Clarkson, "Does this happen a lot?"

"Enough to make the tabloids drool," he replied.

"Will she be okay?"

"Yeah. She'll awaken refreshed. Probably won't remember her outburst."

Cali wanted to protest more, but when Anjali stepped out from the kitchen and sternly said, "Breakfast will be ready in an hour," Cali's rumbling belly demanded her attention.

Breakfast turned into light snacks, then lunch and cocktails, and eventually dinner. Once those not dead or imprisoned made it to the dining room, no one wanted to leave. Cali wasn't sure if it was a communal act of solidarity or the distrust in fellow human beings. Clarkson made assurances that Bhumi was comfortable and receiving meals, but Cali didn't relax until Anjali confirmed.

There was high potential that someone was a murderer after all. Murderer or not, people's guards softened throughout the day. Some guards were dropped. Side-eyes aplenty, but the guests mingled –

Oswald, Annabelle, and Truck sliding through the small crowd to keep everyone's drinks full. Dr. Perricone showed that his persnickety demeanor wasn't an act, sneering at finger sandwiches and rabbit meat pies. The Masterfields and Cousin Pete remained in the dining room – probably Clarkson's recommendation about optics – though they kept to themselves, except for Lincoln. He harangued Cali, trying to figure out how she always had a beer in hand, and she'd be damned if she was going to ruin her fun by revealing her secret. But right when the beers started to suggest that her fun with Lincoln, or Clarkson for that matter, could extend to one-on-one games, she decided to call it a night. As soon as she locked her room door behind her, she flopped onto her bed. And opened her night table drawer, revealing the weird necklace.

How the hell did my tooth get on this thing? The continuous thread of leather had no tie, no clasps. The other teeth were faded, hers the only white one. Well, another tooth wasn't as faded, the one right next to hers. Not quite as shiny as hers, but nowhere near as dull as the others.

"God damn it," she mumbled to herself as she shoved it into the secret compartment of her suitcase, next to her Glock. She finished her beer, and downed a protein bar. Then a second one. She contemplated a third bar, but opted to go to bed hungry, drifting away to thoughts of her breakfast. A mistake, because her dreams were nothing but meat, blood, fur. And knocking. No, the knocking wasn't part of the dream, it was real.

Bolting straight up, she barked, "Yeah?"

"Cali. It's Clarkson."

Rubbing her eyes with one hand, she shifted to get out of bed, putting her hand on something warm and squishy. A slimy lump of fur. "The fuck?"

A rabbit carcass.

One of half a dozen in her bed.

The one in her hand was all fur and broken bones, the belly split open with no guts inside. Very little meat held the crumbled skeleton to the limp pelt. Almost no blood, just some staining around the incision.

Dropping the mess, she scurried out of bed. The other rabbits were in the same state of pulp. *What. The. Literal. Hell?*

The mirror over her dresser reflected Cali's bloody image. Fur and dried blood were caught in her teeth and caked the corners of her mouth.

Clarkson knocked again. "Cali? Did you hear me?"

"Yeah," she called out over her shoulder, unable to peel her eyes away from the tiny abattoir on her sheets. "Gimme a minute."

Starting at the foot of her bed, she pulled the sheet corners free and bundled the rabbit remains and tied it with a tight knot. In between the mattress and box spring for now, until she could think of a better way to dispose of it. *Not perfect, but good enough,* she thought as she reached for her jeans. She pulled up, almost forgetting the fur and dried rust-colored flakes under her fingernails and the horrid state of her face. A quick run to the bathroom to wash up.

Water. Mouthwash. Soap. More water. More soap. More mouthwash. There was no hangover to contend with this morning, but she couldn't remember last night. She went to sleep in her bed – she was positive of this! A sensitive sleeper, there'd be no way someone could have snuck into her room, dumped torn up rabbit carcasses in her bed, and somehow spread fur and blood on her. And she wasn't prone to sleepwalking. "What the fuck?"

No time. Jeans. Black turtleneck. Boots. She whipped the door open and Clarkson's frown greeted her. "Took you long enough."

"Dude, you woke me up. Needed a minute to start my day. Speaking of… Why the hell did you wake me up?"

As he walked away, he gestured for her to follow. To room 301, and the whispered commotion from inside.

"Why is she here?" Oswald asked when Cali entered Lincoln's room – the room of the latest mutilated corpse.

Face up in bed, and just like Webber, Lincoln's arms and thighs were shredded, some areas to the bone. The meat glistened and his blood bloomed the sheets like a macabre flower, but there should have been more. Chest shredded and belly opened, the tangle of intestines were the only entrails remaining.

"To prove I didn't do this," Cali answered. "And neither did Bhumi."

"This doesn't prove shit," Truck said, his teeth gnashed like a hungry wolf. "You could have easily cleaned up."

Annabelle had a dubious squint, as if trying to figure out where Cali was hiding a shiv, and said, "And the hotel room holding the housekeeper isn't exactly a maximum-security prison."

"I was outside room 207 the whole night," Clarkson said.

"And you didn't nod off at all?" Oswald asked, the accusation heavier than the offal smells in the room.

"Hell, maybe it's him doing this. Bodyguard pissed off at the rich family he's guarding," Truck said.

Annabelle glanced from Cali to Clarkson back to Cali. "They might even be doing this together."

Dr. Perricone stood aloof in the corner, knuckles under his nose, staring at Lincoln's body. "Pointing fingers right now isn't very prudent. I think the next step is to leave the room and call another resort meeting downstairs."

A curt nod and Oswald stormed from the room. The doctor hurried after him, the managers followed, sneering at Cali along the way.

As they left, Clarkson whispered, "The empathy from the staff is overwhelming."

"So overwhelmingly empathetic, I'm suspicious of all of them," Cali said.

"Agreed."

Cali took one last look at the body before leaving, and her belly twisted with hunger.

Just like yesterday morning, Oswald delivered the news to a chorus of cries and questions.

Courtney disappeared into herself, a shaking mess of tears and gulping sobs. Sabrina and Everest took turns hugging their sister, then themselves, then each other, seemingly offering what was needed when it was needed. Cousin Peter sat next to them, hugging his shins with his knees pulled to his chest.

The rest of the guests attacked Oswald, Annabelle, and Truck like piranha. Even Slick Andrews had to field some questions. Wide-eyed, Dr. Perricone was dragged into conversations by Oswald. Anjali disappeared into the kitchen, and Cali thought about following, but saw a different opportunity when she noticed that Clarkson wasn't included in the Masterfield grieving process. Perfect.

Cali strolled over to Clarkson and used her beer bottle to point at Peter. "How close is Cousin Pete with the siblings?"

Clarkson glanced at Cali, then her beer bottle, then back to her eyes. "They all get together a few times, coming here once or twice a year. He'll hang out with them separately here and there."

"Anything to warrant his reaction? He's taking it worse than Courtney."

Arms crossed over his chest, Clarkson inhaled deeply. "No."

"Is it just me, or does he look scared?"

A twist of his lips and a whooshing exhale.

"So," Cali continued, "now that the oldest two siblings are no longer with us, who's next in line to run the businesses?"

"Sabrina."

"Does she have it in her to do something like this?"

Before he could answer, a woman's scream grabbed everyone's attention. Two men scuffled – pushing and shoving born from displaced frustration. Accusations of murder being tossed about like a football, but no punches thrown.

"Do you really think one of the other guests are involved?" Cali asked as Slick and Truck separated the men. Oswald and Annabelle raised their voices in an attempt to cool the boiling situation. "It seems more personal, doesn't it?"

"Clarky!" Sabrina called out. One arm around her sister, she reached her other arm toward their bodyguard as if he were a teddy bear. "We need you!"

Clarkson turned to Cali, a surreptitious move to hide his actions from the siblings. He slipped six keycards into her hand and whispered, "Be quick, be quiet, and don't make me fucking regret this."

Cali nodded, then slipped away, everyone else too busy to notice.

All the room keycards were plain white with a gold hologram. Numbers were handwritten in black marker, obviously Clarkson's way to keep track. 307 was Webber's, 301 Lincoln's. There was a 302. Cali didn't know who was staying in 302, but they were next to a grisly murder and didn't hear a thing. Suspicious. One last glance over her shoulders and she slipped inside.

A dude's room – opened suitcase in the corner told her as much. She assumed it was Cousin Pete's because she guessed that Everest would have leopard print banana-hammocks strewn across the place. Yep, Peter's room since the outfit he had worn the night before was bunched in a pile in the room's far corner. A quick peek through his suitcase, drawers, under the bed, between the mattresses, the bathroom cabinet, the closet… Wait. The safe in the closet was shut.

A digital lock, four-digit combination. Had she any of her equipment and an hour or two, she'd have it opened. But Peter seemed like a dude, so she had only one combination to try.

6969.

The safe clicked open.

"Jesus Christ," Cali laughed. She stopped when she pulled out a manila folder and perused the papers within. "Well, fuck."

Safe closed, folder in hand, Cali hurried from the room, but stopped dead in the hallway. The door to 307 was open. And someone was inside.

Cali slipped the folder under the back of her pants and shirt, and approached the room with clenched fists. Pugilism wasn't on her to-do vacation checklist, but neither was waking up with a dead man. But now someone was in his room. Fists still clenched, she relaxed from her boxer's stance when she walked in on Annabelle and Truck on either side of Webber's bed, both wearing thick work gloves. All the room's windows had been opened, chilling the room something fierce, obviously to slow the decomposition process. The smart-ass comment she had queued up puffed out of her mouth unspoken when she looked at Webber. More meat had been torn away, more of his rust-colored skeleton exposed. Suddenly, she was hungry and gulped down pooling saliva loud enough to garner the managers' attention.

"Can't stop yourself, can you?" Annabelle asked.

Cali's stomach hurt when she pulled her eyes away from the corpse. "What do you mean?"

Truck unfurled a blue tarp. "Sticking your nose in everyone's business."

"You're moving the body? To where?"

"Christ, you always got questions. Outside in the snow by the animal coup. Open windows aren't enough and it ain't right to put them in the kitchen's freezer. So, unless you're gonna help, how about you get the fuck outta here."

Aiming for the stairs, Cali left, if for no other reason than to make her stomach stop rumbling. She'd ask Anjali if she had anything for her to eat... Not rabbit, since Cali had a bunch of carcasses under her mattress. She needed to address that, but first thing's first.

As Cali passed through the lounge, she gestured to Oswald and Clarkson to follow her. Dr. Perricone was close enough to overhear and followed along to where the Masterfields were sitting. The three siblings and Cousin Pete sat on a bench seat more plush than most couches, eyes and noses still red from crying. Since Sabrina was now the family head, Cali dropped the folder on the table in front of her.

"What's this?" Sabrina asked as she opened it.

"Evidence that Bhumi didn't do what she'd been accused of," Cali answered.

Sabrina's siblings sat up and crowded around her. Clarkson eyed Cali before he leaned over the table. Cousin Pete started to quake.

Everest must have been the fastest reader, because he whipped his wide-eyed glare at Cousin Pete. "Dude. What the fuck?"

Tears. Snot. Warbling voice, Cousin Pete said, "I thought it'd bring us closer together."

"Closer to our family money, you mean," Sabrina said loud enough to garner the attention of others milling about the lounge.

"No!" Cousin Pete said. "That's not true at all."

"What's going on?" Slick asked, approaching with half a dozen guests gathering behind him.

"Seems that Cousin Pete recently learned that he's Half-Brother Pete," Cali answered. "And judging from the minimal information I know about the family, it puts him next in line to control the family businesses."

Cali had pulled the proverbial pin and tossed the grenade. The explosion of accusations was what she'd hoped for. The siblings yelled. The guests demanded he be locked up. Oswald and Slick did their best to appease everyone. Clarkson got in between Half-Sibling Pete and the burgeoning mob. Someone yelled that Pete should be locked away until the resort figured out a way to contact the outside world, and that reduced the emotional heat from a boil to a simmer. Good enough.

Cali grabbed Oswald's arm and pulled him from the pack. "Alrighty, now that I figured out the who and why, I think we can let Bhumi go."

Indignant, the resort owner yanked his arm away. "I think I should be the one to make such a determination as to—"

Oswald was the same height and outweighed Cali by a couple dozen pounds, but his excess weight was stored in the middle. For almost a decade, Cali completed two-hour-a-day workout routines that developed enough muscle and deadly skill to hunt and kill monsters. The differences between the two were abundantly clear as she grabbed a fistful of his shirt and let the fire burning behind her crystal blue eyes heat her words. "It wasn't a request."

With shaking hands, Oswald handed Cali the key to room 207. Giving him a pat on the cheek that certainly stung like a slap, Cali said, "Good choice."

Up the stairs and to the room, Cali knocked, and then opened the door. "Bhumi, good news. You're free to go."

Instead of jumping from the couch with happiness, the housekeeper slid to the far corner and folded in on herself.

Something wasn't right. To keep from upsetting Bhumi any further, Cali sat in a chair far away from the couch. "Sorry to have startled you, but did you hear me?"

Eyes like a spooked horse's, Bhumi nodded.

This wasn't good. This wasn't good at all. Cali had suspicions about what was really going on with the murders and Bhumi's reactions were confirming them. "Why did you willingly accept being sequestered to this room?"

"The more one protests against guilt, the guiltier they appear," Bhumi whispered with limp confidence. She was probably hoping Cali would believe her weak lie.

"Nah, not buying that answer."

Bhumi shifted on the couch. "I felt safer in here."

"From… the killer?"

A shrug.

"It's not a who, is it?" Cali asked. "It's a what."

A nod.

"I apologize for using this word, but… We're dealing with a wendigo, aren't we?"

Bhumi's cringe was answer enough.

"I found evidence that it's Cousin Pete."

"It's not him."

"Do you know who it is?"

"Yes. It's you."

Cali's peripheral vision tunneled, her world now a pinpoint of light. No. It couldn't be her. But the hunger. The gnawing sensation in the back of her mind grinding her thoughts to powder whenever she thought about Webber or Lincoln or the rabbits. The fire in her gut burning hotter with every hour that went by. The way she salivated when seeing the viscera. No. There had to be another explanation. The necklace. Somone had to have given it to her, attached her tooth to it. It didn't matter, though, did it? The hunger was going to consume her. Not yet. She had one last idea.

"Bhumi? I need a favor…"

Darkness pulsed to the rhythm of Cali's heartbeat. Fast. Hard. The rhythm of pulsing blood. The rhythm of hunger. *I need to eat.*

"No," she whispered to herself, tossing the covers aside and flinging her feet over the edge of the bed. "No, I don't."

Yes, I do! I really fucking do!

Not sure if she had any control of her fingers as she reached for her suitcase. She made no attempt to fight them as they snatched the necklace of teeth and slipped it over her head. "God damn it."

The blood from the coup called to her, the many heartbeats of chickens and pheasants and quails pulsing through her head like an orchestra of the condemned. They knew she was coming and they were frightened. *Hurry up,* her hunger screamed as she paused to put her boots on. "I'm not gonna traipse through the resort barefoot."

Cali had the foresight to stay in her jeans and turtleneck after the social last night. With Petey locked away, the guests and employees breathed a collective sigh of relief. No one cut loose, but it was the first time in over a day that there'd been smiles, especially since the snow had stopped and the sun shone brightly. Bhumi assisted Anjali in the kitchen, the two Ojibwe keeping a watchful eye on Cali. They weren't the only ones – at least one member of the staff was watching her at all times. In between mingling with the guests, Truck leered, Annabelle stalked, Slick skulked, Perricone observed, and Oswald seethed. It didn't bother Cali. She fought against her unnatural hunger, hoping the beer would numb it. It didn't. She decided to call it a night when Clarkson started to look delicious in more ways than one.

Sleep hadn't come easily and now that she was awake, padding to the kitchen, she wasn't sure how she'd sleep again with this hunger. In the darkness, she sensed all the food sources. Nothing in the pantry appealed to her imploding guts. Few things in the refrigerator or walk-in freezer would be satisfying. There was only one thing in the kitchen she wanted to sink her teeth into.

Anjali.

Yes! Yes! Fucking eat her! My teeth are sharp enough to tear through her skin. Cali knew it'd be difficult at first, but she was confident that when the cook's blood coated her tongue, her frenzy would make the rest of the feeding easier.

"No," Cali whispered against her sticky thoughts, loud enough to warn Anjali.

The cook jolted at Cali's presence and ran out the back door, through the covered pathway to the coup. Pots and utensils clanged to the floor as Cali grabbed the largest butcher knife and tore through the kitchen in pursuit, the necklace of teeth bouncing against her chest as she ran.

Cali wanted to encourage Anjali to run faster or fight, but that'd be useless. The years of hunting and killing monsters had made Cali a relentless machine. The poor cook stood no chance of escaping even when she ran through the coup. The smells of living bird meat were intoxicating, Cali wanting to eat every thumping heart behind fragile ribcages, but her ultimate target was Anjali. And nothing was going to stop her, even when the chase led outside.

Near the bodies of Webber and Lincoln – Cali wanted to eat their remains as well – she tackled Anjali. The cook grunted as she squirmed in the snow, a natural fighter. Not enough. Cali straddled

Anjali's hips and tore open her jacket. Teeth first, Cali lunged forward and chomped down. The meat. The blood. More. She needed more.

Laughter. The giddy kind that could no longer be contained.

Dr. Perricone.

"Oh, thank God!" He laughed again, clapping as he exited the coup and stood next to the dead Masterfield brothers. "I am finally rid of this curse!"

Cali whipped around, growling as she licked blood and small chunks of meat from her lips.

"The curse of the wendigo is all yours now." Another laugh. "I had it for too long. I tried to work with it. Two weeks ago, I poisoned a half dozen skiers right before they had left for one of the mountains. Everyone thought they went missing, even the authorities. I thought it'd be enough for me, for the accursed spirit, but it wasn't. I then learned how to pass it on. To you."

Cali snarled.

Dr. Perricone stepped closer, stopping next to Lincoln's body. "You were such an easy target. A few too many drinks and I was able to slip you my special cocktail right before you and Webber went to his room."

Cali glanced at Webber. She wiped her mouth, then sat back on her haunches. "For me to eat?"

"Yes! Well, for you to finish since I started. I had to feed, afterall. Just enough to sate my hunger. And remove your tooth for the necklace."

"So…" She lifted her necklace. "Your tooth is the one next to mine."

Dr. Perricone pulled his upper lip enough to show the gap.

"That's why I never saw you smile," Cali said. "So, the news of Webber's death gets out and then you trash the radio."

Dr. Perricone's gaze shifted to Lincoln's body. "That was Oswald. The fool that he is, he didn't want to report another death on his property so soon after six people went missing."

"If you had passed it to me, who killed Lincoln? Because I know it wasn't me."

Growling, Dr. Perricone snapped, "I did! I had to because you didn't play your part well enough! I had hoped you'd have been enticed by Webber's blood to want to feed. Alas, I was wrong. Then you had rabbit for breakfast."

"Why does that matter?"

Reaching down, Dr. Perricone grabbed Lincoln's hand, skin gray, the exposed muscle a burgundy hue. "Because your hunger for one food source is constant until the wendigo deems there is no more to be had before moving to the next food source."

"Which was why I ate all the rabbits from the coup the next night."

"And why I finished consuming Webber during the supposed autopsy," the doctor said.

"And Lincoln?"

"Again, you didn't play your part. I had hoped that after feasting on the rabbits your libido would guide you to Lincoln's room to find a veritable smorgasbord."

"But you didn't finish him," Cali said.

"It no longer matters. Now that you've tasted human flesh, you will be driven by the nonstop urge to feed on the cook until the wendigo deems you should move on."

"I don't think so."

"I've passed the damnable spirit to you!"

It was Cali's turn to laugh. "Then why are you eating Lincoln's hand?"

As if awakening from a nightmare, Dr. Perricone looked at the fresh bitemarks, newly made divots exposing skeletal fingers beneath. After a couple more uncontrollable bites to remove the last bits of dead skin and cold meat, he dropped the finished meal to the snow. "No! No! I passed it to you!"

"Sort of." Cali stood and stepped away from Anjali, allowing the cook to sit up and wave to the doctor. Cali then held out the rabbit carcass she had torn through, her fingers and lips still warm with its blood. "Looks like I didn't eat all of the rabbits last night."

"No!" Dr. Perricone screamed again. Fingers curled, ready to strangle, he reached out. "I'm going to kill you!"

"No, you won't. Because you're not done eating."

A quizzical look on his face, he pulled up. And focused on his fingers.

"Once I figured out that poor, dumb Petey had nothing to do with this, I added two plus two to equal douchebag. I asked Bhumi about my options to fuck you over. She explained the curse, the rules. And then gave me a master key card to all the rooms. Before I left last night's party, I made sure you were occupied enough to sneak into your room. Your beard is so perfectly sculpted that I assumed you trimmed every day or two. I was right, so I collected your freshly trimmed, free-range, non-GMO, locally sourced face pepper to season Lincoln's hand."

"You bitch!" Dr. Perricone yelled right before tearing his left pinkie off with his teeth. He screamed and it fell to the snow. Cutting himself short, he shoved his wounded hand into his mouth. Orgasmic grunts of satisfaction mixed with ear-splitting shrieks as he ripped, chewed, swallowed. In between gulps, he tore away his clothes; the faster he chewed his flesh, the faster he shredded the fabrics. Cheeks slicked with gristle as ligaments poked from his beard, now dripping with scarlet, while he tore away at his forearm and bicep. Cali doubted she'd be eating any turkey legs at the next county fair. Though, she wasn't sure she'd ever eat another grape after his twitching twig of a left-hand with enough muscle and tendons plucked out his left eye and tossed it into his mouth between screams. Curious, Cali tossed the butcher's knife, and he caught it with his right hand. Anjali moved closer to Cali to get a better view. And smiled.

"No! God, no!" he screamed, unable to stop from pointing the tip at his naked waist. Cali made a mental note to ask about the brand of knife as he sliced from bellybutton to sternum in one pass. Entrails flopped free in a puff of steam as his insides hit the outside air. Letting go of the knife, he dropped to his knees and dug in with both hands. Shaking his head, he blubbered, "No! No! No! I won't! I won't!"

As if trying to detach itself, his head snapped back and forth, side to side as his hands gripped a length of pink tubing, body-slime oozing over his arms. His remaining eye bulged as his jaw snapped open to accept his own intestines. Gurgling whimpers faded into harsh breaths through his frothing nose as he force-fed himself by the fistful. Maniacally shoving his entire hand into his mouth with each slorping thrust, he was a slimy ouroboros. As the sloppy rope disappeared, the bloodied gray pouch of his stomach expanded, stretching to accommodate the tubing it led to. Cali had never tried haggis before, and she never will.

After a few more phlegmy gurgles, his eye rolled into his head. Hands falling to his sides, he finally toppled over. Jaw still moving, he lay dead in the snow.

Anjali put a hand on Cali's shoulder. "How do you feel?"

Cali removed the necklace and handed it to Anjali. "Better. Much better. Thank you for helping me. And trusting my crazy-ass plan."

Anjali accepted the necklace. "Thank you for returning to us what is ours."

Cali smirked. "Thank you for sneaking me a steady supply of beers when no one was looking. It's fun irking the entitled."

A soft chuckle. "I'll see you for breakfast. Of course, I need to find something other than rabbit since you ate them all."

Cali wanted to add a sarcastic note, but as she opened her mouth, the wind gusted, then swirled into an utter whiteout. Unable to see, breathe, or hear anything other than nature's howls, her heart raced, panicked. But in a blink, the pandemonium ceased. No extra snow, no colder than it'd been seconds ago.

Anjali was gone. In her place, nestled on top of the snow, was an opened bottle of Chimay. Wrapped around the neck was a thin leather strand sporting one white tooth. Cali's.

Smiling, she tucked the necklace into her pocket. So many years of hunting monsters had left her with plenty of trophies and even more scars – the necklace was just one more of each. Taking a swig from her beer, she walked back inside and wondered what other trouble she could get into on this vacation.

STORY INSPIRATION: Calista Lindquist, Cali, is our monster hunter in *The Killer of Devils* novel series and she relentlessly works on ridding the world of evil creatures, but even she needs a vacation now and then! Of course she can't get a moment's peace. Even though she faces down many supernatural threats, they always start with human motivations. There is no greater monster than a human with power. Enter the all-consuming spirit, a perfect allegory about the human condition. Cali has been known to be vicious and has the propensity to go too far with her methods, she still knows who the real monsters are.

Mannegishi Rising

Robert E. Waters and Jason M. Waters

Along the Sunwapta River, Alberta, Canada

Maskwa and Atim, members of the Cree Nation, stared at the plush, elaborate cabin. The sound of the Sunwapta River was strong, relentless. Maskwa smiled.

"What a beautiful cabin," he said, touching the exterior. "Wouldn't you agree, Atim?"

Atim nodded. "Yes, very beautiful."

They stared into the windows and reveled in the wonderful furniture within the cabin. Beds, tables, kitchen cabinets, and a marvelous fireplace of rock and plaster.

"I will be delighted when Lawrence Morton arrives," Maskwa said.

Atim turned and stared into Maskwa's eyes. "Who?"

"The lawyer, Lawrence Morton."

Atim shook his head. "I do not know this man."

"Ah." Maskwa raised his finger. "But, you should, Atim. You should."

Maskwa walked around the cabin, still enjoying the view within. "I had a vision," he said. "Law Morton and his family will be here, and they will suffer greatly."

Atim grabbed Maskwa's arm, turned him, and said, "Tell me. What is this all about?"

Maskwa sighed and said, "I used to live in Montana."

"Yes, I know that."

"But then, Mr. Morton deported nearly a thousand Cree from Montana. From Butte and Bozeman. They forced us out and into Canada." Maskwa shook his head. "What a tragedy."

"But, you're back in Canada," Atim said with his hands open. "Isn't that important?"

Maskwa nodded. "It is, but we loved Montana. Loved every bit of it." He pulled his arm away from Atim. "Something must be done about him... and his family."

Atim paused. "What do you intend to do?"

"I intend to make that family suffer greatly. I intend to make Lawrence Morton pay for his mass deportation."

"How?" Atim asked.

Maskwa turned and stared at Atim. He smiled. "We'll use the Mannegishi."

He turned from the cabin and walked away. Atim followed.

Lawrence Morton sighed with delight as he brought their car up the gravel driveway leading to their cabin. He listened to the gravel crunch as the wheels rolled over it. It was the only sound he heard. The car was quiet. Next to him, in the passenger seat, sat his wife, Elizabeth, sleeping. Her head rested comfortably against the window. Lawrence looked in the rearview mirror at their children, Robbie and Gina, in the backseat. Robbie scrolled on his phone while Gina slept, her mouth open, drool pouring out. Lawrence smiled. That was something that Gina had done since she was a baby.

Lawrence applied the brake. The brakes squeaked, and the car came to a halt. He turned off the ignition.

"We're here!" Lawrence said as he nudged his wife. She stirred and Robbie yawned behind them. Lawrence nudged Elizabeth again.

"I'm up, I'm up," she said weakly.

Lawrence smiled. "Right, dear. Sure you are."

As Elizabeth stretched to wake herself up, Lawrence removed his seat belt and got out. He stretched. His aging bones popped and protested, but he didn't care. He took a deep breath and breathed in the cool Canadian air. Lawrence loved their vacations to Canada. Elizabeth had always wanted to vacation some place *warm,* but she was outvoted by Lawrence and the kids.

The gravel crunched as Elizabeth walked to the back of the car and opened the trunk. Robbie got out of the car and looked around. Gina was still sound asleep, as if she hadn't heard three doors slamming shut.

"You didn't wake Gina?" Lawrence said to Robbie.

Robbie laughed and patted his father on the shoulder. "You're funny, Dad."

Lawrence chuckled as Robbie went to help his mother take their luggage out of the car. Lawrence opened Gina's door. Still asleep, she was covered in drool. He understood why Robbie hadn't wanted to wake her.

"Gina, we're here." Lawrence nudged her drool-free shoulder. "Wake up, sweet pea."

Gina grumbled and opened her eyes. "I'm fifteen," she mumbled. "Why do you still call me that?"

"You're still my young lady. Now, get out, and help your mother. And wipe that drool away."

The cabin was large and brilliantly decorated. Family pictures hung on the walls with taxidermy animal heads: a deer, a bear, and a wolverine. At the back of the living area was a fireplace that hadn't been lit since the last time they were there, a little over a year ago. The furniture was crisp and clean. It was a quaint, yet luxurious cabin.

Robbie walked over to the couch, dropped his luggage, and jumped onto the cushions. He sighed and put his arms behind his head.

"It's good to be back," Robbie said with a wide smile.

"Robert Joel Morton," Elizabeth snapped. "Pick this up right now and take it to your room!" She kicked his luggage aside.

Robbie sighed. "Fine."

Eventually, Gina entered the cabin and went to her room to put her things away. Once everyone was settled, they gathered around the living room and discussed their vacation plans.

"I was thinking the kids and I could go whitewater rafting tomorrow," Lawrence said as he looked over at his son and daughter. Their faces lit up. "And then after we could—"

"You can take Robbie," Elizabeth said, "but Gina stays."

"What!" Gina shouted. She glared at her mother, anger in her eyes. "Why do I have to stay?"

Elizabeth returned Gina's glare. "Don't you remember what happened *last* time you three went whitewater rafting?"

"That wasn't *my* fault!" Gina snapped.

Elizabeth turned to Lawrence for help. He could see she was determined to keep Gina safe. They had cut their trip short last year when Gina fell off the raft and broke her arm. Lawrence had been hoping to spend equal time with his kids together, but he knew he wouldn't be able to persuade Elizabeth. Her will was hard as iron.

Lawrence sighed and nodded. "Okay. Gina? You'll stay here with Mama."

Gina grumbled and crossed her arms. "This isn't fair."

"Life isn't fair," Elizabeth said.

"Teenagers," Robbie said, rolling his eyes, lazily scrolling on his phone.

Gina balled up her fist and struck him gently on his back. "You're seven*teen!*"

Lawrence raised both arms in intervention before things escalated. "That's enough, everyone. Settle down. We'll be here for two weeks, so we have a lot of planning to do. Let's make this a vacation we'll *never* forget!"

"Whitewater rafting!" Robbie squealed. "Whoohoo!"

Lawrence was happy about it, too. It had been a while since he had kayaked on a river, the rush of water and the swirl of the chop. Robbie was so excited about it that he couldn't contain himself.

"Hey, can I get my own kayak?" Robbie asked.

Lawrence was skeptical. "I don't know. Wouldn't it be best if we shared a raft?"

"Ah, come on, Pop," Robbie said. "I want to ride my own boat. Please?"

Robbie batted his puppy dog eyes. Lawrence nodded. "Okay… we'll look into it."

Robbie rushed down to the edge of the water, the Sunwapta River roaring like a lion. "You keep close to me, okay? I want to make sure we are safe."

"Okay, Pops."

While Robbie walked among the boats available for rent, Lawrence nodded and smiled at those preparing their kayaks, slipping arms into life vests, rolling tubes into the water. Funny, but Two Native Americans eyed him as if he were some kind of monster. Lawrence glanced at them briefly. He felt their stare on his back and wondered if he somehow knew them. He had deported many Cree back to Canada, justifiably, and they weren't legal U.S. citizens.

"Can I take this one?" Robbie asked. It was blue, long, sleek, and quite sturdy.

Lawrence nodded. "Sure, you take that one, I'll grab another."

He studied the remaining kayaks, found a red one, and paid the man.

Near the bank where it was calm and quiet, Robbie put on his helmet, gloves, and eyewear. He put his throw bag and pocketknife in the cubby, his paddles into place. Lawrence followed suit.

"Okay," Robbie said, "Let's go."

"Hold on now. You stay near me, understand? I don't want you to get in any kind of danger."

Robbie shook his head. "No worries, Pop. I'll stay near you."

They pushed offshore with their paddles and into the river as the water began to rush and swell.

Robbie slammed into a rock.

"Hey, watch it!" Lawrence shouted. "Be careful!"

Robbie made his way down the river, the current fast and treacherous, Lawrence paddling alongside. "This is fun!"

"Yes, it is!" Lawrence said, keeping close to his son.

They navigated further down the Sunwapta River. Because of his muscles and joints, and the long drive had tired him more than he realized, Lawrence was hoping they'd soon find a place in the river where the water was calm. But Robbie was purposefully slamming into rocks, laughing and hooting.

Lawrence was worried. Every time Robbie struck a rock he would raise a paddle in triumph, as if reveling in the riffles.

Finally, as they navigated down a series of boulders and narrow passageways, the Sunwapta River grew calm.

Lawrence and Robbie drifted down the river, paddles out of the water. The current was still strong, but Lawrence floated beside his son and said, "We've got about a quarter mile until we hit the waves again."

"Yeah." Robbie breathed deeply, a smile on his face. He dipped a paddle in the water as the current pushed him forward. "This is the greatest rafting I've ever done. I like how… Whoa!"

His kayak suddenly rolled, and Robbie was dumped into the river.

"Robbie!" Lawrence screamed wondering if his paddle had caught in a rock or in a submerged branch. Robbie tried to pull back up, but many small hands were on him, dragging him back down.

Lawrence grabbed his knife, then dove into the water.

And then he saw them. Dozens of tiny creatures with small arms and hands and legs. Their eyes were big and bulbous, but their heads looked like peanuts. He couldn't tell if they had mouths, but Lawrence swam to them and slashed at their faces.

A creature screamed and pulled away like a tortured soul. Lawrence slashed at another, and another as Robbie was pulled to the bottom of the five-foot-deep river. Lawrence came back up for air. "Robbie!" he yelled, splashing and stabbing wildly, until red blood from these tiny creatures began to flow with the current. "Robbie!" he yelled again as the creatures backed off and swam away. His son bobbed to the surface, and Lawrence grabbed him.

He held him above the water and swam to shore. Lawrence's heart was pounding, his shoulders burning as he swam, worried that he wasn't going to make it, but he did. He dragged Robbie onto the bank.

His son wasn't breathing. Lawrence pumped Robbie's chest and breathed into his mouth, again and again, until Robbie coughed and spit up water, opening his eyes wild with fear. "Thank God," Lawrence said.

"Keep breathing, Robbie," Lawrence said. "Breathe."

Robbie spit out more water, coughing and gagging until he caught his breath. Robbie turned and looked at his father.

"What were those creatures?" Robbie asked, gasping.

Lawrence had wanted to believe that he hadn't seen them, that his imagination had got the better of him when his son fell in the water, but if Robbie had seen them too, then they *had* to be real. *But, what the hell were they?*

Lawrence shook his head. "I don't know, Robbie. I don't know."

"You sure you're okay?" Lawrence asked as he followed Robbie up the gravel pathway to the cabin, both of them soaking wet and sloshing in their waterlogged shoes.

Robbie shrugged and nodded. "Yeah, I'm fine. Still crazy, though… what happened."

"I know…"

They continued toward the cabin in silence. What would he tell Elizabeth? What would Robbie say? What could Robbie possibly say?

Lawrence entered the cabin, Robbie close behind on his heels. The smell of roasting chicken filled the air along with the *tap tap tap* of chopping. Elizabeth stood at the kitchen island, chopping away at a carrot. She looked up and smiled at Lawrence as he approached.

"You're back!" Elizabeth said. "How was rafting?"

"It was… fine," Lawrence said quietly.

Elizabeth placed the knife on the cutting board. "Law, what's wrong? Why are you all wet?"

Lawrence sat on a stool opposite Elizabeth. She watched him, waiting for his response.

"Something happened when we were rafting," he said.

"Did something happen to Robbie?"

Lawrence heard the panic in her voice. He shook his head. "No… Well, yes, sort of."

Elizabeth raised her brows and cocked her head.

"We were kayaking, when his kayak turned over," Lawrence said. "I went after him, but when I got to him these…" He would sound insane if he told her what he thought he saw. But what else could he do? "These *things* were pulling him into the river."

"Things? What things?"

Lawrence shrugged. "I don't know, but they were small and there were a lot of them." He looked into her eyes. Hers were blue, not unnaturally yellow like those creatures in the river. "I want to get the hell out of here!"

Elizabeth smiled weakly and leaned forward, taking his trembling hands in hers. "Are you sure? Maybe you were just seeing things?"

Lawrence shrugged again. "Maybe I did. Maybe I didn't. Robbie says he saw them, too. Either way, I think we should go. Let's leave in the morning. Catch a flight back to Montana."

Elizabeth sighed and nodded. "Okay, if that's what you want. The kids might not like it though."

"Robbie will understand, and Gina will throw a fit. Where is she anyway?"

"In her room. Want me to tell Gina we're leaving?"

Lawrence shook his head. "I'll tell them both during dinner."

"Speaking of dinner, it should be ready soon. I'll call everyone when it's done?"

Lawrence smiled and nodded. He kissed her on the cheek. "You're the best."

He left her in the kitchen making dinner. *I'll feel better when we're back home.*

Back in the den, drying in front of the fireplace, goose bumps on his arms, he closed his eyes, worrying.

They were sleeping. Gina and Robbie were in their rooms while Lawrence lay sprawled on the couch alongside the warm crackling fireplace. He was trying to forget about the water creatures, thinking they had to be something explainable. They had to be. Elizabeth was in her room too, snoring loudly.

Gina heard a knock on her window. *Tap tap tap,* as if it were that stupid robin going after its reflection. Gina awoke, rubbed her face, and turned on the light. She blinked a few times and stared at the window.

The creature tapped again and again, its face pressed against the glass, eyes saucer-wide, head small with no nose or mouth. Gina sat upright. Her mouth dropped open… and she screamed.

Lawrence sat up with a startle. "Gina?" he said.

She screamed again, and he ran to her room.

Robbie was there and Elizabeth too, her with a wooden kitchen mallet in her hand, both of them staring wildly at the large, bulbous eyes of those creatures, their empty faces. "My God!" Robbie said, as one of the creatures cracked a rock against the window, the glass splintering.

"What are those…?" Elizabeth asked.

Gina started crying.

Lawrence watched the creatures crawl up the window.

"Are they going to the roof?" Elizabeth asked, her voice cracking.

"Maybe," Lawrence said.

Lawrence scooped up Gina and said, "Come on! Let's head to the basement."

"They tried to drown me!" Robbie said, running into the living room.

Lawrence chased after him. "What are you doing?"

"We *must* kill them, "Robbie said. "It's the only way." Robbie, fearless and determined, grabbed a piece of smoldering wood from the fireplace. He held it up. "We burn them."

Lawrence nodded as he heard the window in Gina's room shatter. She screamed. Elizabeth pulled her toward the fireplace. "You keep an eye on them." Lawrence said. "Hit them hard with that mallet."

Robbie held the enflamed wood high; Lawrence grabbed another piece of wood. Gina did as well.

They huddled around the fireplace.

The creatures had tumbled in through Gina's room and now scurried into the living room. Small and insignificant, Lawrence knew they weren't as weak and incapable as they looked. He didn't have the wits to count them, but they were maybe a dozen or more. They surrounded the fireplace, their massive eyes glaring at the Mortons.

"Wait!" Lawrence said. "Let them get closer."

Robbie shook his head. "I'm not waiting."

He lashed out, swinging the flaming fire stick, jabbing one of the creatures. It caught fire and groaned like a howling beast, falling on the floor, burning to a crisp.

"Aah, that smell!" Lawrence said, shaking his head at the foul odor of the creature.

They moved closer, avoiding the jabs of logs, reaching out for the legs of whomever stood closest. One of them grabbed at Gina's leg. She screamed.

Mannegishi pounced on Robbie.

Robbie was completely covered in Mannegishi. He lay under their pile, his log singing the carpet. Lawrence pounded several of them off of Robbie with his burning log.

The carpet was set alight. Smoke and flames filled the cabin, and the Mannegishi caught like paper, burning incessantly. The little monsters ran into the couch and the drapes, some of them stumbling out of the cabin.

Gina coughed. Elizabeth coughed. "Come on," Lawrence said, the Mannegishi in flames, as he ushered his family through the cabin door. "Let's get to the car."

"Let's go," he said, diving into the driver's seat. Elizabeth hopped in the front; Gina and Robbie jumped in the backseat.

Lawrence gunned the engine, tires squealing.

"We're safe now," Lawrence said. "We're safe."

They drove for miles, with the sun rising. Lawrence was happy about that. Both Gina and Robbie sat in stunned silence in the backseat.

Along the side of the road, under a canopy of trees, Lawrence saw two men standing as if awaiting his oncoming car. He slowed down as he passed. They were the same familiar men he'd seen at the river, the Cree Native Americans. They stared blankly at the car, watching as they drove by. Lawrence shook his head, sped past them, accelerating.

They're gone, he thought. *Gone forever.*

Then something hit the windshield, shattering the glass and making Lawrence swerve.

Elizabeth screamed.

"What's happening?" Robbie shouted.

Gina was screaming in his ear.

Lawrence tried to maintain control of the car. "I don't know!"

Something struck the hood.

"The creatures!" Robbie yelled.

Another slammed into the windshield. Another and another. Lawrence couldn't see the road. He swerved again, trying to shake off the nasty little creatures, but they were blocking his view.

Lawrence swerved and tapped the brakes trying to throw them off but lost complete control of the car.

He slammed into the guardrail, and the car toppled down the escarpment.

Gina screamed. Robbie screamed. Elizabeth screamed. Everyone screamed while the car shot off the escarpment and into the boulders below.

We're dead, Lawrence thought. *I love my wife, my children. I love them all.*

The Mannegishi held onto the car. The car hit the boulders… and exploded.

STORY INSPIRATION: The inspiration regarding Mannegishi Rising is glorious. The Morton family - Gina, Lawrence, Robbie, and Elizabeth, in addition to the Cree Nation Native Americans, require curses, trouble, and death in all cases.

JUST ONE BITE

DIANNA SINOVIC

Just as Patrick fastened his seat belt in row 24, he identified the hunger rumbling in his stomach: It wasn't for anything prepackaged in the galley of the JAL jet. It was for his seat mate. Specifically, her leg – sweet and meaty.

Suddenly nauseated, Patrick tried to think of anything else but the woman's shapely thighs and calves, only inches away from his middle seat.

"Are you heading home?" the young woman asked, buckling her own seat belt. Mid-twenties, a friendly smile.

"Home?" Patrick pushed his thoughts onto a safer track. "Yeah. From a business trip with my boss. We did some sightseeing, too. And you?"

"Trip to see family. I live here now, but my parents are in Detroit."

Doug, his boss, elbowed Patrick from the righthand seat, pulling him from the conversation. "What do you say we work on the proposal together? We can brainstorm and probably get the draft hammered out over the next hour. Then we can kick back and enjoy a movie."

While Doug continued talking, Patrick kept a hungry eye on the man's arm, well-muscled flesh exposed below his polo sleeve. *'Course he'd have to pick all that hair out of his teeth like chicken feathers…* He shook his head. What the hell was wrong with him?

"Pat?" Doug's raised eyebrows made Patrick frown. Had his boss seen something odd in his gaze?

"I told you we should have stopped at one bottle of sake," Doug said, chuckling. "You're awfully pale. Hangovers can do that to you."

Patrick had no sleep the previous evening, their last night in the small inn outside Kyoto. The tour guide leading him on foot through the glade to the shrine… the eerie lights that flickered around him… the startling scream out of nowhere… the guide acting nonchalant while hurrying the small group back to the inn. "It's nothing," the guide had said while glancing over his shoulder.

"Maybe," Patrick said just to respond. He closed his eyes and clamped down on the increasing urge to take a bite out of Doug's arm. Even over the odors of BO, cloying perfume, farts, and smelly feet that drifted through the cabin, the scent of nearby flesh stood out. Silently he chanted: no, no, no, no, until the jet was airborne and they were streaking east across the Pacific.

He tried to sleep during the endless movie *Avatar*, but a recurring nightmare of chewing and swallowing Doug's ear and then munching on his other seat mate's leg left him even more drained than when he'd boarded. When the flight attendant came by for drink orders, he almost blurted, "Bring me a bloody spritzer." And one look at the light snack on his tray table made his stomach flip.

Finally, he locked himself in a cabin bathroom, claiming to be ill when an attendant inquired through the door if anything was wrong. It was the only way he knew to keep his teeth to himself.

Once through customs at San Francisco International, Patrick followed Doug through the concourse and out to the street. Doug's wife picked him up at the curb, and he waved a farewell to Patrick. "See you Monday morning," Doug called, looking a hell of a lot more rested and relaxed than Patrick felt.

An image flashed in Patrick's mind. *His boss's browned body horizontal and spinning slowly. Barbecued.* He started, realizing he'd been daydreaming of Doug on a spit. *Jesus, this is sick.*

With no one to give him a lift, he waited for an Uber. *Yoshi arriving in six minutes in a blue Honda Civic.* He was eager to get to his condo, where he could try to sort out the craziness that seemed to have enveloped him. The cacophony of taxi horns and shouts of drivers around him receded, and he was acutely aware of a meaty smell right behind him. He turned, expecting to see someone chomping on a hotdog or sausage roll, but saw only a thin woman, backpack over her shoulders, also waiting for a ride. Her heart, muscular and perfect, fragrant with substance, beat in a rhythm that he subconsciously adapted to, until their pulses were in sync. It wasn't possible for him to smell that, and yet he could.

"Pervert," the woman hissed, moving quickly away from him.

He wiped the drool from his mouth. He realized he'd been staring at her hungrily. *Lucky she walked away.* He'd been ready to grab her and somehow rip her chest open. Bile in his throat, he looked at his phone to track his ride, his mind racing. *What is wrong with me?*

The navy blue Honda arrived a moment later, and relieved, Patrick swung his luggage into the trunk. Sliding into the back seat, he took a deep breath. Inhaling slowly, he vowed to ignore the driver – at least his physicality – during the twenty-nine-minute ride.

"Home from vacation?" Yoshi the driver glanced at him in the rearview mirror before pulling out from the curb.

"Business trip," Patrick said, still breathing deeply. *In through the nose, out through the mouth.*

"Good time? Make good sales?" Yoshi's accent placed him from Asia.

"Sure." The meaty smell Patrick had noticed at the airport drifted through the car. "No," he groaned softly.

"You all right?" Yoshi's concerned look mirrored the look Doug had given him on the flight.

"Have you ever been to Japan?" Patrick asked, sounding strained as he breathed through his mouth, not his nose while trying to ignore the mouth-watering aroma.

Turning onto the freeway, Yoshi laughed. "Born there, near the old capital of Kyoto. Lived there longer than here."

"Maybe I picked up a bug," Patrick said. "I've never felt so… weird."

"Ah," Yoshi said. "Sorry to hear. What do you feel?"

It had been Doug's idea to travel to the countryside north of Kyoto to visit the Omagatoki shrine. Patrick was happy staying in the city – *known* for its shrines, he pointed out. But Doug had pushed his plan, arguing that, according to his research, the side trip would be unforgettable. Once they got to the inn near the shrine, though, Doug had been called into a long virtual meeting, leaving Patrick to either sit alone and bored in his room or check out the shrine.

"It was an 'after dark' tour," Patrick said. Five people from the inn, including Patrick, plus the guide. "One of those ghost tours, I guess you'd call it."

"*Yokai*," Yoshi said, nodding. "Spirits, usually not good ones."

"Whatever," Patrick said. "They said we might see a night bird that glows or fireballs or even a skeleton. I thought, why not? I don't believe in ghosts, but maybe they had some kind of Disneyland setup." He shivered, remembering the walk in the darkness. The guide spoke little English, and his lecture covered much more than the few phrases of Japanese that Patrick knew. The trees seemed to hug Patrick at every turn, and the silence was so eerie, he felt his skin crawl.

"No pretend ghost in Japan," Yoshi said fervently. "Real. Always real."

"We made it to the shrine, but the guide's flashlight didn't illuminate much. All around the place were these little lights, in the trees and bushes. Some floated. The guide said they were benign." Or, that's what Patrick thought he said.

"When we were leaving the area, we heard a shriek. The guide seemed frightened by it, but if he said what it was, I didn't hear or understand him. Maybe it was a wild animal." In that instant, Patrick recalled, something had covered him like a thin blanket, but when he reached to pull it off, he had grasped air. "When we got back to the inn, I started to feel… different."

Yoshi's eyebrows were halfway up his forehead and his eyes bore into Patrick's. Terror, Patrick realized. "*Oni,*" Yoshi whispered.

"What?" he asked the driver.

"*Oni,*" Yoshi said again. His driving slowed, and suddenly he pulled to the narrow shoulder on a busy, four-lane road, still a distance from Patrick's condo.

"Oni is a demon." He turned around to face Patrick. "And how do you feel now?"

Patrick caught that raw scent again, his nostrils flaring. He pinched his nose. He began to sweat, warm beads rolling down his back. He chose his words carefully, not wanting to be thrown out of the car miles from home. "I'm a vegan, but since last night I've craved meat of a… special kind. And my sense of smell has gone wonky."

Frowning, Yoshi picked up his phone and swiped through a few screens. "Not good," he said when he looked up again. "*Onihitokuchi*."

Patrick's head began to throb. "Which is what?"

"Demon that kills and eats humans."

"What does that have to do with me?"

Yoshi rubbed his chin. He gestured to the car door. "You must leave. So sorry. It's too dangerous."

A car whizzed by, followed by another. "I can't get out here," Patrick protested. "There's no sidewalk, no place to walk."

"*Oni* has you." Yoshi waved Patrick off like a pestering fly. "Please get out."

"*Has* me?"

"It has taken over. You and *Oni* share your body now."

"Bullshit," Patrick said. "Ghost stories are great for tourism, but they aren't real. This is some norovirus I picked up over there, and now it's wreaking havoc on me."

"I will call 911 if you don't leave. Tell police you are crazy man, try to hurt me." The driver held his phone with his finger poised to start the call.

Patrick fixated on that finger, attached to the hand, attached to the arm. The tang wafting off Yoshi was tantalizing. *Just one bite.*

Two weeks later, Patrick sat in a small waiting room, pinning his hands firmly under his thighs.

One other person, a blond woman with short hair, fleshy with enough meat on her to feed him for days, sat across the room. Patrick couldn't chance what his hands might do if he let them loose. He also kept a close watch on the woman. If she was here for an exorcism, he had to be ready to fend off whatever lay hidden within *her*.

The Hososhi, or exorcist, catered to a Japanese clientele and apparently had a thriving business. No surprise, considering the vast number of otherworldly beings listed under Japanese folklore on Wikipedia. *Why couldn't I have been possessed by a common American ghoul – one less difficult to exorcise?*

He hadn't slept well since his return from Kyoto, with a never-ending revulsion at what he craved. Yet he ate veggie burgers and tofu cheese and tried not to think about the random arms and legs and hearts he'd also consumed. The bones and other undigestible leftovers he disposed of. When his news app pinged a local story about a new serial killer, he hurriedly scrolled right past it.

After fantasizing about biting into a co-worker's exposed shoulder in the company break room, Patrick requested a leave of absence from his job. Doug had been sympathetic without knowing the details.

And now he was waiting to have a demon – which he didn't really believe in, did he? – removed from his body – or was it his soul? – so he could get back to eating roasted walnut pate.

In the quiet of the reception area, Patrick longed to scroll through his phone to take his mind off the other client's unwitting temptation, but he didn't dare free his hands. At least she sat across the room, farther from his traitorous nose.

When he glanced at her, she narrowed her eyes. "What are *you* here for?"

He hesitated. *If I tell her, will she flee?* "It's a long story," he finally said. "How about you?"

She touched her neck and smoothed her hair. "I should have known better than to trust my brother." Her smile was thin. "He and my sister-in-law dragged me along to Kyoto so I could watch their 4-year-old – my niece – while they partied on the town." Again, she touched her neck. "I came back with…"

"Rokurokubi." The receptionist, seated behind a half-open glass partition, filled in the pause. "Kind of like a long-necked vampire. But your problem is not as severe as his." She glared at Patrick. "You are next." She slid the partition closed with a thud.

He was led into a darkened room furnished with two wooden chairs and a small round table on which sat a metal basin filled with water. He hoped it was only water. The exorcist shuffled into the room a moment later, an ancient man dressed in an ornate green silk gown. He did not shake Patrick's hand, but his smile was encouraging.

"I have reviewed your case. I will say first that this rite is usually performed at a Shinto temple by a priest. I am not a priest and we are not in Japan, so we will make do with what we have here. Any questions?"

"Where does the *Oni* go once it leaves me?" Patrick envisioned a spirit trap – like in *Ghostbusters*.

"Once released, the spirits usually disperse and vanish. They no longer have a host." The exorcist pointed to the basin. "Wash your face and hands with the saltwater while I prepare the order of chants."

With his face and hands clean, Patrick sat on the chair, jiggling one leg to distract himself from the smells in the air while the exorcist recited from a book of prayer. He felt foolish as the foreign words swirled around him. How could this possibly work? The man's babbling went on for what felt like a half hour. Boredom was settling in. So was the hunger. Then, with a tug that felt like something was being ripped from his core, a breath of illuminated fog rose from Patrick's chest. Instead of vanishing, it hovered over the exorcist, whose face contorted briefly. When the man's features smoothed, Patrick recognized the avid look in his eyes. Patrick lunged for the door and managed to slip through before the exorcist could react.

"Run!" Patrick called to the woman in the waiting room. He fled the building and was up the street in seconds. When he paused, panting, to look back, the feeling of revulsion had vanished.

The woman caught up with him. "What happened?" She was gasping for breath.

"The Hososhi—" He stopped, distracted by the woman's neck as it began to stretch upward a foot, two feet, six feet. *Kind of like a long-necked* vampire, the receptionist had said.

The woman called down to him with a wicked grin. "Come a little closer, dear."

STORY INSPIRATION: This story was inspired by a class writing assignment on spiritual possession – and a friend's recent trip to Japan.

Step on a Crack

Jacque Day

Dylan stared at the phone, which lay flat on the table in front of her.

She had already entered the number – just as she had at least a hundred times in the ten years since her stepmother's death – and her finger hovered over the green CONNECT icon. One tap, and every closed door between herself and her stepsister would reopen. But was Dylan ready for that? It was a question she had turned over in her mind for the past decade. And well, now, no closer to an answer, she decided to leave it to the universe. *I'll do it blind, like Pin the Tail on the Donkey*, she thought. *If it's meant to be, it's meant to be. And if not...*

Squeezing her eyes shut tight, she drew a circle in the air with her fingertip, and brought it down to the screen.

At first, nothing. Dead air. Gasping, Dylan forced her eyes open – *I missed* – then the line connected and the indicator read, "Calling."

No turning back now.

It rang once, twice, three times. *One more ring and I'll end the call*, she told herself, and when the fourth ring began, she allowed herself to exhale, more than a little relieved that nobody was picking up. "I tried," she said, and reached for the red button.

A wail of static and music blasted out of the phone. Dylan yanked her hand back as if pulling it away from an open flame.

"Thanks for calling Cici's Sassy Sauces," a male voice boomed from the other end. "Will this be delivery or takeout?"

Dylan blinked, her mouth hanging open.

After a pause, the voice came again. "Anybody there?" After another pause, he continued. "I'll give you to the count of three. One... two..."

"Wait!"

"Waiting is what I do best," the man replied, entirely without irritation. Dylan could practically hear him smiling. "Can I interest you in today's special – a sassy fusion of Cici's pancit with saucy Fina'denne and your choice of chicken, pork, or beef?"

Bemused, Dylan squinted at the phone number on the attorney's letter, comparing it with the one she had dialed. They were a match. "I'm sorry," she stammered. "I was given this number for Cecelia Donnelly, but that was a long time ago. There must be some mistake."

"No apologies necessary and no mistake," the man roared over the din. "You got the right place. Cecelia is the owner. Hold on. Let me see if she can talk." There was a clattering as he laid the phone down, and Dylan heard him holler, "Hey, Cici. Can you take a call?" A minute passed before he picked the phone back up. "We've got a line out the door. She'll call you back in a little bit."

"Wait," Dylan put in, cringing at the mousy squeak of her voice.

"Waiting is what I do best."

"I… I want to make sure I've got the right person. Just one question."

"Shoot."

"Is she beautiful?"

He brayed a laugh. "Oh yeah, she's beautiful."

The line went silent.

Shortly after eleven that night, Dylan's phone buzzed. The name, Saucy Cici, appeared on her screen. Counting backward from three, Dylan accepted the call.

Cecelia's voice came low, throaty. "Is it really you?"

"Indeed it is."

"Sorry I'm so late. Friday night dinner rush."

"You have a restaurant."

"Two, actually. I figured you burned that letter."

"I considered it."

"I'm sorry," Cecelia said.

The air hung thick between the sisters as Cecelia's apology settled over them like a heavy blanket, as if to smother the smoldering flames of past wrongs. Dylan opened her mouth to say something, anything. *It's okay*. Or… *I'm sorry, too*. But the words stopped short.

Cecelia snickered. "No need to kill yourself choking up an apology you don't mean. You called. That's enough – for now. Before we go on, I have two questions."

"Okay," Dylan replied tentatively, skeptically, drawing out the last syllable.

"First, cross me off your list?" Before Dylan could respond, Cecelia cut back in. "And don't tell me you don't have a list, because I've seen it. You still keep it taped to the wall, all Steve Buscemi-like?"

"Busted. I'll even cross it out with a red marker, just like in the movie. Next?"

"Is your Real ID up to date?"

"Another Champagne before we land, Miss Dylan?"

The flight attendant stood at Dylan's side, smiling, a platter held skillfully in one hand. They were the only two people in the cabin of the Gulfstream G550, a private business jet that could easily occupy eight, and Dylan lounged on a sofa that she guessed would cost more than the furnishings in her entire Squirrel Hill condo. Enjoying the buzz from her first two drinks, she eyed the tall, sleek Champagne flute. The flight from Pittsburgh International bound for Chicago Midway had been uneventful, thus far, but even the smoothest flight came with the inevitable bumps and lurches. Yet in the hands of this perfectly put-together flight attendant, whose name tag read Layla, the sparkling drink didn't so much as ripple.

Dylan reached for the beverage, shook her head, and drew back her hand. "I need to be thinking clearly."

"Perhaps a club soda, then?"

"That would be nice. Thank you."

Layla withdrew into the galley, and Dylan turned back to the television, which sat on a sideboard across from the sofa, the sound turned off. Lulled by the hum of the jet engines, she allowed herself to get lost in the noiseless images of happy snorkelers, diving and resurfacing in an oceanic pool enclosed by high cliffs.

"The Grotto."

Layla's voice wrenched Dylan from her trance, and she glanced up into the striking face of the flight attendant, who held an uncapped bottle in one hand and a frosted glass in the other. "Should I pour?"

Dylan pushed herself up from a slouch. "I'll take it straight from the bottle," she said, reaching for it. "No need to dirty a glass."

"Just like your father," Layla said.

"You knew my father?"

Layla smiled and nodded, handing the bottle to Dylan.

She accepted it and wrapped both hands around it, enjoying its cool touch on her palms and fingertips.

Layla set the glass atop a coaster on a small table next to the sofa. "In case you change your mind… about the glass," she said. "Your father was a nice man, a kind man. I met him when I was a little girl and he was stationed on Saipan. My Auntie Virginia worked in the officer's club where he often ate."

Dylan sat up, gaping at Layla, who she estimated must be ten years her junior. "Virginia, my stepmother. She was your aunt?" Even now, after all these years, Dylan thirsted for details of her father's love story with Virginia. This was a part of the story she had never heard.

"She was a cook," Layla went on. "Quite talented. One night, after a particularly delicious meal of Kelaguen, he asked to meet the chef. That's how it all began, according to family legend."

Dylan settled back, took a long swig, and turned the bottle to study thc label. "I don't know this brand."

"Topo Chico," Layla said. "Only the best for Cici's sister."

"Stepsister," Dylan corrected, pointing to the television screen, where a man in a yellow tropical shirt spoke, his mouth moving soundlessly. Behind him, snorkelers plunged and resurfaced, then disappeared once again into the lapping waters. "What is – what's that you called it? The Grotto?"

"Oh," Layla said, waving a hand as if such a sight were nothing much at all. "It's a popular swimming hole on Saipan." She tipped a nod to the man on the screen. "Hector there, he likes to talk up the Grotto. You know, for the tourists."

"Looks like fun."

"It is," Layla said. "But it's also treacherous. A steep climb, and there are no steps. Easy to slip and fall."

As they watched, the man turned and dove headfirst into the Grotto. The video cut and rose up and over the ocean, soaring toward a bluff high above the surf. Dylan's breath caught in her throat. "That's spectacular. What is it?"

"Suicide Cliff."

Dylan leaned forward again, interested. "Why do they call it that?"

Layla touched a control, bringing up the volume on the TV. "Let's let Hector describe it," she said, settling into the sofa next to Dylan. "He has more practice."

At first, the flatscreen gave off no sound at all, just drone footage gliding lazily over and around a majestic overhang of jagged rock topped by green grass. The camera stopped, hovered, then dropped suddenly and raced down the cliff. As the view descended, sinking faster and faster toward certain doom below, Dylan grabbed at the arm of the sofa. Then, just in time, the image pulled up and away from the rocks, and cut to an overlook of the ocean from the cliff's edge. A peal of a strong wind combined with the whooshing of the surf rushed into Dylan's ears. She placed a hand over her heart. "Good heavens."

"Hector shot all that drone footage himself. He's quite the gifted pilot."

Dylan's mind flashed back to the video of Hector, diving into the Grotto. "A bit of a daredevil, is he?"

Layla grunted a laugh. "Auntie always said Hector was born without the gift of fear."

At this, Dylan warmed. She had a feeling she would like this man, Hector. "Do you know him well?"

"As well as anyone can know their sibling," Layla said, pointing to the screen. "Listen."

A male voiceover rose softly into the vista.

"Death duty," said the narrator, his tone deep, soothing. Ominous. *"That's what they called it. July 1944, World War Two. As American forces closed in, certain to overtake the Japanese imperial stronghold of Saipan, thousands of Japanese soldiers and civilians came to the edge of this rock face and leaped to their deaths. Some held children as they jumped. Some say they can still hear the screams of the children in the winds over the bluff and in the hallowed jungle and rocks below Suicide Cliff."*

"Okay, enough of that," Layla said, muting the volume. "Hector does have a flair for the dramatic."

Dylan tamped down her disappointment at the abrupt absence of his voice. And what was it about his easy, buttery timbre that rang familiar?

"So, will I get to meet Hector?" Dylan asked.

"Soon enough." From her perch on the sofa, Layla crossed one smooth, brown leg over the other, slung her arm onto the backrest, and stared at Dylan. "Is that really what you want to talk about? Landmarks and swimming holes and my lug of a brother? I mean, you're thirty thousand feet in the air headed to Chicago, where in exactly –" she glanced at her watch. "– thirty minutes you will lay eyes on a sister you haven't seen in more than a decade."

"Stepsister," Dylan corrected.

"Right," Layla said, tapping her impeccably manicured nails on the sofa back. "Steps." She retreated into her own thoughts, and when she emerged, she said, "You know what they say about steps? They belong in a house…"

They finished in unison "…but not in a home."

Dylan sat back and took another long draw from the bottle. "Virginia used to say that. Any time she heard me, or Dad, or Cecelia, call each other 'stepsister' or 'stepdaughter.' She really tried to break us of that."

"Auntie Ginny was an old soul, and wise." Layla's lips turned up in a sad smile. "Do you miss her?"

Dylan's throat knotted into a lump, and she fought back the flash of tears that sprang into her eyes. "Of course I do," she said, the "s" in *course* hissing through her teeth. She closed her eyes and tried to quell the old anger, the old darkness that threatened to creep in. That feeling of being… *excluded.* Here was this beautiful woman and her brother – someone who by all appearances lived for adventure. And Dylan had never, not once, been introduced to either of them. The old questions nudged at her shell, attempting to break through. *Whose decision was that, Virginia's, or my father's*? But it was moot, because neither were there to ask.

So instead, Dylan asked a question that *could* be answered. "I feel bad that you're waiting on me," she said, draining the bottle and nodding toward the galley. "How about I get the next round?"

"Don't be silly," Layla said, rising to her feet. "That's my job. I'm part of the flight crew. Have been since Aunt Ginny christened this aircraft. She made many trips to Saipan before she died, even before your father passed, though he hardly went with us. He hated to fly."

"Yes, I remember. After his time in the service, he never wanted to fly again," Dylan replied, and as she spoke, she scanned the cabin, realization dawning. "This is the plane my dad bought for Virginia."

Layla nodded, collecting Dylan's empty Topo Chico bottle. "It was important to him, that she remain connected with her homeland."

"Amazing," Dylan said, peering around. Eight roomy seats, a galley kitchen no doubt fully stocked and ready to serve, this lounge area with a 32-inch TV. "The bones are the same but it looks totally different from how I remember."

"Yes, the Seedy was more – spartan – when Aunt Ginny and your dad had it," Layla said, glancing around, absorbed in her own memories. "Growing up poor on an island in the middle of the Pacific, Ginny never did get used to having money. Cecelia made these upgrades after…"

"After she inherited it," Dylan finished. *A plane bought for my stepmother with my father's money, and now it reeks of Cecelia,* she thought, but didn't say. Even in her mind, the thought sounded too bitter, too cruel to articulate aloud, especially in the presence of Layla, who had done nothing to deserve hearing it. What she did say was, "The Seedy. I always thought that was a silly name for a plane."

Overhead, a light went on, and a loudspeaker crackled, followed by a thundering male voice. "This is your friendly neighborhood pilot. We have begun our descent into Chicago and will land in approximately twenty minutes. There, we refuel and collect our next passenger for the longest leg of our journey, a direct flight to Saipan, the world's finest tropical island paradise. Please return to your seats and fasten yourselves in. Thank you for flying the friendly skies."

Layla rolled her eyes in the direction of the cockpit. "Such a ham."

For the second time on this short flight, realization dawned on Dylan. "Wait, is that the voice from the video?"

"Hector, yes," Layla answered, gesturing for Dylan to stand. "He's annoying, but hey, I've only got one big brother."

Taking Layla's cue, Dylan rose and followed her through the divider into the bank of seats. "But hey nothing," Dylan said. "He's super talented. Tour guide, drone pilot, airline pilot. You must be proud."

"Don't forget film producer and all-around show-off," Layla said, tucking Dylan into a plush seat, fastening her belt and pulling it tight. "But it's not so big a deal. Living on an island of forty thousand people, you kind of have to be a – what do people in the States call it – a jack of all trades?"

"So you're... Sorry. I just assumed you were..."

"A mainlander?" Layla said, fastening herself in. "It's okay. A lot of people make that assumption. No, Hector and I are from the island, and that's our primary residence." Her fingers brushed Dylan's arm, warm and comforting. The younger woman glanced up, her expression shy, as if unsure whether she should go on. But she did. "Your father, he was so handsome in his uniform. Remind me – was he in the Army Reserves?"

"Coast Guard, Rear Admiral," Dylan replied, feeling the clip, the bite in her tone.

"Where were you at the time?"

"Oh, here and there," Dylan said, trying her best to sound casual, nonchalant, to mask the old bitterness that threatened to surge up and out of its hiding places, to roar up and peck at the shell she had worked so hard, so carefully, to construct around herself. "I was just a little girl myself when my mother died. Dad was… traveling with work, stationed all over the world. I was your basic boarding-school brat."

"You got a good education," Layla replied.

"The best of everything."

Layla smiled and settled back into her seat, seeming to understand that nothing more was to be said on the subject of Dylan's upbringing. "When your dad whisked Auntie and Cici away to the States, how I cried. I thought I'd never see them again. But Auntie came back, many times."

"And she took you with her."

Layla gave off a small laugh, more of a giggle. "When I got old enough."

"And you still live on Saipan?"

She nodded. "I also keep a small apartment in Chicago. Auntie was very generous."

With my father's money, Dylan thought, but again, did not say.

"What about Hector? Is he also a dual resident?"

"Hector, he tends to stay close to wherever Cici is," Layla said with a sigh. "He loved Auntie. When she died, he transferred that love to Cici. But…"

Dylan tried to lean closer to Layla, but found herself stopped, confined by the straps that held her fast to the seat. She laid a hand over the younger woman's. "But what?"

At this, Dylan couldn't be sure, but she thought she saw Layla's smile fade, just a little. "But his love changed. When given over to Cici he became… fiercer. Protective. He made a promise to Auntie that he would always make sure Cici was treated fairly, and he's a man of his word." She straightened, wiping away all traces of melancholy. "In the end, Hector always goes home. He'll die on Saipan." Layla favored her with kind eyes, eyes so much like Virginia's. "Cici came sometimes, you know, back to Saipan with Auntie. But you never did, even though Auntie said you were always welcome. Why didn't you come?"

"I was never asked."

Dylan let this lie linger in the air between them, and they passed the rest of the flight in silence.

When Dylan heard the heavy thumps of luggage being loaded into the cargo hold followed by Cecelia's gravelly voice raised in laughter, she retreated into the bathroom. She needed a moment to collect herself. Standing over the sink, staring into the mirror at her unruly mop of dishwater-blonde hair, she clutched the letter in her fist, wondering if she could bring herself to unfold it again, read it again.

Her stepmother's final wishes.

As it turned out, a moment was all Dylan got. She heard the cabin door open and voices, Cecelia's and Hector's, burst in with them. "Dyl, you can't hide forever," Cecelia called out. "Come out, come out, wherever you are."

The blood rose in Dylan's face, and her fist closed around the letter. *I'm getting off this plane,* she screamed in her head. *I'm sorry, Virginia. I know this is what you wanted. But I can't take this trip, not with her. I'm getting off here and flying back to Pittsburgh, and that will be the end of it.*

At the door came a soft rap. "Miss Dylan," Hector said, concern lacing his words. "Are you all right in there?"

Dylan drew in a deep breath, and her momentary flare-up faded, then died. "Yes, thank you. Wait. I'll be out in just a moment."

"Waiting is what I do best."

For the third time on this trip, realization dawned. Dylan opened the door and stepped out into the cabin to meet the pilot, the maker of tourism videos, and the man who had answered the phone when she called.

But when she saw Cecelia, she stopped in her tracks, stunned.

Cecelia had grown into her beauty. Her dark, silky hair hung long and luxurious over her shoulders, cascading down her back. She wore no makeup and needed none. Like her mother, she was full-bodied. Her Levi's hugged close to her hips, and her plain white T-shirt – which would have looked ghostly on Dylan – accentuated her flawless brown skin.

Only her worried eyes, and the slight flush of red blooming from her cheeks, belied her mood.

She's as scared as I am.

They stood there, the three of them, for an interminable moment, before Hector broke the silence. "I almost forgot. I have something for us." Ducking into the galley, he emerged with three enormous garlands, handed one to each of them, and placed the last one on his head. "No trip to Saipan is complete without the *mwarmwar*."

Cecelia set her garland expertly atop her own head, then looked at Dylan with raised eyebrows. "You want some help?"

Dylan realized that yes, she did. She nodded, and Cecelia stepped close to her, plucked the *mwarmwar* out of her grasp, and arranged it over Dylan's tousled hair. After a few adjustments, Cecelia stood back and admired her handiwork while Hector mounted his smartphone on a clamp designed, it appeared, just for that purpose.

"Let's kick off this vacation with a selfie," he said, slinging an arm around each of them and positioning them in front of the camera.

"Wait," Dylan said.

"Waiting is what I do best," Hector replied with a beaming grin – a grin perhaps a bit too wide – that made Dylan wonder about this swashbuckler of a man. She gestured toward the cabin door.

"Shouldn't we wait for Layla? Get her in the picture, too?"

"Layla's staying back in Chicago," Hector said.

Cecelia stared wide-eyed into the empty cabin, lips drawn tight. Her eyes flicked to Dylan.

"But why?" Dylan asked, trying hard, but failing, to disguise her disappointment.

"Because Virginia wanted you to take this trip together, just the two of you," Hector said, a finality in his tone, as if there were nothing more to say on the topic.

At this, Cecelia relaxed, shaking off whatever seemed to be bothering her.

Hector's arm tightened around Dylan's shoulder, and she felt herself pulled into him. "Say cheese," he crooned. She stood, frozen in a smile, as the camera snapped an assortment of photos. Afterward, they selected the three best shots, and Hector forwarded the pictures to both their phones. He closed and secured the cabin door and stood at the opening of the cockpit. "You know where the food is. Help yourselves. Don't worry about cleaning up, and don't get too drunk. Now buckle up. We're cleared for takeoff in five minutes."

He closed the cockpit door behind him, leaving Dylan and Cecelia alone together. Cecelia turned to Dylan and clasped her hands together. "Looks like it's just us chickens."

"This chicken needs a rest," Dylan said, perhaps too quickly. Cecelia's face fell, and Dylan's heart fell a little with it. Yes, she admitted to herself now that she *had* presumed – taken for granted – that Layla would make the remainder of the flight with them. That Layla would be there, between them, to ease the tension.

Or to serve as a crutch, for you to avoid each other.

But Virginia had wanted this. For Virginia's sake, Dylan would try harder.

The eight empty seats were situated in pairs. Cecelia settled into the first row, removing her *mwarmwar*. Dylan sighed and pulled off her own *mwarmwar*, holding the crown of pink hibiscus leaves woven onto a coconut frond, fingering the soft petals. She strode to the last row, sat, and fastened herself in, placing the *mwarmwar* on the empty seat beside her.

Heeding Hector's request, Dylan got only marginally drunk.

After they reached cruising altitude, she unfastened her belt and meandered back to the lounge. The sideboard that held the television, as it turned out, also housed a cabinet filled with drinking glasses and a refrigerator stocked with juices and miniature bottles of assorted wines and liquor. She poured cranberry juice into a glass, emptied three minis of vodka into it, and retreated to the sofa, where she flipped on the TV. She could have watched anything, but instead she chose to remain on the channel where Hector's tourism videos played, one after another.

She awoke to a violent lurching in the aircraft and Hector's voice in the intercom. "We're encountering a bit of jet stream turbulence, folks. Best to take your seats and belt in."

Above Dylan, Cecelia stood with her hand extended. "Come on," she said. "I'll help you back to your seat."

As the plane bobbed and hitched, Cecelia held Dylan tight with one arm and steadied herself against the wall with her free hand. Dylan wrapped an arm around Cecelia's shoulder and together, they made their way to the back row. Dylan fell into a seat, and Cecelia strapped her in.

"Looks like you've done this a time or two before," Dylan slurred.

"A time or two," Cecelia replied with a nod. She pulled Dylan's belt tight. "You all set?"

Dylan nodded, and Cecelia nodded in return, then turned to head back to her seat in the front. To her own surprise, Dylan reached up and grasped her stepsister's arm. "Stay?"

"You sure?"

"I am."

"Okay." Carefully setting aside Dylan's *mwarmwar*, Cecelia settled into the adjoining seat and fastened herself in. Dylan reached over, and Cecelia clasped her hand. "It's just the jet stream," Cecelia assured her. "This isn't the worst I've seen. On one of the few trips your dad took with us, I had to get him off the couch and buckled in during a particularly violent storm."

Dylan choked back a sob as a memory, vague and dusty like an old trunk stored long in the attic, opened up and revealed its contents. "Virginia did invite me," she said finally. "It was after Dad died. She asked me to come to Saipan with the two of you, and I said yes. It was all planned, and at the last minute I backed out."

"Why? Why did you back out?" Dylan felt more than heard the stiffness in Cecelia's question, the unmistakable resentment. Still, Cecelia kept hold of her hand, her fingernails digging into Dylan's flesh.

"I don't remember," Dylan replied, and in yet another dawning realization, she understood that this was the most honest sliver of truth she had mustered in years. *Must be the damned vodka.* "I swear I didn't know she was sick. If I had known, I would have kept the plans."

But as much as Dylan wanted to believe her own words, she felt the lies returning, leeching back in through the cracks. Wounded, defensive, she turned on Cecelia. "Why didn't you tell me? Why did you close me out? When I finally learned Virginia was dying, I came to the house and I pounded and pounded on the door."

"I didn't open the door for anyone."

"But I was her daughter! She was my mother, and I—" Dylan wrenched her hand away. "I didn't get to say goodbye. You closed me out. Tell me, did she even know I tried to see her, or did you let her die believing I didn't come, that I didn't care?"

"You closed yourself out long before that."

"Oh, no you don't," Dylan spat, crossing her arms in front of herself. "You lost the moral high ground when you left me off her death notice."

"I'm sorry about that."

The aircraft jostled and heaved, but Dylan barely noticed. She turned to the window and stared into the night, seeing only her blind fury.

When the sun peeked over the horizon and the jet had flown into gentler air, Dylan felt Cecelia's touch on her arm. She tensed, but didn't pull away. Cecelia's hand slid down to Dylan's clenched fist and lightly pried it open.

"Is this your letter?"

"What?" Dylan looked down at her open hand, where the crumpled letter lay on her palm. She gaped at it as if she'd never seen it before.

Cecelia went on. "You haven't let go of it since you came out of the bathroom, before takeoff." She reached for it. "May I?"

Dylan shrugged. "Why not? What does it matter now?"

Cecelia lifted the paper, smoothed it out, and read it. Her breath hitched in her throat.

Dylan glanced down at the letter. "Did you get one, too?"

Cecelia nodded. "Dated three days before her death, just like this one. I remember she met with the lawyer to discuss the details of her will, but I didn't know about the letters. Not until I got my own. I wasn't even sure until you called that you'd gotten one, too."

"What does yours say?"

Cecelia handed Dylan's letter back to her, leaned forward, and reached into the back pocket of her jeans. She produced a folded square of paper and opened it, carefully. "It's a little worse for the wear," she said, apologetically. "I've carried it everywhere, close to my body, since the day I received it, ten years ago." Cecelia placed her timeworn, creased letter next to Dylan's crumpled letter, and together, they stared at the identical words on each, written in Virginia's hand.

Dear Girls, it read. *I want you to travel to my homeland together, as sisters. Remember, in a home there are stairs, but no steps. This is my dying wish.*

At the bottom, Virginia had printed two phone numbers, one for each of them.

"If she were alive today, I'd really like to ask her one question," Cecelia said. "How was she so goddamned sure we'd keep the same numbers?"

For the first time since the ordeal began, Dylan felt a smile creep onto her lips. "Do you remember when we were teenagers and you used to tell people we were sisters? No explanation. Just, 'Hey, this is my sister.' What was that you used to call me? *Che'lu.*"

Cecelia chuckled in pure delight. "Yes, *cheh-loo,*" she said, sounding out the word. "For sibling. The looks we would get. I can't believe we waited ten years to honor my mother's request. Ten long years. I'm so glad you made that phone call. I don't know that I ever would have."

For some inexplicable reason, those last of Cecelia's words left Dylan with a tiny sting, a mere pinprick, a pain nearly imperceptible. Something minute, but with an edge sharp enough to pierce a shell and create the tiniest of cracks. *No, no. Shake it off.* She shrugged and forced a smile. "You own two restaurants in Chicago? How do you manage that?"

The clouds lifted from Cecelia's eyes. She nodded, eager. "Hector helps me run them. He does all my social media, too. My first store was downtown, and I opened a second shop in Lincolnwood, just outside the city."

"Let me guess: Cici's Sassy Sauces – Two?"

"Very close," Cecelia said with a wink. "Cici's Sassy Sauces – *Dos*."

"Naturally." Dylan winked back. "And you serve the Pacific Islander cuisine of the Mariana Archipelago, with an American twist. You became a chef, just like your mother."

Cecelia's mouth widened into a genuine smile, and their conversation settled into the kind of small talk that passes time companionably. Eventually, they fell asleep, Dylan's head on Cecelia's shoulder.

They awoke to the sun blazing through the windows. Dylan stretched and yawned. "What time is it?"

"On these long flights, it's hard to tell," Cecelia said, squinting into the light and rubbing her eyes.

As if on cue, the intercom sputtered, and Hector's voice filled the cabin. "Good morning, ladies. I hope you enjoyed quality time together. We have entered the airspace of the Commonwealth of the Northern Mariana Islands, one of the finest territories of the great United States of America, and will be touching down on Saipan in twenty minutes. It's a beautiful morning out there, so for your viewing pleasure I've turned on your seat cams. Simply touch the screens in front of you to wake them up, and you can watch me bring this craft home."

They did as instructed, and Dylan squealed with delight as the scene rolled out before them. A cluster of tropical islands rose up ahead, surrounded by a vast expanse of blue ocean. "Cecelia... Cici," Dylan said. "How did you ever leave here?"

"Simple," Cici said. "My mom married your dad, and we became a family."

"We did," Dylan replied. "We did."

But into that second utterance, that repetition of *we did*, something other than pure affirmation crept in. Something insidious. Something the opposite of *we did*. That old, dark seed sprouted in the cracks of things and began growing, growing, starting innocently enough, with questions, simple questions. *Had* they become a family? Had they really? When Dylan's father married Virginia, had they included her, Dylan, in the ceremony? No. They had explained that they were married on the island, with Cici standing as witness, and that it was unrealistic for Dylan to attend. Too far for her to travel. When Virginia and Cici moved with her father to the States, they abandoned the Squirrel Hill condo for a big house in Fox Chapel. Cici attended public school and got to come home every day, while Dylan remained tucked away at boarding school. When Dylan's father bought Virginia the Gulfstream so she could travel to her birthplace any time she wanted to, Cici had gone often with her, and Dylan's dad, sometimes. But Dylan was never invited, not during her father's lifetime. The invitations came frequently enough in the years following her father's passing, but not before.

Again, always, the nagging question. *Whose decision was that?*

Then there was the elephant in the room. The thing too impolite to discuss. The money.

When her father died, half his wealth went to Virginia, half to Dylan. When Virginia died, Cecelia inherited her mother's share – everything except for the condo, which went to Dylan. *But the apartment would have gone to me, anyway,* she thought. *Dad had lived there with my mother, my own mother, my birth mother, his first wife.*

His first wife who lay in her own solitary grave, while her father was buried with Virginia, together for all eternity.

The seed sprouted in the crack, and the shell split apart.

From far away, a door opened and closed, and Hector's voice reached through the crack in her shell, drawing her back into the cabin. He stood at the open cockpit, holding a folded sheet of paper, his eyes serious, focused. Manic.

"You have your letters from Auntie Virginia, and I have mine," he said, holding up the paper. "To me, she wrote: *Don't land that plane until both girls have apologized to each other*. I've waited a long time to take this flight. I'm a patient man. Waiting is what I do best."

Next to Dylan, Cecelia stirred nervously. "We did apologize."

"You did," he said to Cecelia. "But she didn't."

Cecelia turned to Dylan, then back to Hector. "She did. I'm sure she did. Sister," she said, grasping Dylan's arm. "*Che'lu.* You said you were sorry."

Dylan's gaze fell to Cecelia's hand – her stepsister's hand – clutching her arm, then she looked up at Hector, who glared back at her, stone cold.

Auntie always said Hector was born without the gift of fear.

But his love changed. When given over to Cici he became… fierce. Protective.

Protective of what, Dylan thought. *Of Cici, or of his promise to Virginia*?

In that moment, as they stared one another down, Dylan understood something that Cecelia might have suspected, but that Virginia surely had not. Hector was utterly and completely mad.

The corners of his mouth turned up in a smile.

"What was that Cici said to you over the phone, back at the restaurant?" Hector asked. "*No need to kill yourself choking up an apology you don't mean*?"

"But she called first," Cecelia put in, desperation rising in her voice. "That means she's sorry." She turned to Dylan. "Doesn't it?"

Dylan thought of this plane. What was it called? The Seedy? So obvious now, but how had she missed it before? A mashup of their two names, Cici and Dylan. Ci-Dy. First once again. Cecelia always came first.

Always.

"Here's the thing," Hector said, eyes like daggers on Dylan. "I'm a man of my word. I made a promise to Ginny that Cici would always be treated fairly, and I intend to keep that promise. The flight from Chicago was 7,350 miles. We flew direct, with a fuel capacity of 7,750 miles. Just enough to get us from takeoff to landing, with a few gallons to spare. I have already circled the runway twice. We're flying on fumes."

Next to Dylan, Cecelia screamed at the seat cam. "Oh my god. That's Suicide Cliff. We're headed straight for it. Hector, you have to pull us up. Get back to the controls and pull us up!"

But Hector didn't respond. His eyes never left Dylan's.

In her mind, Dylan rewound to Hector's tourist video of Suicide Cliff, how he sent the camera into a dive and pulled up just before it crashed into the rocks below.

Could he pull up in time now?

As if reading her mind, Hector said, "We have just enough time, and just enough fuel, for me to pull this plane up and land it safely on the runway. But you have to apologize to Cici now, and mean it. So what's it going to be? Are you going to even the score? If not… I left Layla on the ground in Chicago. Just in case your answer is no."

All around Dylan, things roared. The jet engines. Cecelia's frantic screams. Hector's insane eyes. Cecelia, with the capital to open not one, but two restaurants. Dylan's head, howling with her stepsister's words: *I'm so glad you made that phone call. I don't know that I ever would have.*

Dylan peered into the seat cam, and as they bore down on the great bluff, she felt the crack in her soul, splitting apart in the greatest roar of all.

STORY INSPIRATION: "Step on a Crack" grew from a seed planted many years ago, when I mustered the courage to look up and call a woman who, when we were children, took a special interest in tormenting me. She was the class clown, and I was her mark. The moment in the story, during the phone call when Cici says "I'm sorry" and follows by asking Dylan to cross her off her list... that is as close to the true moment as I can reproduce in fiction. In fact it's a story we both still tell. As fate would have it, we became friends, and she once even asked me to travel to Saipan with her, to visit her late mother's homeland. She also happens to be a professional chef. Though we never made that trip together, from time to time I've wondered, *what if*. Unbeknownst to me, at the time I was writing this story she did travel to Saipan for the first time, with her wife. It was a journey as spiritual as it was physical, and a testament that things happen the way they're meant to, when they're meant to be. Unrelated to my old nemesis, the stepmother and sister relationships in this story derive from deeper truths, best left to the ages.

The Last Ride of Freddy Metzger

Diane Sismour

I believe in sales, in commissions, in the smudge of fresh ink on a signed contract.

Metzger Motors boasts a sleek, modern showroom with ruthless salesmen. I believe in the smell of fresh wax on a showroom floor, the gleam of chrome under halogen lights, and especially the thrill when a customer dangles the keys to their new ride in trembling fingers. I don't believe in curses.

For generations, my family has operated the largest car lot in Kona, Hawaii. The Big Island, where I can drive a car off the lot and experience all four seasons in one day, year-round. Today, I mixed business with pleasure, a long weekend on the windward side in Volcano Village, with warm breezes, cocktails on the beach, and the locals going nuts on Hulaween. For the business side of the trip, it's time to squash a thorn in my bottom line, Berlz Motors.

His restored classic cars, with soul, choke our bottom line. Soul doesn't sell anymore. The new islanders want sexy sport coupes and convertibles, or rugged SUVs and family-friendly Grand Waggoneers.

Tonight, on Hulaween, I'm celebrating a conquest. Berlz Motors is dead. Victor Berlz, the last of the rival bloodline, to be exact.

He perished in an inferno that devoured his tiki-themed lot surrounded by Polynesian carved poles. The locals say the Tiki embodies deified ancestors, guardians of thresholds, the divine spiritual essence. They marked sacred boundaries and demanded respect. But no more. They're charred as black as Victor's prized possession.

Vintage won't pay the bills, and his near-beachfront lot will be more valuable if bulldozed. From the ashes will rise a short-term rental with an ocean view.

When the paramedics arrived at his lot, they found Victor's body twisted, with eyes open in terror as though he'd glimpsed something before death took him, something not meant for mortal sight. I don't feel a shred of guilt; business is business.

He was a relic. Just more legend mumbojumbo.

The flames that consumed Berlz Motors were still fresh in my mind, flickering behind my eyelids with every blink. As I watched the revelers, I wondered if any of them really understood the cost of victory in this business. Beneath the bravado and celebration, a chill crept through me, a reminder that every conquest leaves its own mark, no matter the win.

The island's October ritual continues despite his death, a blend of Halloween and tropical heat. Wearing my customary Hawaiian shirt and a gold chain, I lean on the bar with a mai tai in hand, extra heavy on the rum, about to tinge my lips. A hidden speaker buried beneath the tiki thatched roof drones Billy Idol's "White Wedding" as the speakers warble from decades of play.

Flaming pineapple jack-o'-lanterns litter the boardwalk and beach bar, their flesh glistening, sticky-sweet, incandescent in the night. Partygoers drift in piratical skeleton masks, zombie surfers, and skeletal hula girls. The crowd ebbs and surges like the tide a mere fifty feet away. Laughter rises and falls like windblown fronds, and overripe fruit mutinies with the sea breeze misting off the beach.

The last of my drink slugs back, and the bartender sets a fresh mai tai on the bar, this one stronger than the last by the almost clear color. His grin flashes. "A Freddy Metzger special."

Holding the drink in an appreciative salute, I give him a nod. "Thanks, Mano."

He inserts a new thumb drive into the player and cranks the music.

My heart clenches as "Let's Groove" by Earth, Wind & Fire fills the air. The song tugs at me. The nostalgia, thick and vibrant, belongs to another era, Victor's. An age of velvet nights and popping tunes, reminding me of what I've done to win, no matter the cost.

My head swells with rum and victory. I know exactly what happened, and that prime beachfront property is now mine. The signed deed to the Berlz Motors makes my wallet appear fat with cash when I toss three twenties on the bar to cover the tab.

The Talking Heads' "Burning Down the House" plays through the humming speaker. The aroma of roasting pig wafts from the grove. The sickly stench of burning fruit and flesh engulfs me. I won't forget the acidic stench of burning hair, sharp against the gasoline fumes. The flames licking the flesh smelled much like pork, savory, fatty. His skin shriveled like an over-cooked roast on a grill, twisted and black.

Trying to shake off the lingering ghost of fire and fortune, I lift my glass and let the music wash over me. Beats thump in time with my pulse. Laughter and island rhythms blend with the distant crash of waves.

Mano pours another drink. The party swirls. The night tilts, unsteady. Even surrounded by costumed strangers, I catch myself searching the shadows for something I can't name, unsettled by the sense that the island itself is watching, waiting to see what price I'd pay for having won it all. As the last chords fade, the party's pulse swells, and I drift away from the smoldering remnants of memory.

The music shifts, and somewhere beyond the tiki lights, laughter peels above the din. Pineapple lanterns flicker, their ghostly glow reflecting off sand and spilled rum, while costumed revelers surge and recede like breakers in the night. The scent of char and sugar clings to my clothes, mingling with the salt air. I raise my glass again. The rum bites.

Forcing myself to join the celebration, even as the shadows press closer and the island's rituals persist, undisturbed by the smoke curling in my recollection.

I duck past a circle of fire dancers and let the murmurs wash over me. Weaving among the vendors, rumors drift of Victor's demise float in fragments of conversation. Speculation and half-truths, the island's gossip swirls as relentless as the increasing breeze. An accident or arson? The air changes, heavy with possibility and dread.

The music takes on a sharper edge. The beat echoes my heart's uneasy pace. Michael Jackson's "Thriller" draws people off the beach to dance. I let myself be carried along by the crowd toward the bar, drawn onward by the promise of another drink or answers hidden in the flicker of tiki torches or the glint of wary eyes. The music blares through the speaker. A line of zombies, stiff moves, and snarling faces mimic the iconic moves.

All around, the celebration barrels on, indifferent to the growing shadows. The heat swells as the rum swims in my head. That's when I notice her parked behind the bar. A 1957 Plymouth Fury repainted to a black darker than a starless sky, the chrome polished to a mirror shine, and tailfins sharper than daggers. Under the hood: a V8 engine packing 290 horsepower, fed by dual four-barrel carburetors. The exterior gleams immaculate; the new paint radiates like it holds embers from the torchlight.

Shock pins me. My vision doubles. The Fury stays in my sightline. My inebriated buzz dissolves. That car, Victor's pride, should have melted.

I edge away from the crowd, set my drink on a table, and rum sloshes across my hand. The wind gusts, rattling the torches and making their flames dance in unpredictable currents, as if the night itself senses my unease.

I'm drawn toward the muscle car. The distant laughter and glow of lanterns promise comfort, but I'm transfixed, standing before the Fury, its presence impossible and undeniable.

I touch the hood.

Cold as bone.

Despite the humidity, a shiver races down my spine.

A few hours ago, this demonic car was in Victor's showroom.

Through the open window, a faint hula melody trickles out, soothing yet haunting. I swallow; my hand lingers on the frigid hood.

My spine crawls.

For a moment, the world narrows to the space between me and the car, as the party's pulse fades to a dull echo behind me and shadowy memories stir. The driver's door yawns open, slow and deliberate, inviting me into a mystery I'm not sure I want to solve.

I step closer, compelled.

Lightning flashes. The wind gusts without warning. Thunder crackles. The torches hiss and flicker. Volcanic steam spouts from Kīlauea.

The party still pulses behind me in blissful ignorance. Laughter grows louder, and the glowing lanterns brighten as the sky darkens. The pineapple's flesh burns to a sickly sweet.

I glance inside. The radio knob is off.

A whisper comes over the speakers; one I feel more than hear. "Freddy."

My skin tingles.

Whipping my head around to whoever called out, nobody waits for an answer. It was just the wind and too much rum.

Arrogance, stupidity, or curiosity clutches me. The car seems alive, waiting. I slide in. Leather seats, unburned, smelling faintly of gasoline. A hula tune warps like dripping honey over vinyl. Sad, distorted.

The door shuts.

The keys are in the ignition.

The engine growls alive.

I hadn't turned the key.

The horn's V emblem glows molten red.

With my feet flat on the floorboard, the engine revs. I clutch my shirt as the D on the push-button transmission depresses. The tires squeal.

I grab the steering wheel.

The wheel sears my palms.

I can't let go.

I slam the brake.

Nothing.

Outside, the world fractures. Tiki torches smear into comet trails. Revelers ripple into red and orange blurs. Roads shift under us. Palms stretch into alleyways I don't know.

Polynesian Tiki statues, deified ancestors, the carriers of mana with carved faces, teeth carved in grins, eyes bulbous with warning, line the way.

I've never seen them before.

The radio snaps through static. A voice: "You didn't win, Freddy."

The Plymouth barrels toward Berlz's ruined dealership, black and smoking. Embers flicker ghost bright.

Thunder rolls like tribal drums. The festival pulses still beyond, but I'm tethered to a darker heartbeat.

Speed climbs, and the tach blinks like a beating heart in red. I choke in the ichor of the car: burnt rubber, sea salt, roasting pineapple, scorched flesh. Each breath tastes of ruin.

In the rearview mirror, I see him. Victor Berlz.

Face melting, skeletal grin stretched wide. Lips blackened, eyes glowing embers. Heat radiates. He whispers ancient Polynesian syllables, curses older than the island.

I scream.

I yank the wheel.

It's no use. The car has a will, a purpose.

Victor's laughter flickers over the engine's roar as the horizon warps, a spectral sound, hollow and consuming, echoing the fury of the storm outside. My hands tremble on the wheel as the Fury careens forward, unheeding of my white-knuckle grip.

The world convulses in crimson and shadow. The tiki statues blur, their faces twisted into silent scorn. Stern faces with watchful eyes and frozen, toothy smiles leer through the windshield, hailing the car's possessed flight.

The blackened dealership looms, flames reflected in the gleam of Victor's hollow gaze. The line between nightmare and reality blurs. The ancient words linger in the air like smoke, promising that this unholy ride will not end with steel and ash, but something deeper and far less merciful.

The Fury roars into the skeleton of Berlz Motors.

Flames rip upward.

A final glance at Victor's ember-grin.

In that frozen second, time snaps. Dawn bleeds in coral and gold. The festival stirs again, the pineapple lanterns still burn, the party rises from its narcotic haze.

But I'm not there.

There is no wrecked Fury.

No charred steel, no engine smoke.

Instead, a new wooden tiki statue stands, locked in a silent scream, eyes wide, mouth gaping. Around its carved neck is my gold chain, melted into the grain of its torso.

The island breathes oblivion: the partygoers mill past, costumes shedding horror into routine. Life goes on.

Some say I fled, a terror-made sailor disappearing at dawn. Others whisper of a curse, a car consumed of soul, not steel.

Yet as the revelers drift away and sunlight stretches across ash-stained sands, some still sense the chill, a memory that lingers, unseen yet waiting, as the world resumes its careless dance.

But deep in a jungle's hush, beneath tangled banyans, a black car waits. Chrome glints like sharpened teeth, engine silent.

Waiting.

STORY INSPIRATION: When asking for ideas about a story with a tiki travel twist, Moaner Lawrence suggested a play on Poe's "Metzengerstein" a tale of two monarchs in an age-old feud. The Hulaween spin includes the tropics, pineapple carving, eighties tunes, and Halloween traditions that made "The Last Ride of Freddy Metzger" a fun write.

A Kiss Is Not A Kiss

Catherine Jordan

I had yet to be tamed. Not that I was a wild animal in need of a handler, but I had an edge. Rules were not for me. I was a contrarian at heart, meaning if anyone told me I can't, then by God I would. "No," means yes when presented with a palatable argument.

I liked to have fun. My husband, Chuck, was more of a homebody. We were opposites in many ways – him the introvert and me the extrovert. People had warned me of our differences before we got married. As if I didn't know. Some asked how we even wound up together. He's handsome, handy, funny. Call me practical.

Chuck and I had been at each other's throats the past year. He constantly eyeballed me when I said I was going out. He wanted me to stay home more; I wanted him to go out more. Okay so his idea of going out was him and a few beers at the local bar while watching the game. Yawn. Mine was a big concert and a tailgate with friends.

The Mediterranean cruise had been exactly what he and I needed – time apart. And now the ten-day vacation with my friends was almost over. I figured we'd make our last night worth remembering. Croatia was our last port before heading back home to New Jersey. Spending the final night drinking with the locals was my idea.

We were happy to hear that a local bar was within easy walking distance of the ship.

The beach bar in Dubrovnik sat on a precipice of the city walls, facing the sea. Though it was dusk, outdoor lights glimmered from roofs, hung from trees, and trimmed windows. The full moon was out. White lilies glowed in its bluish light. The salty sea and sweet over-ripened plums mixed perfectly in the air. I inhaled deep. Ahh – I wanted to bottle that smell.

The hotty at the bar made my crotch throb the second I laid eyes on him. He sat alone, occasionally glancing up into the bar mirror at the small crowd behind him.

Of course, I steered my friends right to three open seats at the bar. We spotted our ship from afar, the silhouette of a giant floating tube all lit up in flickering yellow. Thin vases lining the polished wooden bar held a lone lily and a menu advertising tapas and beer – my kind of place. Sweaty and thirsty, I ordered us a round of Zmajsko Pale Ale. The cold bottle felt good in my hands, better against my wrists. I'm a *pivo* drinker – I love an ice-cold beer, especially on a hot night. After making a big deal of admiring its "thick white head", I chugged, then loudly declared it "lip-smacking good."

I sat two seats away, watching him, hoping he'd think I was cool and strike up a conversation. But once the familiar rumble moved from my stomach to my throat, I lowered my head and stifled what could have been an applause-worthy belch. Still thirsty with sunburned skin throbbing under my flimsy dress, I wasted no time on the next selection, an Osječko, allegedly the oldest Croatian beer in the country. After that, the pretty bartender suggested a dark, malty Tomislav. "7.3 percent alcohol," she warned with a greedy smile. She plunked the bottle in front of me and I took it as a challenge, and chugged.

My hot neighbor took a swig of his beer, long fingers choking the bottle's neck. He looked thoughtful, serious, yet I bet he had a wicked sense of humor.

I tuned out everything, couldn't even hear my friends who were hunkered in, stern mouthed, glassy eyed, and mascara smeared. That's what alcohol does to those women. They were discussing their boring lives, the ones we were headed back to. Three drinks in and they hadn't changed the subject. And though these Eastern Europeans sure as hell knew how to drink, we just couldn't keep up.

I caught a glimpse of my half-cocked smile and my lowered eyelids in the bar-mirror. My chin rested seductively in my palm. I was wearing my sex face. The bartender flicked her eyes at me and my hot neighbor, then winked at me.

Hotty looked my way nonchalantly, then did a double take. He raised a brow, smiled, turned away and took another swig. I got up and strolled to the bathroom. When I returned, I plopped on the empty stool beside him. Pretty smooth, huh? I thought so, too.

"Bok," he said with a nod.

For a second, I thought I'd heard him wrong. Then I realized he was just saying hi.

"Bok," I replied, flipping my long hair over my shoulder, trying to flirt, but I wound up dizzy from the sudden move.

"What country you from?" he asked, smiling. "United States?" His lips were slightly chapped. It gave him a seductive edge.

I nodded. "What gave it away?"

"How long you here?" he asked.

"We've been here two days. This is our last night."

"Da? Where you stay?"

"On the boat." I turned and pointed into the open air across the sea at our docked ship.

"Very nice. I never been on cruise. You like?"

I twirled a few hair tendrils. "Da. What's your name?"

"Josip."

Fast forward about an hour, a couple lagers later, and a shot of plum rakija. Rakija is a lot like brandy in the states. It's made from fermented fruit and it'll kick your ass. This stuff is potent hard liquor, and we had already learned that you're not to wolf it like a shot even though it's served in a tiny glass. It's supposed to be experienced.

Over the course of our trip we'd "experienced" honey rakija, cherry, grape, pear, apple, apricot, quince, raspberry, peach, and juniper. The juniper tasted like pine needles. Smelled like it, too.

I was leaning into him. He slurred foreign sweet nothings in my ear. He kissed my neck, and nibbled, giving me a little prick on the neck, a love bite. Chills ran down my shoulders, my chest, and my thighs. *I want some more, please.* I curled into him, thinking about grasping his dark hair and pushing his wet *pivo* lips on mine.

My friends kicked the back of my stool. Sigh. I had practically forgotten about them.

"Hey, Meghan. Time to go."

"What time is it?" I asked, turning to face them. They had clearly sobered.

"It's ten o'clock," my one friend said, showing me her cell's display. My other friend nodded in agreement. "We have to be on board by ten-thirty."

Anyone who's ever cruised knows that if you're not on time, they *will* leave without you.

"Ship sails at eleven," one of them said, both friends nodding like bobble heads.

"Come home with me." Josip's warm, yeasty breath tickled my ear and his flaky lip brushed my neck.

I thought about Chevy Chase clapping his hands together right before he dove in the pool with a naked Christie Brinkley while chanting, "This is crazy, this is crazy..."

As Josip kissed my neck ever so softly, I started to think, *This idea isn't so crazy. I can catch a plane back.* I'd miss out on girl-fun; big deal. They'd get my suitcases and crap back home. I could tell my husband, *"Hey, I missed the boat."* I've missed planes before. I've missed buses. Why not a cruise ship? And who would know? No one. Besties don't tattle.

But both of my friend's faces said, *Oh, hell no.*

"Molim," Josip whispered, Croatian for, "please". Please can mean many things. His passion-filled hand trembled as he pressed on my lower back. Another kiss followed by a light, trailing tongue. "I have good plum rakija." Croatians making their own rakija is like Americans making their own beer or wine. It's a pretty common thing to do. So I'd been told.

But I wasn't so sure. I really, really wanted to. I even went so far as to rehearse my excuse to my husband: *I had too much to drink and went to use the bathroom and the girls had left thinking I'd gone on ahead…*

Then rationality hit. Nope. No way. Huh uh. Can't do it. I'd never let one of my friends go home with a stranger in a foreign country. And my husband would never forgive me.

Josip grabbed my hand – his were cool to the touch – and squeezed it. He ran a quivering finger lightly along my jawline, up towards my ear. He tucked a lock of my hair behind my ear. "You are beautiful," he said. His breath – it wasn't yeasty so much as it was foul.

I still felt dizzy. I got that mouth-watery-salty taste you get in your mouth right before you throw up. "I have to go," I suddenly said.

He released my hand and reached for my napkin. He mimicked writing on it. "Pen?"

"Ah… yeah, got one." I pulled an engraved pen *(Adventure Awaits*) from my purse. I handed it to him.

After a quick scribble, he handed me the napkin. "This my hotel. You tell your friends goodbye and come to my room."

"You're not from here?"

"Ne. I'm Croatian on vacation." He smiled wide and kissed the back of my hand.

My friends rolled their eyes.

Regardless, a hookup wasn't gonna happen. I tucked the napkin in my purse along with my pen. "Goodnight," I said, sliding off my stool.

He pulled me close and nuzzled my neck again. A small jolt of electricity burned through me. I sighed, then turned and walked out of the bar with my friends.

The Josip fantasy stayed in the forefront of my mind. Every piece of delicate fruit had a sexual connotation. Every drop of water and drip of condensation brought me back to the bar and his tongue. I didn't want to rehash last night with the girls; I wanted to close my eyes and fantasize.

Benadryl, aloe, scopolamine, and residual booze left me doped and tired by the time I landed in LaGuardia.

Chuck picked me up on that blistery Saturday morning. He commented on my burn, kissed me gently on the cheek, and then loaded my bags in the Jeep. I promptly fell asleep on the ride home.

I slept straight through the next day.

At work on Monday, I scratched and squirmed at my desk.

I do data entry for a medical team, a little HR, too. Nurses and doctors pop in my office on a regular basis to say hello and drop off papers.

"Your burn looks bad." Janie, a gastroenterology nurse, plopped a file on my desk.

Eyeing her smock, I read it out loud. "*Coffee, scrubs, and rubber gloves*. How the hell do you get away with wearing those? Pediatrics wear cartoon scrubs, the derms wear black with hot pink details and rhinestones. But you gastros? I remember you wearing, *You can't take this shit seriously* the day before I left for my trip."

Janie smirked, then walked around my desk and pulled at my collar. "Our doctors have a great sense of humor." Her smile had faded. "Have you been scratching?"

"Yeah, of course. It itches."

"Hmm. I wonder if you got sun poisoning. Stop by upstairs before you leave. Doctor Blankenship is here today." The head of dermatology.

I figured he'd take a gander, then give me ointment samples and a hefty oral steroid with an antibiotic. Instead, he had me hop up on the table. He removed his glasses, took a deep breath, and drilled me with questions: Where? When? and What?

"You all know I've been out of the country on vacation," I said.

He pulled a marker from his breast pocket and drew on my neck. The ink smelled sharp. Must've been a new marker. "Not consistent with sun poisoning," he said. The doctor motioned for me to turn my head, then examined the other side of my neck. "Has it been getting better or worse?"

"Worse. That's normal, right? It's only been a couple days since I got back. I'm not even peeling yet."

He threw the marker in the *biohazard* can. "Is this red patch anywhere else?"

I squirmed, the table's tissue paper crinkling underneath my legs. "Uh, no."

"I want to open one of those blisters, take a blood sample, and a biopsy."

"Blisters?"

"You're blistering."

"Since when?"

"Your skin is warm and moist. That scab is yellow." He leaned in and sniffed me. "It's got a foul smell."

I put a hand to my neck.

"Stop touching it," he said. "And wash your hands here at the sink. I'll be right back."

I gasped. "Wait, a skin biopsy? Will it leave a scar?"

He disappeared down the hall.

I hopped off the table, wanting to look at myself in the mirror over the sink. My neck was all I saw while washing my hands. Dark purple ink circled two inflamed, scabbed sores. My heart pounded in my throat.

Blankenship returned with an instrument-filled tray and a resident.

He poked and prodded with the resident looking on, hands gloved. "Can you wait here?" Blankenship asked me. "I'm going to send these to the lab next door. I'll have the results within the hour."

"Um, my husband and I have dinner plans tonight. We…"

Blankenship flared his nostrils and straightened his shoulders. He wasn't *asking* me to stay. He was telling me.

I mashed my lips together. "All right. I'll wait. Should I call someone? You're scaring me, Doc."

He smiled sympathetically and patted my hand. "Sorry. We'll know more soon, Meghan. Call your husband and tell him you'll be late."

Of course, my thoughts went to Josip and his mouth on my neck. Yet I hoped this was a reaction to the new body cream I bought overseas, or the turtleneck I wore yesterday, or something I unwittingly picked up on my hand and transferred to my neck while scratching.

I didn't want to have to tell Blankenship about Josip. He knew my husband, though not well. We weren't friends and we didn't hang out, but he'd met Chuck several times.

My face burned as I devised an explanation for my husband. Truthfully, I didn't have anything concrete to tell Chuck and didn't want him to know I was worried. I dialed his number from my cell. No answer. Phew. I left a message saying my sunburn had worsened and I was waiting for the doctor. Then turned my phone to silent.

I closed my eyes, but couldn't relax, my thoughts on my neck. Bedbugs? We'd had them before – a hazard of traveling. The little bastards had preyed on my face, neck, and arms. I was super careful ever since that incident. My suitcase from the cruise still sat in the garage, my clothing waiting for me to launder.

This certainly wasn't eczema or psoriasis. Chuck had eczema; I knew what it looked like. And Blankenship wouldn't subject me to madness over some condition he could treat with a prescription. What about cancer – melanoma? God knows I spent enough time in the sun.

"Okay." Blankenship stood in the doorway, hands on his hips. "Do you remember cutting yourself? From a necklace, or a scarf tag, or…?"

Josip had nuzzled on my neck. His lips had been rough, but I liked it. I'd been drunk, numb and content. I replayed the night over and over. He *might* have broken the skin.

Blankenship cocked his head. "You look guilty. Talk to me."

"Patient-doctor confidentiality?"

He nodded.

I took a breath. "I, um, guess I should tell you…" My shoulders crumbled. He kept glancing at my neck as I confessed everything. When I finished, he made no judgement comments. Just whipped out a pair of goggles – microscope glasses.

"Well. This blister…" He poked at it with a long Q-tip. "It's deep." His voice dropped. "Deeper than I thought. We found infectious proteins in the biopsy. Prions." He removed his goggles. "Ever hear of a prion?"

I shook my head and held my breath.

"It's a type of protein spread by infected meat products. It can affect humans and animals. You've heard of Mad Cow Disease?"

I became lightheaded. "You kidding me?"

Blankenship raised a brow. "Mad Cow Disease is a neurodegenerative disease in cattle. Cattle contract it by eating infected processed animal brains. Humans can get Mad Cow when infected cow brains are mixed into the meat supply. But Kuru is a twisted protein that develops on its own after—"

"Kuru?"

"Kuru. It's rare. A disorder caused by infectious twisted proteins called prions. It causes tremors, lack of coordination. It's degenerative, incurable."

I held up my hand for him to stop. "Wait. You're talking too fast. I don't understand. What the hell are you saying? I have Mad Cow Disease?"

He shook his head. "You don't have Mad Cow Disease."

I released a nervous laugh. "What do I have?"

He gave me a stern glare. Apparently, he didn't think this was a laughing matter, nervous or not. His face said I wasn't going to like what came next. My husband often gave me a similar look now and then. But I quieted my thoughts and listened to him explain.

"We found an infectious prion in your blood sample, *and* you have Necrotizing fasciitis. A flesh-eating bacterium." He crossed his arms and leaned back. "It's a fast-moving soft tissue infection. You can contract it from even the tiniest opening, like the one on your neck, though it's not so tiny anymore. Platelet aggregation blocks blood vessels, depriving your vital organs of oxygen. Good thing we caught it early. That's why I was concerned – early detection is key. We called in an infectious disease expert."

"Shit. An expert? Can this spread?"

"Oh yes. It can infect your muscles. Like I said, we caught it early. We'll treat it with a strong antibiotic. Unfortunately, we're going to have to perform a graft, which means we'll remove the infected skin and replace it with skin from your thigh, or your stomach."

I cleared my throat. Josip – Croatian on vacation, was sick and didn't know it. Or did he? Thank you God I did not go home with him and those crusty lips that I thought were sexy, shit shit shit. "So," I cleared my throat again. "Josip – he ate a bad burger? And now I've caught a bacterial infection?"

"Meghan, this Josip – you mentioned his chapped lips. You said his hands were cold, and they shook. I'm telling you he was sick, that he had tremors. This isn't the first case of Kuru coming out of Croatia. And no I am not jumping to conclusions here. You were infected by someone who has consumed a massive quantity of human brains."

That Indian Jones movie came to mind, where they sat around a table while presented with chilled monkey brains for dessert, a spoonful of bright red slurped into the mouth. "Do people in Croatia eat brains?" I asked. I don't remember learning that little factoid on my trip.

"Excuse me… I'm confused. My head hurts."

"I'm sure it does." He neared me and cocked his head, eyeing me suspiciously. "The point of origin on your neck – it's a bite mark. It was loaded with prions. Tell me dear, are you… hungry?"

Food was the last thing on my mind. I was repulsed and irritated and physically drained. "Not in the least," I said with a croak.

He nodded in an agreeable manner. "You'll let me know if you are? Hungry, that is?"

A shot of alarm followed by understanding. "Okay, doctor. Are we talking about what I think we're talking about?"

"Necro sapiens."

"The fuck?"

"He invited you to his place?" Blankenship took a deep breath and leaned in. "You're lucky to be alive."

Another visual hit of me with my head carved open and Josip digging into it with a spoon, like a soft-boiled egg, him going all Hannibal Lector on me. I imagined my brain would taste like liver, because I hate liver.

Blankenship caught me before I fell off the table. "Whoa, whoa. You're okay." He propped me up. "Hey, look at me." He gently pushed against my shoulders, so I'd lie down.

"I'm gonna throw up, doctor. I need the garbage."

I didn't make it to the trash in time and vomited all over the floor. Not much, since I'd only had coffee and a bag of chips from the vending machine. But enough.

"We'll get you a gown to change into," Blankenship said.

"No, I wanna go home."

"Did you call your husband? You can't go home. I'm sorry, but we have to quarantine you."

"I have the napkin he gave me. His address."

Blankenship squeezed my shoulder. "Good. I consulted not only with infectious disease, but Interpol. Like I said, you're not the first case."

I don't know how long I hovered in a state of panic.

I only know that I woke up confused and achy to the sound of a zipper rip. I was lying in a hospital bed, in an enclosed plastic room.

Alcohol, ammonia, bleach – neither was strong enough to mask the distinct sickly odor in the room. White curtains provided privacy and buffered the distant beeps next door. There were no windows in the bright florescent-lit room. A bulky figure stood at the foot of my bed reading the ticker printing from a computer. He was fully gloved, capped, and masked in his bio-suit. He raised his head. "You're awake." The mask did not hide his eyes. You could learn a lot from a person's eyes. His were bright blue with bags and pronounced crow's feet. They moved up and down the length of my prone body. "How are you this morning, Meghan?" His voice was muffled, but clear, precise, and stoic.

"Where am I?" My voice scratched like it was roughed with hard-grade sandpaper. Numb lips, throat sore and dry. My back hurt.

"New York Presbyterian Hospital." He stepped closer, eyes on my midsection, hands clasped behind his back. "I'm Doctor Udre."

I felt drugged, sluggish. "Where's my husband?"

"I regret having to tell you this: your husband has also been quarantined."

Quarantined. A cold shiver moved down my spine. Trying to digest that idea was like trying to digest a stomach-full of cement. Udre's head stayed focused on my torso. He would not make eye contact.

"You both contracted a rare strain of Necrotizing Fasciitis."

"So I was told." I lay motionless as I mouthed, "Necrosis." Meaning rot. And fascia was skin tissue. I reflected back on what Blankenship had told me however long ago it was when I saw him in his office – *Necro Sapiens.* Cannibalistic undead. But those creatures aren't real. They can't be. All that stupid talk of prions, kuru, brains. My stomach growled. Shit. Had Udre heard?

He leaned away. Yep, he heard.

"We have you under observation," he said, which sounded like a warning to me. "You've been in a medical coma for about two weeks. We kept cutting away skin, but the bacteria spread too fast."

The ammonia smell. Not a cleaning agent; the smell of bacteria. "My disease spread?" Incoherence had me questioning everything.

He nodded somberly.

My chest felt like it had been squeezed. I was breathing fast. The room seemed to fill with haze. The beeping machine beside me got louder and louder. Another machine hissed. Too many noises. I had to slow my breathing before I hyperventilated. I closed my eyes, counted backward from ten, and prayed harder than I ever had in my life that this was a bad dream.

Except it wasn't.

I blew out a breath, swallowed hard, and opened my eyes to a dystopian world. Can't be real. Stay calm, I told myself, trying not to imagine the worst, not knowing what could be worse.

I glanced at my blanket-covered arms, my covered legs. "Can I see it?" I wanted to know the depth of my infection. I thought he would tell me no, that it was best to keep me under wraps.

Dr. Udre frowned. "What part of your body would you like to see?"

Imagine trying to process that – *what part*. He had a hard demeanor, and the insinuation that I had more than one choice of tainted body parts struck me hard.

Dr. Udre pulled my blanket down to my stomach.

I tilted my throbbing head – it was difficult to move, like lifting a bowling ball at the neck. My upper torso was mummy-wrapped. Blood and yellow leakage had seeped through the gauze. It looked like red paint had been half-hazardly splattered across me.

Then he moved the blanket farther down my waist to my ankles.

My thigh was thick and black, like charcoaled meat on the grill, flayed open, the skin pulled and held open by a wicked contraption, exposing the bone. "Aggressive acute wound debridement. I removed necrotic tissue from your thigh."

Necrotic. Decayed, dying, dead. I cleared my throat and tried to swallow, but it was nearly impossible. "I want to see my other leg." I thought it was under the blanket.

"We did our best to stop the progression."

"Progression." I whispered the word and chewed on it. It tasted sharp and pungent, like my rotting limbs. Then it dawned on me – I couldn't wiggle my toes. "Where are my feet?"

He sighed, then dragged the blanket to the end of the bed.

Purple ankle thick as a seal. No skin on top of the foot, no flesh, every ghastly sinew on display. "I can't feel anything."

"Your nerve endings are dead." Still, no eye contact. "I had to amputate the other leg."

A great indigestible nugget of truth. I was tired and slightly nauseous. Realization and dread had exhausted me. My stomach sunk into the bed. Gazing at the ceiling, I saw images of ruin. Spoilage. Deterioration. A private hell reserved for me. Everything I had ever hoped for in life was gone. Over. "How am I supposed to live like this?"

Overcome with anguish, I slid further into desolation. How to react – what was expected of me? My reasoning tumbled into free fall. And then I realized I had yet to see my face. "My face! A mirror?"

The doctor shook his head. "Your nose is gone. So is your chin. You don't want to see that."

What kind of continued horror was this? Where would it end? Would it end? There was no one to ask. I felt so alone.

Yet I wasn't alone. Chuck – my husband. "Is it possible to see my husband, Doctor?"

"Certainly."

The doctor pivoted towards the plastic partition and pulled open the white curtain.

I stared at my husband through the plastic haze. Chuck was as broken as a failed promise. He lay in a hospital bed with his head turned away from me. His left arm was skinned and suspended high above his head, like a piece of displayed meat in a butcher shop. A gauze-wrapped stub took the place of his right arm. Waist and stomach appeared normal, not yet infected. Thankfully, neither did his legs or feet. Was this my fault? How far would the disease travel on him?

I broke into sobs. I'd never seen any man so pitiable. "Chuck?" I called his name over and over through gulps of air and snot. He didn't answer or turn to my voice. "Can he hear me?" I asked the doctor.

"He should be able to, yes."

He was asleep, or in a drug-induced slumber. Hopefully he wouldn't wake to a shock, like I had. "Please tell me you got him," I managed to choke out through the tears.

"Who?"

"The bastard who did this to me. Josip."

"I wish I could."

"Did anyone bother to look for him?" I asked, infuriated by his indifference.

"Yes. Of course. Dr. Blankenship called the police. But he was long gone. He left no trail, other than a few others like yourself, your husband, and…" He paused for a moment, then rolled his shoulders. "Poor Dr. Blankenship."

"Ohhh." Right. I was contagious. So not only Chuck, not just my doctor, but my friends, co-workers, anyone I had come in contact with those past few... days. Weeks. "How many people has this spread to?"

The doctor shrugged. "Enough. It's a pandemic. We're not exactly sure what we're dealing with, but the statistics are not in your favor."

"Nice bed side manner, Doc. Thank you for the sympathy."

He gave a slight, "humph".

I took his response exactly as he intended it. *My* conduct deserved revenge. I deserved my loathsome state. Chuck, the doctor – they did not. I had slithered up beside Josip like a snake. My whole body – what was left of it – shivered violently with self-disgust.

The weight of my entire life sat on my chest, deflating me. Childhood memories flooded my mind, playing to my favorite song, and I was an impartial observer. My parents, the holidays, school, vacations, boyfriends, besties. Maybe they were all sick. Maybe they were all going to rot and die.

Other than intellectually, I'd never considered death. Death was a fact, but I hadn't worried about it, until now. "Am I going to die?" I looked at Chuck, then the doctor. "Are we?"

I'd had no time to plan for death. I'd never made a will. Neither Chuck nor I had life insurance. Who would come to my funeral? Anyone? Should I make video journals? I guess I could, but why? Who'd watch it? Who'd tune into my vanity platform and listen to the last story I'd ever get to tell?

"I don't know," Doctor Udre said. "We're dealing with a lot of unknowns. I wish I had more to tell you." He unzipped the partition flap, about to leave. He turned to me, then fixed his wrinkled, scowling eyes on the printing ticker. "If it's any consolation, your *bastard* is probably dead."

Chuck – he sat up and stared straight at me. He grimaced with either pain or hatred, I wasn't sure which. Maybe both. He had no words for me. He couldn't hold my hand to console me. Those eyes of his – they were inflicting retribution. And I deserved it. Even if I could get better, I didn't want to.

"No," I said. "No consolation at all."

STORY INSIRATION: A longer version of this story came from a friend: "My hairdresser told me about this woman on vacation in another country and she made out with a local. He gave her a sore, a flesh-eating disease that you only get from corpses. The police got involved and turns out the local guy is wanted for murder and cannibalism." Ew, right? Can't be true, right? It's not. The rumor made it to Snopes.com and goes back to 2001. Anyway… it inspired this story.

AUTHOR BIOGRAPHIES

JONATHAN MABERRY is a NYTimes bestselling author, 5-time Bram Stoker Award-winner, 4-time Scribe Award winner, Inkpot Award winner, editor, writing teacher, poet, playwright, and comic book writer. He writes in multiple genres including thriller, horror, sci-fi, mystery, and fantasy. V-WARS (Netflix) was based on his books/comics; Alcon is developing his Rot & Ruin novels for film; and Chad Stahelski, director of JOHN WICK, is developing his Joe Ledger thrillers for TV. Marvel's BLACK PANTHER: WAKANDA FOREVER was partly based on his work. He's written more than 50 novels, 200 short stories, 30 graphic novels, 1200 feature articles, and two dozen nonfiction books. Jonathan has also edited 30 anthologies, including Aliens, The X-Files, the official tribute to Scary Stories to Tell in the Dark, and many others. He's the president of the International Association of Media Tie-in Writers, and the editor of Weird Tales Magazine. www.jonathanmaberry.com

STORY SYNOPSIS: Hannah Smoak wants to enjoy a vacation in Kaua'i. Her happiness is short-lived when disaster strikes: chaos erupts with fires, violence, and society's collapse. Facing terror and loss, Hannah ultimately seeks peace by recalling her best day.

LISA MORTON is a screenwriter, author, and editor whose work was described by the American Library Association's Readers' Advisory Guide to Horror as "consistently dark, unsettling, and frightening." She is a six-time winner of the Bram Stoker Award®, the author of four novels and over 200 short stories, and a world-class Halloween and paranormal expert who has appeared on CNN, NPR,

The History Channel, Discovery +, and dozens of other sites and shows. She also hosts the popular weekly "Ghost Report" podcast and a newsletter about the paranormal (The Whole Haunted World). Lisa lives in Los Angeles and online at www.lisamorton.com.

Photos: https://lisamorton.com/about-2/gallery/

Facebook: https://www.facebook.com/lisa.morton.165/

Instagram: https://www.instagram.com/lisamortoninla

BlueSky: https://bsky.app/profile/lisamorton.bsky.social

STORY SYNOPSIS: When Gabe tires to reconnect with his brother and distract himself from grief by attending ConTiki25, they visit a tiki pop-up where mysterious aquarium organisms seed their drinks with strange gelatinous spheres.

GWENDOLYN KISTE is the four-time Bram Stoker Award-winning author of *The Rust Maidens, Reluctant Immortals, Boneset & Feathers, Pretty Marys All in a Row,* and *The Haunting of Velkwood*. Her short fiction and nonfiction have appeared in outlets including Lit Hub, Nightmare, Best American Science Fiction and Fantasy, CrimeReads, Titan Books, The Lineup, and The Dark. She's a Lambda Literary Award winner, and her fiction has also received the This Is Horror Award for Novel of the Year as well as nominations for the Shirley Jackson, Premios Kelvin, Ignotus, and Dragon Awards. Originally from Ohio, she now resides on an abandoned horse farm outside of Pittsburgh with her husband, their excitable calico cat, and not nearly enough ghosts. Find her online at gwendolynkiste.com

STORY SYNOPSIS: A recently divorced woman arrives at a decaying seaside motel for a consolatory girls' trip, where she encounters unsettling theme-rooms and a town that entices the lost to stay. As Sarah's isolation deepens, she sinks into the motel's

strange mythology—and is absorbed into a new, strange sense of home.

CHRIS MCAULEY is a best-selling, award-winning, New York Times Best-selling writer who is most famous for creating the popular StokerVerse franchise with Dacre Stoker (Bram Stoker's great grand-nephew). This continuation of Bram's work has proliferated from graphic novels, books, audio dramas, table-top games into the world of television and film. He has also created a successful science fiction franchise with Hollywood actress Claudia Christian (star of Babylon 5) called Dark Legacies. Chris has recently been nominated for the highest award for writing in tabletop games – The Ennies for his Three Musketeers vs Chthulu RPG which has also become a comic book series. He is also known for his work on Doctor Who, Star Trek, Star Wars, Battlestar Galactica and Terminator franchises. Away from writing duties, he is also a multiple award-winning screenplay writer and executive film producer. He has formed a new production company Trinity Studios, a film and television production company focused on developing and producing Hollywood-level projects with A-list talent along with Owen Cotter and Brooke Woods-Bechtol.

STORY SYNOPSIS: A couple visits a lake to mend their relationship, but a supernatural force disrupts their evening, leading to violence and a disappearance that renews the cycle for future guests.

Meteorologist turned novelist, **MARIA V. SNYDER** has been writing since she was bored at work and needed something creative to do. Over twenty-four published novels and two short story collections

later, Maria's learned a thing or three about writing. She's been on the *New York Times* bestseller list, won a dozen awards, and has earned her MA degree in Writing Popular Fiction from Seton Hill University where she's been happily sharing her knowledge with the current crop of MFA students. When she's not writing, she's either playing pickleball, traveling, taking pictures, or zonked out on the couch due to all of the above. Maria welcomes readers to learn more about her and her books at https://www.MariaVSnyder.com
Instagram: https://www.instagram.com/mariavsnyderwrites/
Facebook: https://www.facebook.com/mvsfans/

STORY SYNOPSIS: A leisure cruise turns dangerous after a passenger dies and a rescued crew brings a Polynesian spirit (an Aitu) into contact with the ship; a group of retired women led by the first-person narrator and aided by crew must outwit the supernatural threat before the talismans protecting the vessel fail and the ship is lost.

JO KAPLAN is a Shirley Jackson Award nominated author whose work has been described as "immersive, chilling, and compelling" by Library Journal and "delightfully creepy" by Booklist. She is the author of *It Will Just Be Us, When the Night Bells Ring,* and *The Midnight Muse,* as well as short stories which have appeared in publications such as Fireside Quarterly, Black Static, Nightmare Magazine, and award-winning anthologies. In addition to writing, she teaches English and creative writing at Glendale Community College and is the co-chair of the Horror Writers Association's Los Angeles chapter. She also plays cello in both the Symphony of the Verdugos and the indie Spanish rock band Guerra/paz.

STORY SYNOPSIS: On a jungle zipline trip, a vacationer is stranded by an unexpected blockage and finds signs of danger in the

canopy, forcing her into a desperate escape from a monstrous creature.

AARON ROSENBERG has been accused of cloning himself, of being a robot, and of signing a pact with dark powers. How else could he have written over fifty novels and a hundred short stories in just over twenty years? (There's also the dozen or so children's books, the equal number of educational books, and then the seventy or so roleplaying games—let's not even go there.) His work ranges from epic fantasy to space opera to superheroes to mysteries to thrillers, even Regency romances and Westerns, and includes novels for *Star Trek, World of Warcraft, Shadowrun, Warhammer, Sherlock Holmes,* and *Eureka,* and stories for *The X-Files, Zorro, World of Darkness, Joe Ledger,* and *Stargate,* as well as a veritable ton of original fiction. When he's not writing, Aaron can be found on the streets of New York City, hanging out with friends and family, watching movies, or reading. He's heard about this whole "sleeping" thing and means to give that a try some day, too. You can find out more about him at gryphonrose.com and follow him on Facebook at facebook.com/gryphonrose, on BSky at @gryphonrose.bsky.social, on Instagram at the_gryphonrose, and on X (formerly known as Twitter) @gryphonrose.

STORY SYNOPSIS: Irradiant (Bobby Gaynor), an all-powerful superhero, attempts to get needed rest after constant world-saving but faces public backlash from his long-overdue vacation.

HILDY SILVERMAN writes and edits in multiple genres. In 2020, she joined the Crazy 8 Press authors collective, which publishes novels and anthologies. In 2013, her short story, *The Six Million Dollar Mermaid*, (Mermaids 13: Tales from the Sea, French, ed.), was a finalist for the WSFA Small Press Award. She was the publisher and editor-in-chief of Space and Time Magazine for 12+ years. She is a past president of the Garden State Speculative Fiction Writers and frequent panelist on the convention circuit. For more, please visit www.hildysilverman.com.

STORY SYNOPSIS: A trauma-damaged woman boards a luxury cruise seeking peace but quickly comes to believe that real, violent pirates have infiltrated the ship. The story explores revenge, survival, and the protagonist's delusions as she pursues external predators that may or may not exist.

MIA DALIA is an internationally published, Crime Writers Association-nominated author of all things fantastic, thrilling, scary, and strange. Her short stories of horror, noir, science fiction, mystery, crime, humor, and more have been featured in a variety of anthologies, magazines, literary journals, online, and adapted for narrative podcasts. Her work has been voted top ten of Tales to Terrify 2023, shortlisted for the CWA's Daggers Awards 2024, acclaimed by Booklist, and praised by authors and editors such as Michael Marshall Smith, Stephen Jones, Marie O'Regan, Clay McLeod Chapman, Neil Sharpson, M.R. Carey, A.C. Wise, Edward Ashton, and more. She is the author of the novels *Estate Sale* and *Haven,* novellas *Alakazam, Tell Me a Story, Discordant, Arrokoth,* and *Do You Know The Muffin Man?* and the collection *Smile So Red and Other Tales of Madness.*
https://daliaverse.wixsite.com/author
https://linktr.ee/daliaverse

STORY SYNOPSIS: Before his wedding, a man and his college friends visit O'ahu for a last hurrah. Obsessive curiosity about local legends leads them to Nu'uanu Pali Lookout, where they confront deadly supernatural Nightmarchers – forcing a fight for survival and a reckoning.

VILTOR BLOODSTONE is one of the pen names for Brian Koscienski, Chris Pisano, and Jeff Young, three guys trying to make the voices in our heads pay rent. We cultivate entropy and skulk the arcane realms of south-central Pennsylvania. They have logged many hours writing novels, stories, articles, comic books, reviews, and the occasional ridiculous haiku. To find out more about what the voices in their heads told them to do, visit www.novelguys.com. If you happen to see them at one of the various conventions they participate in, feel free to stop by their table and say, "Hi." They're harmless!

STORY SYNOPSIS: Calista "Cali" Linquist wakes up at an isolated luxury ski resort beside a mutilated corpse with a necklace of human teeth and a missing molar of her own, thrusting her into a murderous mystery where suspicion, supernatural contagion, and hunger collide. As guests are slaughtered and communications are cut off, Cali must investigate to clear the innocent and survive while battling an internal, monstrous hunger and a manipulative antagonist who reveals the truth about the wendigo curse.

ROBERT E WATERS is an author with over 70 stories published. Also, he has written *Ring of Fire* novels, including *1636 CALABAR'S WAR*, and *1637 THE TRANSYLVANIAN DECISION*. In addition, he's written novellas for ESpec Books, *including EYES OF THE WOLF, ICE*

MUSIC, and *GHOST OF THE DAWNLANDS*. Robert has also written novels for Winged Hussar Books, including *THE LAST HURRAH* and *THE FINAL RUSH*, all based on the game of Dreadball. Robert lives with his wife Beth and son Jason, and a cute cat called Ash.

STORY SYNOPSIS: A vacationing lawyer and his family come to a remote Alberta cabin only to be attacked by small, malevolent creatures called Mannegishi, sent as vengeance for past wrongs. The story juxtaposes the family's initial comfort and safety with escalating, supernatural violence beginning on the river and culminating in catastrophe.

DIANNA SINOVIC is an author of speculative fiction, horror, and mystery, as well as a certified book coach and editor. She's a member of the Horror Writers Association, Sisters in Crime, and the National Association of Memoir Writers. Connect with her via her website www.dianna-sinovic.com, or on Instagram @dsinovic94

STORY SYNOPSIS: A man returns from a trip to Kyoto infected or possessed by a meat-craving Japanese demon (an *Oni*), which transforms his senses and drives him toward cannibalistic urges; his attempt to be exorcised briefly seems to succeed but the menace escapes containment, leaving a final twist of danger.

JACQUE DAY is the founding co-editor-in-chief of Carnage House Publishing, a staff member for Crystal Lake Publishing, and the former longtime managing editor of the New Madrid journal of contemporary literature. Her fiction and nonfiction can be found in the wild. She lives in her home state of Pennsylvania with her childhood-sweetheart husband, Art.

STORY SYNOPSIS: Dylan finds herself haunted by a decade of grief and unresolved tension as she attempts a fateful phone call, wanting closure. What begins as a nervous hope for connection devolves into a chilling, disorienting encounter, leaving Dylan stranded in uncertainty.

DIANE SISMOUR is an award-winning screenwriter and author of suspense, thrillers, and grounded horror. She is the founder of The Doll Keeper Productions LLC, where she develops original projects for film and television. Her feature screenplay, *The Doll Keeper*, a psychological horror about abduction and survival, is currently in development with industry partners. Diane's work is recognized for its matter-of-fact voice, layered characters, and themes of resilience. Her award-winning short stories appear in publications and anthologies, and she is a member of national and local writing and screenwriting groups. Whether writing about love, suspense, or horror rooted in everyday life, she explores how ordinary people face extraordinary choices. Learn more about Diane at:
https://www.dianesismour.com
LinkedIn https://www.LinkedIn.com/in/dianesismour
Facebook https://www.facebook.com/dianesismour

STORY SYNOPSIS: A ruthless island car dealer celebrates crushing a competitor and seizing beachfront property only to be haunted by the rival and ancient tiki guardians; the triumph of business ambition becomes a catastrophic downfall.

Raised in the Pennsylvania Pocono Mountains, **CATHERINE JORDAN** is inspired by gothic and weird movies with unusual settings. She loves to browse antiques, travel at a moment's notice, and take pictures of food and flowers. She's a mom of five, an avid gardener and traveler, and a caregiver. As a horror novelist with many anthologies and articles to her publishing credit, she holds an active role within the HWA and HorrorTree.com as a volunteer and a mentor. Ms. Jordan also facilitates creative writing courses and critique groups.

https://catherinejordan.com/

https://www.amazon.com/Catherine-Jordan/e/B00A3BVMEO

STORY SYNOPSIS: A woman's reckless night and flirtation abroad leads to a catastrophic medical outcome. The story traces the collapse of her ordinary life into devastation and horror.

OTHER EXCITING PRODUCTS FROM FORTRESS PUBLISHING, INC.:

The Killer of Devils series:

NEED SOME MORE CALISTA "CALI" LINDQUIST? SHE HAD TO FIGHT AND DESTROY AN UNKILLABLE BEAST. NOW, A FINAL GIRL WITH PTSD, SHE AND HER MOTHER HUNT MONSTERS. JOIN HER IN

THE KILLER OF DEVILS, BOOK 1: CLOWNS

ISBN: 978-1-959797-01-2

The Legacy of Devils series:

Hammer and Blood

ISBN: 978-0-9887991-6-5

ODE TO DAMNATION

ISBN: 978-1-959797-06-7

The Dream Eaters

ISBN: 978-1-959797-90-6

The Progeny of Devils series:

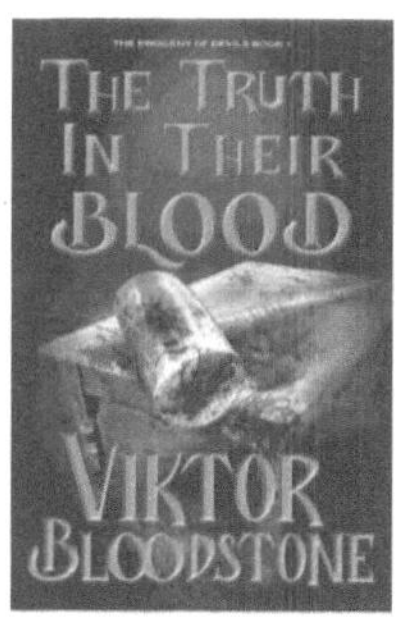

ISBN: 978-0-9887991-8-9

ISBN: 978-1-959797-04-3

CULTIVATE ENTROPY!

www.ingramcontent.com/pod-product-compliance
Lightning Source LLC
LaVergne TN
LVHW091039080826
845145LV00002B/556

* 9 7 8 1 9 5 9 7 9 7 0 8 1 *